THE ZAMBEZI CODE
THE AGENCY OF THE ANCIENT LOST & FOUND
BOOK SEVEN

JANE THORNLEY

PROLOGUE

August 18, 1840. southern Africa, near the Zambezi River

Terrence is so beset by fever this morn that no dosage of the medicines we have brought will appease what plagues him. Jacob remains by his side, as steadfast a manservant as any man could want, and at times I hear him chanting over my brother as if to exorcise a demon that has taken hold of his mind and body. The man believes his master to be possessed, claims that we have angered the river god Nyami Nyami by asking questions and seeking the staves of the three fabled kings.

Have we, have I? It is true that I ask many questions, that I probe deeply into the oral history of these people in order to better understand the mythologies that ensorcel these tribes. Should I continue my search or abandon it, and thus begin to move our party homeward? Terrence well may not make the trip but should I permit him to die here far away from our papa, who must be deeply worried that we may never return? The enormity of the decisions overwhelms me.

Later this same day

The witch doctor will often appear on my path as if he has manifested from the air and light, from the very soil beneath our feet. Every time he appears, our men attempt to chase him away as if he were a rabid dog or worse, though

Jacob warns them to treat the man with respect for he is most powerful. I, in turn, admonish the men for not allowing the man to approach me unaccosted. He is my friend, I try to explain, my *shamwari*.

Today, I was following the village women down to the river to collect water when suddenly the witch doctor jumped out from behind a baobab tree, scattering the women who deeply fear him. Again, the man bid me to stay, to attempt to understand his strange mutterings, and to decipher the sketches he makes upon the earth with a stick. I try, I truly do, but the closest I have come to comprehension seem to emerge like fully formed thoughts in my head. Is that possible? Can I understand such complex matters without the use of language? Sometimes I believe that, yes, it is the only way.

This time, my shamwari repeated the story he has oft told me through interpreters and now, through this strange deep connection that we share: if I am to find that which I seek, I must be brave. I must leave the body of the woman I am to become *other*.

What other? I ask without words. *How do I leave the woman I am to become someone I am not?*

You will know, he tells me. *When the people come, you will understand and follow them wherever they lead, even if it is to the edge of the precipice and beyond.*

What people and am I to consider this message in the literal sense? At the instant of my knowing, I glimpsed an image of a huge cliff, an overwhelming thundering, the glint of something sharp and feral far in the distance, and, truly, I was afraid. I asked whether I must die to find the truth but he did not reply. Perhaps it is because I already know the answer.

CHAPTER 1

The last time I had seen my brother in the flesh was shortly before I assisted Interpol in putting him behind bars for art theft three years earlier. For some reason, traveling across the ocean from London to Canada to pay him a spot visit that day in August felt like the bravest thing I'd done in ages.

Our eyes locked across the prison waiting room as he wheeled himself through the barred double doors, guard in tow. Though I tried keeping the shock from my expression, I knew it was useless. As the guard moved the chair out of the way so that Toby could position his wheelchair across from me, the plate glass between us may as well have been as deep as the stratosphere.

Picking up the phone, I whispered, struggling to control my voice: "You look good."

"Liar. I look like shit and you never could tell a lie though I've heard you've gotten better lately." He smiled. Same smile, at least. "But, damn, you *do* look good, Phoeb. My little sister has grown into quite a woman." There was emotion there, something like love visible in his eyes. It gave me courage.

"Thanks." I said.

"You'll have to speak up."

I pressed the receiver close to my mouth and leaned deeper into the wooden cubicle. "Right," I said more loudly. "So I came with a list of questions and here I am practically tongue-tied."

"Questions, hey? Fire away. I'm just happy you're here. Wondered how long it would take. Why now?" he asked.

I swallowed. "I wanted to find the brother I'd lost but was always terrified that I'd find a stranger instead." My heart galloped in my chest.

"You'll be finding a bit of both, Phoebe. Prison changes you, gives you too much time to think, but part of me is still here where you left me. God, it's good to see you. I've been keeping up with your escapades."

My escapades. I cringed at the word.

"I know you nailed Noel in the end, Phoeb. Good on you," he said, filling in the silence. All around us, the guards stood watching as other prisoners in other cubicles talked with their visitors. A few occupied tables in another section that seemed to be accommodating whole families, including kids. This wasn't the maximum security wing and Toby wasn't handcuffed, but since he was in a wheelchair, he was shackled just the same.

"I did," I told him, "finally."

"But he won't stay there for long, Phoeb. The only way to stop that bastard is by killing him. You had the chance, what, twice now? But you never took it."

I shot a quick glance towards the guard standing no more than six feet away. Every conversation was probably scrutinized. "I don't kill people, Toby, even those who make my life hell. I prefer to put him in jail where he is now."

"Like you did me?" He said it softly. No bitterness detected.

"Yes, like I did you." That came out a hell of a lot stronger than I felt.

"Thanks for that. I mean it. You probably saved my life and I'm willing to accept my punishment because I deserve it. Besides, I intend to make parole someday soon, even rejoin society as a productive member. Noel never will do that, won't even try. He'll come after you the moment he's free."

I shook away the thought. "Then I'll keep throwing him in jail."

My brother sat across from me wearing some pained expression I'd never seen before. It's as if wherever it came from, anything he said seared his soul on the way out. "You can't win against the corruption that runs the world, Phoeb. Look around: the bad guys know how to play the system even when they're behind bars. The world works on pay-offs and favors returned. Noel's been in bed with the higher ups for a long, long time. He'll get free someday and when he does, I'm hoping I'll be out of this place to protect you."

That shocked me. "Protect me Toby, seriously? I've been protecting myself for years, remember? Ever since you threw me under the bus." That slipped out. I lifted my hands and took a deep breath. "Sorry, sorry. Look, I didn't come here to recriminate—that's all in the past—I came to talk about who I am, *who we are*. I need answers."

THE ZAMBEZI CODE

"I'll tell you anything you want to know and I didn't intentionally throw you under the bus, okay? You know that, don't you?"

He had been Noel's partner once, had knowingly lured me into situations where I could have been killed. What else was I supposed to call it? "I need to you to tell me everything and I mean every. single. thing."

"I said I would."

"Go back to where it started, back to Nova Scotia, back to Dad. I was a kid, our father was a lobster fisherman, and sometimes we lived well, other times not so much. It all depended on the catch. Spin forward a few years to when suddenly there was this rich Australian standing in our tiny kitchen talking treasure hunts with our dad. The day Max entered our lives with that son of his, everything sucked us into this vortex. You disappeared; I took after you and fell down this rabbit hole of art crime and treasure hunters. Noel insinuated himself into my life and I've been chasing down stolen art and him ever since."

"That bastard used you like he used me."

I leaned forward, pressing my palms flat on the counter. "Used you how? That's the part I'm struggling with. Over the years, this, this …'gift'" I put the word in air quotes "—has been strengthening in me, my 'lost-art sniffer dog' tendencies, as Noel called them, has become a pack of baying hounds. That's why Noel wanted me, because I could find things, see things I shouldn't be able to, like lost art and missing artifacts."

"That was the draw, all right," he said softly.

"So things keep happening to me, even more unexplainable events that are becoming increasingly difficult to handle. Now I'm seeing things, experiencing past lives—timewalking, we call it." I paused, staring towards him. "Sometimes it feels like I'm no longer in the driver's seat of my own life. I'm afraid I'll touch something and go spinning off into another realm."

I expected him to be startled, shocked even, but he continued to watch me steadily, pausing only long enough to rub his eyes. For a moment he looked just like the brother I'd lost, the one I'd sometimes catch in an unguarded moment while he was deep into painting one of his elaborate fantastical scenes. "Yeah, I know," he whispered.

"Know what?" I demanded.

"Know what it's like to see things you shouldn't, find things others can't— the shipwrecks, the pots of gold at the end of a toxic rainbow." His eyes met mine.

I stilled. For a moment I couldn't speak. "You, too?"

"Me, too. How'd you think I got mixed up with Noel and Max in the first place? How'd you think I got spun out on drugs? Yeah, me, too. I was the teenager that got invited on treasure hunts with Dad because I had an uncanny ability to find things no one else could—the shipwrecks, the buried gold. Then the big Australian rich guy wanted to partner with the lobster fisherman."

"They always took you with them, never me," I whispered.

"You were too young. Max made on that they wanted Dad's boat and local knowledge of the Nova Scotian waters but really he wanted me. Dad didn't know about the drugs. Neither did Max, by the way. That was all Noel's doing. He was in his early twenties by then and passing me stuff that sharpened my abilities, mostly magic mushroom and psilocybin at first but then the hallucinogens grew stronger, more dangerous. What did I know? I was a kid."

"Oh, my God!" Tears were rolling down my cheeks. "Noel injected me the night I found Cleopatra's hoard."

Toby slammed his fist down on the table. "Bastard!"

The guard shot us a warning look.

I whispered: "What did he do to you?"

"Made me into an addict, and then went after my little sister. Isn't that enough? Thank God you got away from him in the end, Phoebe, at least for the short term. Sure, I'll own up to my part in the crime binge, but considering how it started, I'll lay most of it at Noel Halloran's feet. I didn't want to hurt you, Phoebe. My brain was so addled most of the time, I didn't know what I was doing."

Shock was hitting my system. It was all playing out before my eyes, the whole damn panorama of corruption and deceit. My family, my life, the lies. How wrong I had been about everything. "Are you sure Max didn't know about the drugs?"

"Pretty sure but Dad sure found out in the end," Toby continued. "That's why he broke all ties with Max and son but by that time it was too late, too late for me, too late for Dad. I was long gone and soon enough, Dad would be gone, too, along with everything in the world I loved...like you."

"Can you timewalk?" I whispered.

"Yeah. Had some experiences once or twice."

"Why didn't you tell me this sooner?" I asked, crying in earnest now.

"When—somewhere in our five minute phone calls, the laundered emails, maybe? No, Phoebe. I've been waiting for the day when you'd come to visit me in person and here you are. I knew that you couldn't face me after what I did and I accepted that. I tried to send you code in my letters, made it look like I was doodling in the margins—I doodle all day long so the guards don't suspect anything—but you hardly ever responded."

"All those scribbles were making me crazy! Besides, I didn't want puzzles, I wanted straight answers for once."

"So now you've got them."

"But what am I supposed to do with this timewalking ability?"

"Bury it," he said. "As long as there are crooks out there, they'll want to use it and you. That's what I've been struggling to do these past years—kill the ability inside these gray walls. I'm almost there."

"But I can't just turn it off."

"Try, try real hard," he warned. "And don't trust anyone."

CHAPTER 2

They were waiting for me in the parking lot of Terminal 2, Rupert's glossy Rolls Royce purring in the warm August rain. By then, I was stumbling from exhaustion but so eager to see the two of them that I let go of my roller bag and leaped into Evan's arms as he came to meet me. The resulting kiss was much briefer than I preferred but Peaches was already calling to us from the car.

"Okay, break it up, you two. You can gob each other all you want once we're home." A few seconds later, she added: "Where are you taking us, Ev—your place, mine, or Phoebe's?"

Snug in the front seat, I buckled my seatbelt and glanced at Evan as he slid behind the driver's wheel. He often borrowed his father's car and since he had once played his chauffeur, always looked so natural behind the wheel.

"What if I drop you off at your flat and carry on to mine with Phoebe?" he asked, a little smile tugging on that fine mouth of his. Evan had commandeered the top floor of his father's house where he had lived since he began working with his dad as an underground operative.

"Bad idea," she remarked cheerfully. "Our girl here needs to decompress. She's got things to tell us and we have things to tell her. Great, so it's settled: my flat it is. I'll dose her with my anti-jet-lag tea. Would you mind turning up the aircon back here, Ev? Oh, never mind. Of course this thing has independent controls."

I could have argued, of course. What I really needed was sleep and plenty of it, preferably the alone variety, but Peaches was right: I also needed to talk and since it was still only 9:30 p.m., I obliged. Besides, the half hour trip into the city gave me a chance to nap. By the time Evan pulled up outside Peaches's Notting Hill flat, though hardly refreshed, I knew I could soldier through a few more hours. We left Evan to find a parking spot while I followed Peaches through the door.

Peaches was renting an upper open-plan two bedroom flat around the corner from Portobello Road. I teased her that she chose it only because the exterior was painted purple but she swore that wasn't true. In any case, the yellow and bright pink ones had already been taken. The interior, on the other hand, was an assault of bright open plan white, something that my friend had countered with plenty of art posters, African textiles, and wooden carvings. Carvings, mostly of faces and masks, was the only thing she seemed to collect.

"Oh, you've really punched some color into this place since I was here last," I enthused, dropping my sweater over the bannister and striding behind her towards the kitchen. "Love it."

"My latest acquisitions are the framed vintage Jimi Hendrix poster which hangs right over my Jamaican happy bird tree in the lounge, and that." She pointed to the tall oval item propped on a table halfway down the hall.

I paused, staring. That was an intricately carved mask made of some strange pale speckled wood. "African? Wow, it's so expressive. And looks old, too." Actually, it was strangely beautiful. "Looks like she or he is shocked."

"She, pretty sure it's a she. The face is quite small, almost delicate, see? Not typical of African masks."

"Which region does it come from, then, and where did you get it?" About twenty-four inches high made of some pale wood, the mask wore a round open mouthed expression that just showed two little ivory teeth but it was the fringe of orangey dreadlocks that really got me. "She looks startled."

"Maybe she just saw an evil spirit," she said, plugging in the kettle. "Masks like that are designed to scare away bad magic but maybe that one's supposed to look startled or something. As for where it originates from, I have no idea, but who left it is another story. It's valuable. Collectors would give their ivory teeth to have a piece like that and here I found it propped inside my front vestibule two days ago."

"As in a gift?"

"More like a bribe embedded in a clue."

I turned and met her eyes. "From whom?" It took two seconds to figure it out. "Surely not?"

"Surely yes. Sonny Baldi put that piece on my doorstep delivered anonymously but, really, I knew who put it there the moment I laid eyes on it. That mask is her way of getting to me. She's pushing my button."

"You have a mask button, Peaches?" Evan asked as he stepped into the hall, shutting the door behind him on a blast of misty air. That man had incredible ears and as usual, took in everything in an instant.

"I have an African art button, period," she replied. "Big, multicolored, and the size of a continent. In fact, it's almost as big as your Phoebe button, Ev, if that's possible."

"Which is shaped like an enormous beating heart, a bit enlarged at the moment and exceedingly distracting, I admit," he said, casting me a dazzling grin. He paused by the closet long enough to hang up his jacket—Evan didn't do the draping over the bannister thing. "But Sonny Baldi did attempt to push a few of my buttons, too, which I refused to permit."

"And I hope you didn't let her anywhere near them, either," I said. "Seriously though, what did Sonny Baldi hope to gain?"

He turned, his gaze warm when it touched my face. "Her intent was to prevent me from running interference in what she hoped would be the agency's next mission."

"Our next mission?" Something about that inspired both dread as well as excitement.

"She has a proposal for you, one upon which she did not elaborate. However, by reviewing her role in my rescue during the Pompeii debacle, she implied that I was in some way indebted to her for assisting in my escape, as if 'her services', as she put it, weren't totally self-serving."

"And you said?"

"I assured her that I would do everything in my power to prevent her from coercing you or the agency into doing something illegal."

I crossed my arms. "Coercing, really?"

"That's the correct term." His mild tone belied the tensile strength beneath his words. "If it involves attempting to pressure a person to perform an act by using force or threats, it is coercion."

"What if said person performed those acts by mutual agreement in order to benefit humanity in some way or to protect the ones she loves?" I said it teasingly but he knew where I was coming from. We'd already had many long tense discussions about my dealings with Sonny Baldi.

He had chosen to look the other way during the Cleopatra affair mostly since he had been unconscious most of the time so really couldn't offer much of a firsthand account. The fact remained that I had bargained for clues to lost art in order to save his life and ultimately find Cleopatra's hoard. In exchange, I paid by sharing part of the proceeds with a criminal and hinted I would be willing to do it again. Yes, I know.

"If the intent is to ensure that person ultimately commits a crime, it's still a criminal act," he said softly. "And, bringing matters back to the first-person singular for a moment, I promise I'd do anything in my power to protect you and prevent you from continuing your dealings with Sofonisba Baldi and the entire Baldi organization, for that matter."

We gazed at each other, me trying not to melt because he had that effect on me, while thinking how much I did not want this line drawn between us. It was like an invisible wall that I somehow had to get around or over because, in the end, I really despised being contained by any thing or anybody.

Peaches arrived at my elbow and gently unfolded my arms. "Drink this—you need it. Now tell us about your visit with your brother. Since this is the first time you've visited him since his incarceration, I bet you two had lots to say."

I broke the gaze-lock with Evan and turned away, taking a sip of the steaming brew. "He told me things I'm still processing, like the fact that Noel had been passing him mind-altering drugs way back when he was still a teenager. That's one of the reasons why he ended up an addict."

"Damn, really? Can we lock that bastard away ten times over just because it feels so good?" Peaches was brandishing her spoon like a sword.

I smiled. "Let's just hope he stays imprisoned this time around. Toby believes that unlikely but I'm hoping he's wrong."

Evan's temple was twitching. "He'll stay put if Interpol has anything to do with it."

"That's what I said," I added, "but forget about that for a moment. Toby also told me that my lost-art sniffer dog tendency is a family trait that skips generations. He has it, too, or had it. That's what drew him into working with Noel and Max in the first place. Toby's lost-art sniffer-dog abilities gave Noel something to exploit all those years ago."

"Astounding," Evan said. "Has anyone else in your lineage been affected?"

Interesting that he said "affected" like he meant *infected*. It felt like one of those deadly infections that remain in remission before rearing up and wreaking havoc days, months, even years later. "The last one in our family to be stricken according to our mom was her Irish great grandmother. She ran around seeing things and was believed to be the village witch."

"I love witches," said Evan softly. "One, in particular."

I smiled. Really, if I'd lived way back then, I had no doubt that's what they'd call me.

"Hope they didn't burn her at the stake or drown her or any of those things they did to wild, brilliant, supernatural women in those days. My lineage used to celebrate them as soothsayers and medicine women. Is this like a mutant gene or something?" Peaches pressed.

"I'd prefer to nix the mutant part," I replied. "The Celts are known for heightened psychic perceptions so let's just call it a rare hereditary trait. In my case, I'm just going to stifle my timewalking abilities and return to using my brain and intuition. I can't bear anymore of that dying a thousand deaths thing. Dying again and again can be so distracting." It had taken me a long time to recover from experiencing the last day of ancient Pompeii and on no account did I want to repeat anything even close.

"So you've forgiven Toby." Peaches was searching my eyes.

"Yes," I whispered, "and it feels like I have my brother back finally, maybe even my entire family, even though they're still gone. At least my memory feels…healed. Toby told me a few things about Max, too, most of which I already knew. Anyway, I forgave him a long time ago. He's suffered enough."

"Phoebe." Evan slipped an arm over my shoulders and drew me close. "You, too, have suffered enough. Stay near to me." He kissed the top of my head.

This was something new, him wanting to keep me from doing my job in the name of safety. Though sweet, it was troublesome.

Peaches rolled her eyes. "Should I give you two a minute?"

What happened next kept us too busy to reply at first. When we came up for air moments later, Peaches was standing by holding Evan's brew of choice —strong tea, black, two sugars.

"Let's discuss this mask for a moment, you two. Save the snogging for later. That mask is definitely African," she said.

"What do you think it means?" I asked, forcing myself to pull away from the safe nest Evan created by his embrace.

"I suggest we not ask that question but return it immediately," came Evan's response.

"Return it how?" Peaches asked. "I don't know where to send it. Besides that thing is undoubtedly a collector's item so hardly suitable for popping into the post."

The three of us were soon staring at the mask. The oval face was unsettling and oddly powerful. I almost didn't want to touch it and yet I set down my mug and picked it up in both hands, turning it around to study it on all sides. A tremor hit me at once. I set it back down and took a step away.

"Did you feel something?" Peaches asked, picking it up instead.

"Something, yes. Probably nothing more than the resonance of centuries. Masks are one of the oldest forms of art," I said. "There is evidence of their existence on rock carvings over 11,000 years old, which means that they've been important to human evolution almost from day one. They represent our deepest unconscious selves—fear, honor, initiations, love, life, death. This piece has been stolen, by the way."

"How do you know that?" Peaches gasped. "Oh, hell, not another whoo-whoo moment."

"More boring: deductive reasoning. Flip it over."

Peaches turned the back of the mask around.

"See the little black ink markings in the lower righthand corner?"

"SA62?" She peered closer.

"Collectors, even museums, used to mark their holdings by cataloguing them with permanent ink. This one belonged to a collection once," Evan remarked. "Most likely late eighteenth to early nineteenth century, judging by the script. Museums rarely deface their holdings with any permanent markings these days." He'd donned his reading glasses. Let me just say that gasses perched on that perfect nose was a devastatingly fetching look on him.

"Yes, my thinking, too," I agreed, struggling to stay focused. "This piece was probably considered a curio by some early explorer who emerged from Africa bearing trophies of all sorts. It must have ended up in either somebody's personal collection or in a museum somewhere."

"Stolen from its original owners and then stolen again." Peaches had shot up straight. "Damn it all to hell. I hate how African heritage gets plundered as souvenirs. Now they're valuable commodities but the original makers got zilch."

"The record paid for an African mask was $7.5 million, the last I heard, but as far as museums go, holding on to them has become an ethical dilemma," I pointed out.

"For good reason," Peaches said. "Most of them were stolen and now museums keep them locked away in storerooms while they figure out how to avoid repatriating them to their home countries."

Peaches could well explode into a tirade on this subject so I attempted to divert the course. "Why did Sonny send you this?"

"Because she knows that African anything is my hotspot and she's trying to get to me."

"And, if indeed this piece is stolen, she may attempt some level of blackmail," Evan said.

"Coercion," I said.

"Coercion," he agreed.

"Because if it's stolen, she knows that you can't easily return it to its original owner. We'll take it to the lab and begin searching for it in the data banks." I nodded as if it was all that simple.

"And as for our appointment with Sonny tomorrow?" Peaches enquired.

I glanced at her. "Do we have a time and place?"

"We do. I'm actually invited, not you, though, Ev. Sorry." She flashed him a smile. "The British Museum Great Court coffee shop, 2:00 p.m."

"I advise you not to go. Do not take one step further towards this trap she's setting, at least until we know what exactly she's up to." Evan used his steeliest tone. "I implore you."

"'Implore you'—you sound just like your dad, Ev. You're just jealous that you weren't invited and will miss out on one of those cement pastries they sell," Peaches teased.

"I'm very serious." He bit down on the words. "Proceeding with a meeting might make it appear that you are a willing accomplice in whatever she has planned."

"Evan," I said, "we won't know what she's up to unless we at least have this initial meeting. Aren't you curious?" I took a deep breath, turning to Peaches. "We'll be there. Besides, there's nothing illegal in meeting someone for coffee."

CHAPTER 3

The British Museum's southern concourse or Great Court was a huge glass dome that seemed to settle over the hallowed institution like a transparent spaceship. The court was still the largest covered public square in Europe and always took my breath away. Actually, my brain also required a bit of a reboot just to jostle so much modernity with the ancient treasures the institution housed. I strolled straight through the main foyer heading for the circular enclosure without glancing right or left in case I veered towards one of my favorite galleries.

"So where are we meeting her exactly?" I asked Peaches as we stepped inside the circular light-filled space. I averted my eyes from the bookstore and reading room which inhabited the center directly in my line of vision. Many long delicious hours had been spent there in the past.

"Coffee shop," Peaches replied. "This way. I wouldn't be surprised if Ev was having us followed."

He couldn't easily do so in person since our agency tracking map pinpointed exactly where all our members were located at all times. On the other hand, he had the means to make his tracker go dark where the rest of us couldn't. I found that oddly thrilling and simultaneously annoying. "He's made his disapproval pretty clear."

"He'll be listening in to our conversation, at the very least."

"Pardon? He can do that?"

"If you'd read your manual for once, you'd know what other marvels he's embedded into our phones," she replied.

Damn, I had to read that thing as soon as I had a spare month.

We waited for a school group to pass before rounding the circular enclosure towards the refreshment station against one wall. The coffee shop was notorious for its pyramids of what looked to be delicious pastries, each of which often turned out to be vaguely inedible and disappointingly tasteless.

"Avoid the cornbread thingies unless you want to crack a molar. Aim for the sticky buns instead," Peaches commented. "At least you can safely bite into them."

I was too busy scanning the long white tables for Sonny to listen. The only woman who appeared to be waiting for somebody was the dark-haired woman in sunglasses and the white fur jacket. The last time I had seen Baldi, she had been blond, yet there was something unmistakable in the way this woman commanded the space. "Just a bottle of lemon juice for me Peach. Meet you at the table, thanks."

With that I maneuvered my way through the shelves of snacks and seated patrons to the woman in white. "Fur in August, Sonny, seriously? Britain's having a heatwave, haven't you noticed?"

She glanced up and smiled, all brilliant white teeth against crimson lips, which reminded me unaccountably of blood. "It's several degrees cooler in London today and you know I cannot bear the chill. It was searing hot in Naples when I left so I brought my jacket just in case. Ciao, Phoebe. Good to see you, too. How are you?"

I sat down across from her, dropped my bag on the floor, and leaned forward with my arms propped on the table. "Curious, like you know I'd be but I also know what you're up to. By setting our rendezvous in one the most completely CCTV-covered buildings in Britain, you want a public record of our meeting to ensure that we're implicated in whatever you have planned next. Just so you know, it won't work."

She laughed that gravelly chuckle of hers. "So suspicious! And here we are friends! But, really, Phoebe, where in London can we meet that isn't under surveillance? Sometimes I think even the public toilets are watched in this city. So distrustful, these Londoners. We Italians think 'so shit happens. *Non c'è problema.*" Picking up a tiny cup of espresso, she grimaced. "Unbearable coffee, too. Only Italians make a decent brew." She set the cup down.

Peaches arrived at that moment with a tray and slammed a bottle of lemon juice in front of me before sliding a paper coffee cup accompanied by a sticky bun to the space nearby. In seconds she had pulled up a chair and sat down, glaring at Sonny the whole time. "Is that fur real?"

"Arctic fox," Sonny told her in a frosty tone.

"Hope that some activist mugs you on the street with a can of bright green spray paint on behalf of the poor creature skinned for your benefit," Peaches said between her teeth.

"And this will help the fox how?" Sonny asked. "This was a gift from my father and I assure you, no one will get close enough to do it any damage."

I swiftly changed the topic. "Speaking of gifts, I understand that you're sending them anonymously now. The mask?"

The woman grinned. "African art is very valuable on the market, no? That one hails from southern Africa and you can tell your gladiator here that she is welcome for the present."

"It's not a gift, it's stolen goods—the only kind you understand." Peaches had never removed her furious stare from Sonny's face.

"Stolen, maybe, but not by me, or at least not the first time. Second times don't count. I am certain that your agency will find the provenance trail very interesting, if tricky to trace. Still—," she shrugged. "—I will help. You enjoy your drinks first and then we proceed to the African galleries. Meanwhile, we catch up, as they say. Phoebe, how was Toby?"

I stared. She knew about that? "Are you are having me followed, too."

"Not followed, no—not yet, anyway—but as your friend, I keep my ear to the ground. I am interested in your well-being."

"I just bet," Peaches growled. "More like you're interested in what you think she can do for you. Get this Sonabitchi: Phoebe is not and never will be your lost-art sniffer dog."

Sonny turned her shoulder slightly until she was addressing me exclusively. "Noel told me that Toby shares your gift and I know how that bastard exploited you both. Very bad. We must keep Noel imprisoned to prevent further atrocities while working to get your brother released. I have many friends in high places, as you can imagine. Some were my father's contacts, some mine. Through their influence, we can assure that only those who deserve freedom will achieve it."

Was that a threat or a promise? With Sonny, probably a bit of both. Her late arms-dealer father who had been one of the most successful art thieves on the planet and Noel's former colleague, would certainly have connections in high places and plenty in low ones, too. But, I reminded myself, Noel's incarceration benefitted us both. I couldn't see her arranging for his release any time soon, nor Toby's, for that matter. "I refuse to be exploited by anyone, Sonny, especially you."

"But I do not exploit people, Phoebe," she said pleasantly. "I give them what they want as well as something for myself so that we both benefit. Win-win, as you English say."

"I can't see how we can both benefit if it results in a criminal act on my part." I poured my lemonade into a paper cup and sipped deeply. "Just to spare you the effort, I have no intention of discussing my family or anything else with you. I only came to see what you hope to achieve this time." I had always been too curious for my own good.

"Wait and see. I am certain that you will find it very interesting."

"And illegal?" I asked.

"Nothing illegal in visiting a museum," she remarked.

"What about that mask?" Peaches demanded.

"Oh, you will see many similar masks in the exhibit here," Sonny remarked,

Peaches rolled her eyes and looked ready to erupt. I quickly changed the subject and for the next ten minutes we discussed weather, clothes, and the best place in London to do lunch. It turned out that she owned a flat near Harrods just to accommodate her occasional forays to London. No surprise there, though that news seemed to irritate Peaches even further.

"I thought Rupe was filthy rich," she muttered. "Just not as filthy, I guess."

Sonny ignored her.

Finally, we finished our drinks and Sonny got to her feet. "Let us visit the African exhibit now. It is this way."

That's when I realized that I had no idea in which direction to head. I had always been more of a European history to Western civilization kind of girl, something which delivered a sharp pang of shame.

I strode along staring down at the museum map. "I can't figure out where the galleries are located from this thing," I admitted.

"Yeah, that happens," Peaches said beside me. "An entire continent has been shoved into the basement. Just like our African heritage has been forced to the back of the bus. The space is called the Sainsbury Galleries, by the way. Follow me." She passed Sonny and strode around the court like a woman on a mission, the two of us scrambling after.

The Sainsbury Galleries were not easy to find in the huge multilevel sprawl of one of the greatest museums in the world. Africa did appear to be wedged in the basement at the bottom of the stairs, a fact that surprised me, considering the sensitivity surrounding African studies in general. Yet, the color and artistry that greeted me at first eclipsed any shortcomings, which was probably the idea.

First there was an astounding piece of contemporary art hanging at the base of the stairs made with found objects like flattened bottle caps and foil. But no sooner had I spied this but I was then entranced by the life-size ceremonial costumes from Cameroon glimpsed nearby. The exhibits were magnificent, thrilling, even.

"Don't let yourself be seduced, Phoeb," Peaches whispered. "Sure these pieces are stunning but why so much contemporary art in a historical museum? Ask yourself that."

"Because if they removed all the contemporary art, you would soon realize how little ancient African art they really have on display," Sonny said on my other side.

"Their official answer is that they want to show the vibrancy of the existing African culture as well as the historical aspects," Peaches continued.

"But," said Sonny, it is really because they don't have enough historical pieces and they keep other examples hidden for fear of criticism. You see, many of the main exhibits have been stolen from their original nations. A very controversial subject."

They were actually almost talking to one another. I hated to interrupt. "Do you mean like the Benin Bronzes?" I asked. "I always wanted to see those. Take me to them."

The Benin Bronzes had been a festering point for the British Museum for decades. Like many other exceptional pieces of art—the Elgin Marbles being the poster child of the removal of a country's heritage—these masterful pieces of thirteenth to fifteenth century Nigerian art were stolen. Granted, this was back in the Colonial days when British explorers and soldiers figured that trophy confiscation was their divine right. Even so, this story is particularly distressing. In short, the kingdom of Benin resisted colonial takeover, and their city was razed to the ground, people massacred, their king dethroned, and their heritage taken off to England by colonels and soldiers in 1897. Attempts to repatriate the bronzes have been challenging ever since.

The metal plaques and sculptures that once adorned the Edo people's royal palace in Benin have resided in the British Museum and other world galleries ever since. The museum refused to repatriate them at first, suggesting instead that they 'loan' the collection to a Nigerian museum temporarily but other museums began returning the bronzes outright accordingly. The repatriation issues continue to grow increasingly more complex to this day.

I stood staring at the wall of bronzes, which were actually brass alloys mixed with ivory inlay, each plaque an arresting depiction of warriors, gods, and royalty exquisitely rendered and amazingly naturalistic—a whole wall of detailed images.

"Of course, at first the then-experts said that no primitive African people could create lost-wax casting at this skill level. They had to be of Portuguese origin, right?" said Peaches. "White, in other words."

"When they are gone, the British Museum will have no showpiece of African art," said Sonny at my elbow. "The next biggest and best cache of African art resides in a private collection here in London, also mostly stolen. This late local collector had amassed an enormous cache, some pieces acquired just before his death."

I turned to face her. "This is why you've brought us here, isn't it? You're hoping to whet our appetite to go after this stash of African art? But that can't be all there is to it. Even though such pieces are fetching high prices at auctions, I can't imagine they'd interest you much. You prefer gold and precious jewels, right?" I said it aloud, not caring who heard.

"This is true." She laughed. "But I am certain your agency would find this man's collection very interesting and may want to investigate further. Repatriating African art would bring big kudos, yes?"

"I'm not interested in kudos."

"Of course you are," she countered. "Agencies like yours thrive on kudos."

I left her to study the rest of the gallery, which was surprisingly small given the scope of the peoples it represented. An impressive pottery tree, a selection of weapons, jewelry, and against one wall, a breathtaking selection of African textiles that kept me engaged. Sonny never left my side and Peaches didn't take her eyes off the woman for a minute.

While staring at a piece of barkcloth, Sonny whispered into my ear. "He had been planning another heist, this collector, against the original country that holds the lost treasure until his untimely death. Word is that others may be planning to move forward. Do you wish to stop such sacrilege?"

I swung around. "Either you tell us what you're up to or stop wasting our time," I snapped.

"Let us walk outside," Sonny suggested. "I will tell you more."

By then, I thought Peaches was ready to throttle her. "Is the mask you dropped in my vestibule from this collector?" she demanded.

We were on the sidewalk now, the black cabs lining up on Russell Street to pick up the occasional museum-goer. By the manner in which Sonny was gazing at me, I knew that she was attempting to block her face from the nearby CCTV cameras. She didn't care who knew we were talking but she didn't want anyone to lipread her words.

Sonny addressed only me. "The collector's estate will never admit that mask is missing publicly. That would bring too much attention to the family's collection which contains many pieces acquired illegally."

Peaches wedged herself between us. "But you stole it? Surprise, surprise."

Sonny stepped two inches to the left, her gaze fixed on me and continued as if she hadn't heard. "I know this because the mask was sold by a local dealer." She shrugged. "Still, it is what this man has acquired before his death that will be of much interest to you. It is one of the largest private collections of African art in the world, most from countries in southern Africa which are under represented in Western museums., most acquired by this man. Also, there are clues in his collection that lead to another massive secret hoard of African gold. Your agency would find this very interesting, Phoebe, is this not true?"

Peaches glowered. "Why didn't you just tell us this in the first place? Why all the cat-and-mouse?"

I was ready to throttle her myself.

She grinned before suddenly sobering. "Phoebe, you and I both have a vested interest here. This man, the late Lord Hanley Hopkins, had a diary in his collection by one of his ancestors, a little-known woman explorer, a Lady Louise Hopkins. You need to see this diary first and then, if you are interested, I will share with you the missing pages."

"Missing pages? What about the mask?" Peaches exclaimed.

Checking her watch, Sonny beamed a megawatt grin in my direction, stepping in front of Peaches in the process. "It is part of my father's library that I told you about. Don't blame me. I am very respectful of old books. Him, not so much. Here is my card. Call the number when you are ready to talk. Must run."

Peaches laid a hand on her arm to hold her in place. "What aren't you telling us, woman? What is it about this diary that's so important?"

"Careful, gladiator." Sonny stared at Peaches without blinking until Peaches released her grip. A man had emerged from a black car pulled near to the curb.

"One more thing," Sonny said, nudging her aside to face me. "Lord Hopkins estate does not allow people to see this collection—very sensitive, you understand. The gentleman died unexpectedly awhile back—long story—but I am sure you can probably gain entrance to his Belgravia mansion if you ask the son nicely. He lives a few doors down from Rupert Fox who can secure you an invitation, I am sure. After all, Sir Fox was the dealer who sold his father the stolen mask in the first place. Imagine that? Ciao."

She waved and scuttled off to slip into a black Rolls that had pulled up to the curb. A minute later and she was gone.

CHAPTER 4

"*How* delightful it is to have you visit this afternoon, Phoebe—and Penelope, of course—and dare I say that Phoebe, you are looking quite refreshed despite the effects of your transoceanic flight yesterday. I find plane travel so distressing on one's skin. Do tell me more about your meeting with Tobias." Rupert sat across from us in his Belgravia lounge, his prize tea set spread across the mahogany table between the velvet upholstered slipper chairs, a plate of his butler Sloane's sandwiches stacked on an antique serving tray nearby. Peaches had already devoured three, much to her hosts' delight.

Meanwhile, I was getting nowhere. "I've already told you the pertinent details of my session with Toby, Rupert, and we discussed it on the phone this morning, too. Now, about the mask…"

Sloane was fussing, delivering additional treats almost by the minute as if having company for high tea was just the kind of event upon which the household thrived. I sensed rather than saw Mrs. Lee, the cook, bustling away in the kitchen somewhere in the back. My call to say that Peaches and I were dropping over that afternoon must have sent them all into a spin.

Sloane urged Peaches to take another cucumber sandwich, which she managed to find room for on her already overloaded plate.

"Thanks," she mumbled through a mouthful. "Everything's so delicious! You say that green stuff is watercress, Sloane? Oh, I just love it. Got the recipe?"

23

The butler beamed. He was very old school but had adapted admirably to having a tall Amazonian Jamaican periodically visit his employer. "The recipe is exceedingly simple, Miss Williams, truly. Cucumber sandwiches are an English staple and I would be embarrassed to disclose the true simplicity of their preparation."

"Mayonnaise and cucumbers," I offered in the hopes of nipping this conversation in the bud.

"Oh, come on. You're pulling my leg," Peaches exclaimed. "You're keeping it close to your chest because it's some kind of family secret, right? I get it. My granny would have killed to keep the recipe for the fluffiest johnnycakes on the island under wraps."

I shot Peaches a warning glance. *Enough, already.* But the recipe exchanged continued unabated.

Resigned to my fate, I waited until Sloane had retreated before broaching the subject with Rupert for a third time. I briefly reviewed our rendezvous with Sonny (again) and mentioned the mask, in particular (again). "Do you remember it, Rupert? Sofonisba claimed that you had sold it to your neighbor, Lord Hanley Hopkins, who had amassed a large collection of African art and has since passed."

"I'm still getting used to the idea of some parent naming their kid Hanley Hopkins," Peaches mumbled. "There should be a law against torturing kids with awkward handles like that. I would have just gone for George or Frederick—anything to avoid the alliteration. At least the late Hanley named his son Rory which says something."

I tried to catch her eye but she continued blithely on. "But who was the first Sir Hopkins besides being a wealthy toff born with a silver shovel up his…" She quickly averted course, set her plate on the table and gazed across at Rupert. "I mean, if he collected African art, he had good taste but where'd he get all these pieces and why would Sonabitchi drop a mask on me that once belonged to him? She implied that you sold it to him, Rupe. Is that true? Have you ever dealt in stolen African artifacts in your nefarious past?"

From one extreme to another, Peaches rarely traveled the middle road.

Rupert, who had gone noticeably paler, cleared his throat. "I am not certain exactly to which piece you refer but—"

Peaches held her phone out opened on the photo. "This one."

Rupert took a moment to don his glasses and take the device from her fingers. A few seconds of intense study followed where the room was so quiet that the only sound was Peaches munching.

Finally Rupert returned the phone. "Yes, indeed, that looks familiar—a startling example of southern African artistry. I believe the late Lord Hopkins purchased it from me several years past. At that time I had acquired a number of African pieces lacking provenance from an auction house in Berlin. Though admittedly I hesitated from dealing with these initially, I ultimately acquiesced as I was involved in an undercover operation to capture an art smuggling ring. Thus it behooved me to play the part, so to speak."

"Buying stolen art is playing the part?" Peaches asked.

"Yes, of course." Our host set down his tea cup and adjusted the lapels of his silken smoking jacket. "I was an undercover arts and antiquities dealer, after all, and one must add veracity to one's activities. Surely you understand this, Penelope?"

"What I don't understand, Rupe, is why you resold items to this Hopkins when you believed to them be stolen in the first place?"

"Ah," he said with a triumphant smile. "Because, dear Penelope, the provenance ultimately lead right to Lord Hopkins's door. It was a stroke of luck, in truth, because Hanley once attended a dinner party at my country estate and interesting details about his African collection unfolded as we dined. Imagine how delighted I was to discover that the Hopkins family have an ancestor who had brought many artifacts from Africa in the nineteenth century? In fact, he even had sketches documenting each piece, the Victorians being great sketchers since many of their exploits predated the widespread use of the camera. Provenance thus confirmed, I sold the mask to him at a nominal price, just covering the shipping fees, if you must know."

"How magnanimous of you, Rupe." Peaches dabbed a bit of mayonnaise from her mouth with a linen napkin. "And that's where the ownership trail ended, I suppose, with the thieves rather than the original African owners? The British came in, poached the goods, and still ended up the winners. Nice play."

He shifted in his seat as if suddenly perched on a something sharp. "Well, I...what I mean to say is that how could we ever decipher who owned those masks originally? After all, they must have been tribal in origin."

"Tribal? All humans are tribal at the core. Here we call them 'communities'. Only the supposedly 'civilized' refer to extended families in other communities less educated than themselves as being 'tribal'. That implies that those communities are a helluva lot more primitive and inferior to our own, which isn't true depending on how you look at it."

"What I mean to say is—"

"What you meant to say was that since the original owners and makers were indigenous African and beneath you in status and formal education, they're not worthy of being considered significant on the repatriation trail." Peaches had set down her plate again. That didn't bode well.

Rupert's cheeks were reddening by the minute. "That is not my intent at all, Penelope. What I meant to say is that Interpol chose not to pursue those avenues, being more interested in the modern criminals circulating loot than in returning the individual pieces to their original owners, whomever they may have been."

This wasn't going to end unless I intervened. "That's where we come in. Our job is to repatriate lost art and artifacts to their original owners, regardless of where they live or their status. Did you see the late Hopkins's collection before his death, Rupert?"

"*Lord* Hopkins, yes. I have seen his collection which is undoubtedly magnificent but as my interests primarily reside in Greek and Roman artifacts, I admit to not having given the display the attention to which it undoubtedly deserved." He shot Peaches a quick look. Her expression was still in glower mode, he quickly returned his gaze to mine. "It was only the briefest of tours, you understand, and more out of a personal favor than anything else. I was shocked to learn of Lord Hopkin's untimely demise months ago, devastated, in fact. They say he suffered a massive heart attack. You say that Ms. Baldi has since acquired the mask?"

"Stolen it," Peaches clarified now sitting with her hands clasped in her lap. "It kind of runs in her family, if you recall, but she dropped another bomb just before she left us yesterday. She said that we needed to see a certain diary in the Hopkins collection, too. Said you could get us an invitation from the son."

"An invitation, from Lord Rory Hopkins?" Now Rupert had blanched around the gills.

"Ring the doorbell on the old boys' club, in other words, or is it a new old boys' club now?" Peaches was leaning forward now, fixing him with an unwavering stare. "Bet you can do that, can't you, Rupe, being one of those old boys yourself."

Hell. "What Peaches means is that we need to meet the younger Hopkins for an interview and hopefully see his father's collection while we're at it," I quickly clarified. "Can you arrange that, Rupert?"

"Under what pretense?" Rupert enquired, now back to a putty hue. "The young Lord Hopkins is no fool and will know the line of work in which I am engaged, especially now that the agency has reached a level of fame. Your presence in particular, Phoebe, might raise the man's concerns, besides which the family is exceedingly protective of the collection and allows few people access."

"Sure, why would he? Why not keep this gallery of African art all to himself?" said Peaches with a slight growl.

"My point is that the man must know that his father was a private collector and be fully aware of the repatriation scandal involving other African collections of a similar ilk, thus will be reluctant to discuss his father's holdings with a repatriation agency," Rupert pointed out. The term "ruffled feathers" had taken on an almost visible meaning.

"I don't blame him," I said mildly.

"I do," Peaches protested.

Before either of them could lock horns again, I raised my voice a decibel. "I've already given this some thought, Rupert. Tell Rory Hopkins the truth, or part of it. Tell him that our agency has a lead on a possible stolen artifact that may belong to his father's collection. Tell him that we may also have information regarding the missing pages of a certain diary possibly also in that collection. Say that he needs to meet with us in person before we will disclose further details, of course. We won't handle sensitive matters by proxy or email."

Peaches was regarding me with undisguised admiration.

"I would be ever so pleased to handle this matter on behalf of the agency," Rupert said hopefully. "I could set up an appointment myself to meet the young lord."

"No, but thank you anyway. We'll all go. This fell into Peaches's and my lap and therefore as the head of the Agency of the Ancient Lost and Found, I will steer the matter along myself, with the help of our African art expert here."

Peaches shot me a look. "Did I just gain a title? If so, change it to 'expert in indigenous art'."

"Done," I said, remaining fixed on our host.

"Will I need another degree?" Peaches asked.

"And if Lord Hopkins refuses?" Rupert inquired, ignoring her.

"Then I'll assume that he's not interested in retrieving his family's property and that we must look elsewhere for the owners, maybe put something out on social media."

Rupert actually looked affronted. "But Phoebe, that is—"

"Coercion." I grinned and topped up my tea.

* * *

JANE THORNLEY

Lord Rory Hopkins wasted no time in arranging a visit the next morning even if he did so through what I understood to be his late father's private secretary.

To prepare for the meeting, I actually dressed in the closest thing I had to a suit, which consisted of a vintage skirt, leggings, and a somewhat matching jacket accessorized by one of my knitted art shawls. I thought I looked rather professional.

When we met met at Rupert's fifteen minutes before our appointment time of 10:15, Rupert averted his eyes from my attire and even failed to comment on Peaches's purple leather ensemble. Clearly, he was miffed at us for pressuring him into maneuvering an interview with a neighboring peer in the first place.

"I am certain that the young Lord Hopkins was most distressed when I called yesterday," Rupert informed us as we stood in his foyer readying ourselves to stroll down the street. "It is highly inappropriate for a man in my position to imply to one of my social connections that he must agree to meet with my colleagues or there will be unpleasant consequences, let alone to do so through an intermediary, a secretary, of all things."

"There, there," Peaches said, patting him on the arm. "Don't worry about your social connections, Rupe. We'll still be friends with you no matter what."

That didn't help.

"Tell us more about the Hopkinses, both old and new," I requested.

"*Lord* Hopkins. The eldest male Hopkins inherits the title of earl, I'll have you know, one of the highest standing in the peerage after the monarchy."

"Only one son?" I asked.

"Yes, sadly there was a daughter who died at a young age but otherwise no other progeny."

"At least the heir had a spare," Peaches commented.

My research had only dredged up the barest of facts. The father had been eighty-two years old and widowed at his death, his title having been passed down to his male heir by a royal degree dating back to 1354. The family owned considerable real estate in Britain and most male heirs had held seats in the House of Lords. There was no mention of the elder Hopkins's art collecting ways. No relation to Anthony, either, in case you wondered. Admittedly, I hadn't had time to dig too far or too deeply into the man's specifics having gone off on a related tangent. Now I needed to wring out more relevant details from Rupert.

"The late Sir Hopkins had been very influential in his day," Rupert huffed, "and was a proper gentleman."

"I find the improper gentlemen a lot more interesting," Peaches remarked. "Just saying."

Rupert had decided to completely ignore her.

"So when did you first encounter the late Lord Hopkins as a collector?" I pressed.

"Mostly during social engagements," he said. "I knew that he was amassing a collection of African art and we briefly discussed it during various occasions such as parties and at the Royal Ascot. He requested that I keep my eyes open for any interesting specimens in my travels, which I was delighted to do since it behooves anyone in my line of work to stay in good terms with the peerage."

"I just bet," mumbled Peaches, busy adjusting her violet-hued bomber jacket in the hall mirror. "I behoovered my lounge just this morning. Man, was it dirty." A wiggle of her hips straightened her miniskirt.

"Did he mention his ancestors, the brother and sister team of Lady Louise Hopkins and Lord Terrence Hopkins?" I continued. "The brother was a member of the Royal Geographical Society and they were contemporaries of David Livingston, though more of naturalists than missionaries. Like Livingstone, though, the young Hopkins mustered together an expedition to southern Africa for the purpose of observing the flora. He and his sister set sail on the clipper *Away Hoy* in 1852, a few years after Livingstone's voyage."

"Believe me, the slavers beat them all to it," Peaches asserted.

Rupert was gazing at me. "He did mention his ancestors, yes. He stated that they went as far as Victoria Falls and were among the first people to see the extraordinary landmark."

"Oh, wait." Peaches, turned to him, eyes flashing. "You mean the first *white* people to see the falls. The people who lived there knew about it for eons."

"Ah, yes, of course. My apologies. An abysmal slip of the tongue," Rupert hastened to add.

Before we veered off course again, I pushed on. "And did he mention that Terrence returned from his travels without his sister? Lady Louise Hopkins apparently went missing during their travels—missing as in she did not succumb to a fever like her brother, who ultimately died shortly after his return, but one night just disappeared from her tent. *Disappeared.* Her brother's efforts to find her were nil. Since he was ill with malaria himself, he couldn't launch a proper rescue and was soon forced to return to England without her. Louise was never heard from again."

"Yes, well, it was quite a scandal at the time, as I understand, and besmirched the family's reputation since the excursion was seen as a tremendous failure financially, too. The then earl, young Terrence's father, Herbert, put up a large share of the funding himself, you see. Not only did the young lord fail to map the route into the interior of what is now Zimbabwe and Zambia as planned, but returned home without his sister. A nasty turn of affairs all around."

"But there was more to it than that, wasn't there?" I asked. "Lady Louise was actually very accomplished in her own right and convinced that there was a lost civilization hidden deep in the African bush. There is an account of her bursting into a meeting with the Royal Geographic Society, something considered highly inappropriate for a woman at the time, demanding that her theory be heard. She was removed before she could explain her findings and instead of presenting it on her behalf, her brother just waffled about making apologies for her behavior."

"Damn weasel," Peaches said under her breath.

"That's why we need to see her diary, Rupert. If it's true that Terrance returned with her journal as well as the rest of her things, it must contain clues as to this missing civilization as well as to her disappearance. Why else would Alesso Baldi rip out pages?"

"Damn right," Peaches muttered. "And why else would his daughter be pulling our strings now?"

"Ladies, if we do not leave this very minute, we shall be late," Rupert announced, checking is watch. "Damnably late. Let us depart at once."

CHAPTER 5

*H*opkins's house turned out to be around the corner rather than a few doors down. Nevertheless, I had been expecting something similar to Rupert's white stucco townhouse tucked away in the social enclaves of one of the richest real estate areas in London. Instead, Lord Hopkins's abode was even grander, whiter, bigger, and accessorized by its own shared gated garden across the street. The site of several Porches and E-type Jags parked on the curb beyond in varying states of decay was the real shocker.

"What the hell happened here?" Peaches asked, pointing to the black Porsches and E-type Jags sagging on deflated tires directly in front of one of the largest mansions. "Did someone forget to water them or something?"

"It belongs to an oligarch whose assets have been frozen by the British government," Rupert informed us. "He owned the house yonder where you will spy several armed fellows guarding the estate ever since Britain, and dare I say most right-minded countries, decided to freeze foreign Russian wealth as a result of the Ukraine travesty. Lord Hopkins owns the house next door so I can only imagine how galling it must be to have a SWAT team stationed next to one's house for months on end."

I cast a covert glance at the men in question. All were packing serious-looking firearms and chatting amiably among themselves. Though they must have seen us strolling past, nobody paid us any attention.

Several moments later, we were ringing the bell of an enormous house, very much the twin of the oligarch neighbor's but with fresher window boxes blooming with flowers and tidy potted topiaries on the front steps. Since London was still being broiled under a heatwave, discreet sprinklers had to be working overtime after the sun went down despite conservation mandates.

I was half expecting another butler of Sloane's ilk to open the door but instead faced a much younger man smiling, welcoming, and greeting Rupert with a hearty shake of the hand.

"How are you doing, Rupert, old boy? It's been far too long."

"Rory?" Rupert exclaimed. "Why, I did not expect to find you home today let alone to greet us is person. I have not seen you since the funeral."

"I've been here since my father's passing, attempting to put his affairs in order and behave like the new earl." While Rupert uttered his sympathies over his father's passing, Rory turned his full charm on Peaches and me. "And you must be the famous Phoebe McCabe and her colleague Peaches Williams? Very pleased to meet you both. Please come in."

Much handshaking followed while we were ushered into a grand vestibule accessorized by a floral bouquet as magnificent as any hotel's.

"Hope I don't have to call you 'lord'," Peaches said, grinning down at the man I estimated to be in his early forties and dressed in a perfectly tailored pair of lean-fitting trousers and a striped shirt, all very fashionable. All he needed was a suit jacket and a tie to be ready for a business meeting.

"No such formality required here. Call me Rory, please." He smiled up at her before leading us into the lounge.

"And call us by our first names, too," Peaches said. "Though I wouldn't mind being called a lady once in awhile, it hardly fits."

"I'm sure that's not true," he laughed. "Lady Peaches has a certain ring to it."

"Yeah, like a pavlova or something," Peaches countered.

Of medium height, fresh-faced, blue-eyed, and extraordinarily handsome in a clean-cut boyish way, Rory was not what I expected of Lord Hopkin's son, not that I had any expectations exactly.

In the meantime, Peaches was inquiring about the late lord. "I hear he died of a heart attack. Sorry to hear that. Horrible thing."

"Yes, my father's health wasn't the best to begin with. I had been seconded to a law firm in New York when I heard the news and raced back to be by his side, arriving too late, sadly. I've remained in Britain ever since but I do wish I'd resolved to return sooner."

"It's most difficult to decide what is the best course of action, old chap. Death is always sudden, I'm afraid," Rupert murmured.

We were ushered through a set of glass doors into a light-filled lounge area papered with a William Morris Willow print in a startling turquoise and green. Traditional with a modern twist, much like Rory, I realized. Spying a couple of hot pink velvet chairs bright enough to shock the eyeballs, I thought the younger Hopkins had to have been doing some redecorating after his father's passing.

"May I offer you some refreshment—tea, coffee, something stronger?"

Several minutes passed while the social graces were lubricated by mugs of tea and a brief tour of what Rory referred to as the house's "reception rooms" —lounges, lower floor library, conservatory, all exquisitely furnished with a mix of antiques and modern pieces. Yes, the place had had recently had a makeover. The senior lord's collecting tastes were in evidence, too, with the occasional mounted mask—mostly Nigerian according to Peaches who remarked on every one in passing—framed textiles, and the occasional display of insects.

I paused by a butterfly case hanging in a bright green alcove. "That looks Victorian. Would this have come from one of Lady Louise's collections, by any chance?" I was gazing at the display of brilliant winged specimens wishing they had all been allowed to fly away. "I researched a bit about her extraordinary life. Wasn't she a gifted naturalist and as passionate about Africa as her brother?"

Rory, who had been standing by while I admired the collection turned away and opened another glossy wooden door. "Yes, indeed," he remarked.

"What do you think happened to her?" We were now weaving through a conservatory where orchids grew among the glossy foliage and one southern palm tree was so large that it could have come straight out of Kew gardens. I peered up at the sunlight beaming through the fronds while inhaling the moist air.

"Feels like home," Peaches was saying. "Coconut palm, right? Does it produce nuts?"

"Unfortunately not. It's completely nutless," Rory said with a grin. "But that palm is original to the house and its growth means having to enlarge the glass roof every five years. Still, we strive to keep this orangery as close to the Victorian original as possible. My great-great-great grandfather built this extension back in 1839."

"Really? That's amazing," I enthused. "Lady Louise must have been around then. What do you think happened to her?" I was past being subtle. "You must have some idea—kidnapped, dragged away by a leopard, something?"

"We have no idea and it was all a rather long time ago," Rory said, turning away. "It remains a family mystery. Shall we return to the sitting room?"

JANE THORNLEY

"A family mystery that appears to be deepening by the minute," Peaches pressed. "After all, somebody ripped pages from her diary which can only mean that they must contain something important."

Rory abruptly swung around. "Exactly what information do you have regarding that?" He was addressing all three of us. Then just as suddenly, he smoothed down his tone and added with a wry grin: "I'm sure you can understand how eager we are to retrieve our lost property."

"Of course we do, my good man," Rupert assured him.

"Such as the mask?" Peaches asked.

Rory's gaze swerved in her direction, the smooth charm hardening again. "*The mask?* We are missing more than a mask, more even than the diary pages, and they were all stolen from this very house. We want them returned as soon as possible. I'm sure you realize how difficult that will be under the circumstances. What exactly do you know about this situation?"

At last, we had arrived at the crux. I took a deep breath. "Our job is to repatriate lost art and artifacts to the original owners so, of course, we'll help any way we can but you need to help us, too."

"Answering my questions fully would be a good start," Peaches added. "When did this theft occur and do you have any idea who the perps are?"

Rory spun on his heels and marched from the conservatory, the rest of us scrambling after. "Just as I thought. You don't know a thing," he muttered.

"Rory," I called. "Talk to us. We do have a lead on who may be behind the theft."

He was halfway back to the lounge before stopping to face me. "Do you now? And do you have the pieces in your possession or not?"

I hesitated. "How many are there?"

"As I suspected—not." He turned and continued striding towards the lounge.

"I hesitate because it's complicated," I called after him. "We have one piece but not all. We don't even know how many are missing."

That stopped him. He turned again. "Which piece?"

"I received a mask that Sir Rupe here identified as having sold to your dad awhile ago," Peaches began.

"May 15, 2013, to be precise. I checked my records," Rupert added.

"Louise's mask but not the two Nyami Nyami and the diary pages?" Rory demanded.

"The two what what?" Peaches asked. "No diary pages, no, and what the hell is a Nyami Nyami? We think we have a lead to get the pages back, at the least, and we do have the mask. It was literally dropped on my door by the daughter of an arms dealer," she explained. "Now, if you want our help, cough up the details, old boy, or your collection will just stay lost."

Rory stood gazing from one of us to the other. "An arms dealer's daughter dropped off Louise's mask on your doorstep? Is this some kind of joke?"

Shit. I really hadn't planned to disclose that so soon but now had to wade into the sludge. "No joke. Let's talk."

He stared at us for a minute before abruptly striding back the way he had come. "Follow me."

That sent the three of us scurrying after him up the grand staircase and down the top floor corridor, me taking in the mix of contemporary and vintage art along the way. At the end of the hall beside a tall arched window, Rory inserted a key, tapped a code into a wall panel, and led us into a dark room.

I stood breathless waiting for the lights to turn on, catching the scent of aged wood, something spicy, and the stuffiness of a long-enclosed space. The room felt alive somehow but maybe that was just the human-like shapes I sensed standing nearby in the darkness. I shoved my hands into my jacket pocket and counted the seconds.

When everything burst into view at last, I almost gasped. We were surrounded by standing wooden sculptures and mounted masks with frightening expressions flounced with brilliant feathers and rimmed with animal fangs. Illuminated display cases of seemingly every size and shape could be seen in almost every direction. It was an explosion of emotion and color frozen in a film of time and dust, the energy of the makers still pulsing into the air around the objects they'd created.

"Oh, my God!" Peaches exclaimed. "Look at this!"

"It was once a ballroom, now a museum of sorts," Rory said quietly ,"and represents my family's obsession with all things African, which began long ago with Terrence and Louise Hopkins, both naturalists and at least one a gifted illustrator. My father carried the torch almost single-handedly until his death."

"Like wow." Preaches whistled as she gazed up at a life-size ceremonial costume. "Zulu! Look at that beadwork! I mean, how fabulous is that?"

"Yes, well," Rupert said with a cough while shuffling a few inches away from the warrior. "Badly in need of dusting, old chap," he said to the mannequin. "When last I saw this...area—," he gazed at Rory, "—the collection was much tidier."

"The collection, in fact the room itself, has remained exactly as was following the break-in over a year ago, at my late father's instructions, I might add. Or, at least, I believe they were my father's instructions " Rory strode around the display cases running his hands through his short hair. "They did sweep up once in awhile but that's about it."

"This happened a year ago?" Rupert asked.

"Yes. I wanted to call in the police immediately but apparently that was not what my father wanted and since I was in New York at the time, hardly had a say. My father was unconscious directly following the event and suffered a heart attack hours later."

"He was here when they broke in?" I exclaimed.

"Yes, indeed. He had been suffering with bouts of dementia before the robbery but still had the presence of mind to add instructions in his will of which his secretary knew the contents but not I." Rory paused long enough to get ahold of his emotions.

"I'm so sorry," I whispered.

"By the time I'd returned from New York a day later," he said, his voice hitching, "my dad was gone and the room under lock and key. At first I had no idea why the police were not brought in immediately until Sydney Preston-Baron explained the details."

"Sydney Preston-Baron? That was the man to whom I spoke on the phone when arranging this interview?" Rupert asked. "He is still employed, dear chap?"

"My father's will states that his secretary, Preston-Baron, was to remain in charge of his collection until his passing or until he decided to relinquish control. Though I've technically inherited the collection, apparently I get my father's secretary, too."

"What the blasted occurred during the break-in, do you know?" Rupert huffed. "Obviously, your father was assaulted but did he recognize his attackers?"

"I'd rather Preston-Baron tell you himself since he's been running the show on my father's behalf. He just texted to say he is on the way down." Rory lifted his mobile by way of proof. "Feel free to look around in the meantime."

But I wanted answers now. "Did your father recognize the attackers?" I asked.

"He said very little, apparently," Rory acknowledged.

Which didn't answer my question.

"And the robbery occurred in this house?" Rupert enquired.

"In this very room," Rory said with a nod. His gaze scanned the area, every fiber in his body tense.

"And the police have not found the suspects?" Rupert huffed.

"They were not properly informed."

That took a moment to digest. Rupert's busy eyebrows shot upwards. "Dear boy, you must realize that any home invasion and assault is a serious offense. Your father expired as a result! Besides the damage done to your father and his property, the matter is of great interest to your neighbors, also, and the police should have been duly informed to protect us all. This is most irregular and I—"

"Not my decision" was Rory's clipped response as he strode away thumbing a text into his phone.

I felt something vibrate on my own device and pulled it out to read a message from Evan:

> Phoebe, there's more going on here than you realize.
>
> Me: Then fill me in.
>
> Evan: I'll be waiting for you at Dad's house as soon as you're finished, at which point I'll share all.

When I looked up minutes later, everyone had wandered away. To the left, I could just see Peaches studying something down a long aisle. Turning, I stared down another passageway that appeared to reach towards the back of the room. For some reason, I could see a sky blue swath of color hanging over a golden colored haze as if an enormous landscape had been painted on the wall. I moved in that direction as if by some magnetic pull.

Yes, it was a wall painting, I realized, breaking into an open space seconds later. A mural but more than that—a fully realized safari camp constructed to look as real as any museum diorama complete with tent and cook fire. A folding writing desk could be seen inside the tent with an imitation lantern flickering on its surface. All around, the African savanna had been composed to look so real, I could almost smell the grass. I sniffed. Damn it, I *could* smell grass, burning grass, sweet yet acrid all at once.

It was both beguiling and disturbing. My heart fluttered and I found myself tamping down a roil of panic. A blue smoke-like haze hung far in the horizon as if a brush fire was in progress, though the campsite seemed so peaceful. There was even a cookfire with its electric flame burning and a tea set perched on a long trestle table nearby, complete with various plates and wax edibles as if the diners had just vacated the area. A leopard peered through the grass in the distance as if as curious as I was about this vivid scene.

Stepping inside the tent, I gazed around at two narrow camp beds, steamer trunks, blankets, a water canister, compasses, a woman's veiled pith helmet hanging on a peg—everything made to look as if it had just been left by its owners minutes before.

A shiver hit my spine. It was all I could do to stay put. A presence pressed against me as if demanding my attention and I was afraid that merely touching something might pitch me into that life. Slowly, I backed away.

"When Terrence returned from Africa, he begged his father to reproduce Louise's tent just as it had been the night she disappeared."

I turned to find Rory standing behind me.

"I guess it was a kind of shrine," he continued. "Imagine how wracked with guilt the poor bugger must have been. Granted he was gripped by fever at the time but his broken-hearted dad complied with his request and meticulously had the scene reproduced," he explained.

"You mean that the elder Lord Hopkins reconstructed all of this from his son's fevered memory?" I asked.

"Not quite. Since Louise was a talented watercolorist—an artist, in truth—it wasn't too difficult to get the details right and Terrance had her belongings brought home so they used them as a reference. She apparently painted or sketched just about everything that moved and plenty that didn't. This scene was taken from a sketch in her journal and was among the pages some bastard ripped out of that book on the table the night they assaulted my father."

He was pointing to the open leather-bound book the dimensions of magazine sitting on the table by the lantern. Nearby a pot of brushes and a dried-up little wooden travel box of paint tubes sat by at the ready. The senior Baldi had been ruthless enough, all right, and was fully capable of doing anything to get what he wanted but why ruin an object he considered valuable?

"You say 'they'? Do you mean that whoever is responsible for this didn't act alone?"

"Not likely. My father's secretary was there that night and counted at least four separate voices before the bastards wrested him to the ground, not that that would have been much of a skirmish. Still, I seriously doubt that the head criminal would have done the deed himself."

True. Alesso Baldi usually set his henchmen to do the dirty work, that is before he fell off that Florentine roof in the summer of 2021. "When did the theft happened?" I asked.

"February."

"Not long ago, then." Surprising, yet Sonny Baldi still had enough time to get her hands on her late father's contraband library. "But you must have read the diary yourself. What do you think Louise wrote that was so significant?"

"Of course I've read them. There were three, more, really, if you include her early writings, but those weren't included in this collection. The first journal describes her and Terrence's preparation for the expedition along with Louise's theories which, from what I can tell, she gleaned from researching the accounts of captains, explorers, missionaries and David Livingstone himself who had penetrated Africa a few years earlier earlier. You'd be surprised how many journals and letters there are, most of which haven't been widely published because they are either missionary in nature or focused on the slave trade. The second diary was smaller in size and describes the sibling's journey across the sea and through southern Africa to the banks of the Zambezi River."

"It can't be that usual for a Victorian woman to set off on such an expedition but I know there are more who did so than most people are aware."

"Yes, definitely. Since neither Terrence or Louise ever married, they were one another's companions. Terrence considered himself to be a naturalist and was hunting for specimens while his sister recorded his findings through her illustrations but she certainly had ideas of her own."

"What happened to the earlier journals?"

"The first and second books went missing years ago when this wing was in the process of a massive renovation by my mother. We still hope they might turn up some day and didn't get shoved off to the Oxfam somehow but so far no luck. My mother wasn't a fan of what she called 'the family obsession'."

"And the stolen pages?" I stared at the clump of torn paper that bristled like a ragged spine down the center of the splayed yellowed pages.

"That one contained sketches and drawings with detailed notations plus Louise's accounts of their last days in Africa. It was the most telling but as far as deciphering the importance of any of it, nobody in our family or any so-called expert we've engaged over the years can make bloody sense of a thing. If the secret to some lost civilization lay in those pages, damned if we can figure it out. Louise not only liked to talk in riddles but she insisted that all the artifacts she collected were codes in themselves, like the walking sticks and the mask."

"And she didn't hint of their meaning?"

"Then I guess there wouldn't have been any point in coding them in the first place, would there?" He didn't say it with sarcasm but more in a matter-of-fact manner accompanied by a brief smile.

"True." I smiled back. Surprisingly, I actually liked the guy. "I wonder why they didn't take the whole thing instead of ripping out part of it?"

"Because it's braced to the desk." Rory stepped in front of me and made to lift the covers. It didn't budge. "There was a time when my great-great-great grandfather had the idea to open this room up as a museum so he fixed everything that could be fixed. All four corners are tucked into a metal bracket which we've since replaced several times over."

I stared at the torn pages, eager to touch them so badly that my fingers tingled. *No way, no way!* screamed in my head. This tug-pull sensation mounting inside me was getting unbearable.

"So this was a grab and run operation?" I managed to say. From what I knew of Baldi, he had been more careful than that.

"Yes, the bastards took the key objects and made their getaway, knocking my father down and causing his heart attack in the process. As far as I'm concerned, they murdered him."

Of course the Baldi had an army of people to do his dirty work. Maybe even Noel had been involved. "What key objects did they take again, can you describe them?"

Rory turned away and strode down the aisle, me bolting after. "It's time you met Sydney Preston-Baron who may answer your questions to your satisfaction though I can't honestly say he has never done so for mine. In any case, he has arrived."

In seconds, I was before a lean, balding gentleman with a long hawk-like nose dressed in a three-piece suit. Middle-aged, trim, with a high forehead, his expression apparently fixed on some distant point across the room, he nodded briefly to me and waited until Peaches and Rupert arrived from opposite directions.

The moment they reached us, Rory launched into formal introductions. Sydney Preston-Baron had been his father's personal secretary for over twenty years, he said, and was now in charge of the African collection.

As Rory introduced the three of us. Preston-Baron responded to Peaches and I with a curt nod but bestowed a full greeting upon Rupert. "Sir Fox, a pleasure to meet you, sir. Lord Hopkins held you in the greatest of esteem and, if you recall, we met briefly once when he obtained Lady Louise's mask."

"Yes, indeed, my good man, I do recall that occasion and am so very sorry of your late employer's demise. Tragic," Rupert said.

"It is, indeed, yet I have full authority to speak on his behalf according to his wishes so do feel free to ask what you will."

Rory spun on his heels, took several paces away rubbing his hands briskly over his face before returning to his original spot.

"What happened, Mr. Preston-Baron?" I asked.

But the secretary seemed determined to address only Rupert and refused to meet my or Peaches's gaze. Rupert on the other hand was at his finest when taking the lead by virtue of his station and seniority so I decided to let it ride as long as the information began flowing, which it did.

"We experienced a home invasion on February 27th of last year at approximately 11:15 while the earl and I were surveying this collection," the secretary began while clipping his words like trimming a box hedge. "I often accompanied him up here before we both retired for the evening, this being his most favorite place and one which brought him much pleasure over the years."

"You have accommodations on the premises?" Rupert asked.

"Yes, rooms on the second floor. Most of the long-serving servants do. As I was saying, we were standing near the safari camp reproduction when suddenly the house lost power. At the same time, we heard a noise in the region of the mask display. Immediately, I reached for my phone but it was knocked from my hand and at that point I was wrestled to the floor, bound and gagged. My employer suffered a far worse fate as he attempted to accost the attackers with his cane after which he suffered a massive heart attack." The secretary paused, gazing at Rupert from behind thick glasses that magnified his bleached blue eyes.

"Do go on," Rupert prompted.

"Yes, indeed," the man complied. "The thieves evidently knew exactly what they were after as the entire operation was over in a matter of minutes with only the key pieces taken."

"The key pieces being?" Rupert prompted.

"The walking sticks, Lady Louise's mask, along with the lady's journal, or part thereof."

"And this theft took place without warning?" Rupert had assumed the demeanor of a Monsieur Poirot or maybe a carbon copy of some standard old school gumshoe.

The secretary duly continued. "By the time the servants heard the alarm, for we do have a 'silent alarm' rigged to alert the housekeeper and groundsman's quarters, the thieves had escaped. We immediately called the ambulance and later the police but only after we had an opportunity to secure this collection as per my employer's instructions which he had disclosed some time earlier."

Rupert stared. "What the devil do you mean by 'only after you had secured the collection'? I am thoroughly baffled by your hesitation to bring the authorities into this investigation at once."

Preston-Baron stiffened. "Dear sir, I would expect you to understand that we did not want an investigation of that sort. You of all people should comprehend the difficulties of bringing the police into this matter."

"Tell them the rest, Preston-Baron," Rory said through his teeth.

The secretary cast him a cursory glance before continuing. "We concocted a story that assured the authorities that a break-in occurred on the lower floor and that Lord Hopkins was wounded in the process without the loss of any valuables, a matter in which all of our employees were fully complicit."

"I was not," Rory said.

"You were not here, sir, nor are you an employee."

"But the police later grilled me and I was forced to lie along with your and Dad's little game even though the event cost him his life! They didn't believe a thing I said, nor do I blame them," Rory stated.

"It was not a game, sir, but the instructions of your father, instructions which I have upheld to the best of my ability for all my years in his employ. No, the authorities were not satisfied with our explanations but without our assistance could not really proceed further and now that the matter is over a year old, is no longer of police interest. Your father would never have wanted an investigation. He had been adamant that if anything were to happen, we were to bury it at all costs."

"What the devil—" Rupert began.

"Even if it meant that my father's murderer got away with it?" Rory demanded.

"In order to keep you safe, sir," Preston-Baron insisted.

"In any event, the investigation has been dropped," Rory said, turning away.

"But why?" Rupert was clearly not catching on.

Peaches couldn't wait to clarify. "He didn't want the cops involved because half the stuff in here was obtained under illegal means or, at least, is missing its provenance, right, Sydney? You didn't want the cops poking around because it would open another proverbial can of worms, wouldn't it, and would sully your employers reputation and all that?"

The secretary kept his gaze fixed on Rupert. "As I have said, I was acting and continue to act on the instructions of my employer who insisted that if anything were to happen to him, this collection would be protected against scrutiny at all costs. When you rang yesterday, Sir Rupert, Lord Hopkins Jr and I saw this as an opportunity to bring a trusted ally into the fray and to help us retrieve our stolen goods without police involvement. I hope that is, indeed, the case."

"It's not *junior*, but Lord Hopkins, Preston-Baron," Rory reminded him.

"And rest assured I will do anything I can to assist but how the devil do you expect us to find the perpetrators and locate your pieces under such a confounding mangle of both the crime scene and the ensuing circumstances?" Rupert protested.

"Easily," Rory said with a snort. "We already know the identity of the thieves and even have a good idea where the stolen pieces are sitting at this very moment, don't we, Sydney?"

"You know about Baldi?" That just escaped me.

"Who in God's name is Baldi?" Rory turned to me before demanding of the secretary: "For God's sake, tell them, man!"

If possible, the secretary stiffened further. "Yes, sadly we do believe we have that information." He turned towards the large floor-to-ceiling windows shuttered behind drawn curtains. "We have every reason to believe that Ivan Semenov absconded with key pieces of Lord Hopkins's prized African collection and that his men attacked my employer and myself on the night of the theft."

"Ivan Semenov?" This time it was me who wasn't catching on.

"The oligarch next door?" Peaches gasped.

"Exactly!" Rory exclaimed.

CHAPTER 6

*E*xtracting the full story from Sydney Preston-Baron was like prying barnacles off the sides of rocks at low tide. Luckily Rory provided extra leverage where necessary.

"Bear with me while I get this straight: Sir Hopkins was actually friends with Ivan Semenov, the oligarch next door?" I asked.

We were back in the sitting room, the remains of our tea things from earlier still sitting on the coffee table.

"I would prefer to say that they were acquaintances," the secretary stated, sitting straight as a post with his hands folded in his lap.

"More like business affiliates but friends, too, isn't that right, Sydney?" Rory said while pacing the room.

"'Friends' is going a bit too far, in my opinion, sir. When Mr. Semenov purchased the old Sanderson mansion next door, Lord Hopkins was, of course, reluctant to make his acquaintance but the Russian was forever hosting events at his home and issuing invitations to the creme of society, invitations that my employer refused at first."

"That is until the Russian claimed to be an avid collector of all things African, too—what a coincidence—at which point my father agreed to attend a private dinner party at the man's home, correct? That's where it all began," Rory said, halting in his path long enough to send the secretary a sharp look.

"What all began, my good fellow?" Rupert prompted when a chilly silence followed.

"The business dealings, the undercover purchases," Rory said. "Call their relationship what you will, but my father became a close contact of Ivan Semenov."

"This was before Russians invaded Ukraine, you understand," Preston-Baron hastened to explain, staring at a point on the far wall. "Lord Hopkins certainly did not believe that his involvement with the Russian was in any way suspect."

"Oh, come on, Sydney. You know damn well that everything about it was suspect and you were in the background prodding it along," Rory accused. "With your help, my father became involved in the some scheme to find the lost civilization that Louise wrote about in her diary. Semenov offered to help finance the operation. I came home for Christmas and that's all Dad could talk about—launching some secret African operation to find lost gold like something out of an *Indiana Jones* movie."

The secretary's expression remained unchanged. "Your father has always been fascinated by the possibilities, yes."

"More than fascinated, more like obsessed. He and Semenov were researching southern Africa attempting to put the clues together to retrace Terrence's and Louise's steps during their expedition—bloody madness, the whole thing! Luckily Covid was still making matters difficult and when that lifted, something changed Dad's mind."

"The Russian invasion of Ukraine, to be exact," Preston-Baron said. "Your father no longer wished to have dealings with Semenov or any of his ilk."

Rory turned around. "He came to his senses finally, in other words, broke off all relations with Semenov and that's when the shit hit the fan."

The secretary winced at the profanity. "He refused to receive calls from the Russian from that point forth, yes."

"But Semenov wanted to move quickly on the scheme with or without my father's involvement, isn't that right? Specifically, he wanted that diary so he could study it more closely, as well as the mask, and the two Nyami Nyami sticks."

Catching Peaches about to ask a question, he added: "Those are two priceless carved wooden ceremonial staves once owned by a league of African kings. Louise brought two back from her travels and believed there was a third somewhere and that the three together held clues to the existence of a lost civilization located somewhere in southern Africa."

"Seriously?" I asked.

"My father would never let them out of his sight, not for a moment, though Semenov urged him to put them through X-rays and other technolog-

JANE THORNLEY

ical tools to see if they held some secret. They argued about it, sent letters back and forth on the matter. I've read some of them and they were heated. Semenov even threatened my dad."

"Your father was very protective of his collection." Something like a hitch caught in Preston-Baron's throat. "I hold myself responsible for the dreadful set of circumstances that followed."

"And so you should," Rory barked. "Good Lord, man, my father has been suffering from a form of dementia these last few years and you encouraged him to delve into this lost civilization fantasy with a damned oligarch!"

"It brought him pleasure, sir, and excitement," the secretary explained, "something which he had little enough of with everybody he loved gone."

"Wait, wait." I held up my hands not wanting to dissect this happy gathering too far or too deeply until the pertinent facts were on the table. "Rory, back to the diary pages, mask, and walking sticks for a moment: why do you think Semenov stole them?" Especially considering that I had been so certain that Baldi was the perpetrator and nobody had even mentioned his name. What was I missing?

"Because Sydney heard the thieves speaking Russian the night of the theft, didn't you, man? Of course, that information might have helped the police identify the suspects had they been informed. Besides, only our friendly neighborhood oligarch knew of those items in the first place."

"Did you ever accuse him outright?" Peaches asked.

"Certainly not," Rory told her. "I didn't want to wind up floating dead in the Thames, did I? Besides, Semenov covered his tracks and made certain that he was out of the country on the night of the heist, no doubt planning to return as soon as the deed was done. But before he could get back from his skiing holiday on February 24th, the British government seized the assets off all of Putin's closest figureheads residing in England and guess who was included?" Rory shook his head. "Now, part of my father's collection is locked away inside that bastard's house and nobody can get to them."

"And where is Semenov now?" Peaches asked.

"In Belarus, from what I've heard," he replied.

"But how do you know that he really took those items let along hid them the next door?" I demanded. "So far, everything seems circumstantial."

"Where else could they be and who else could have done it?" Rory demanded. "Nobody else knew of the value of those particular items but Semenov, and could there be a more perfect hiding place than his mansion? The bastard has a basement secured like a vault."

Preston-Baron cleared his throat. "Additionally, the Russian did threaten

Lord Hopkins. I was instructed to respond to a few unfortunate pieces of correspondence from the man on behalf of my employer. His words were, for they are forever burned into my memory: *If you do not continue our plan, Hanny, I will proceed with or without your assistance, and make you damn sorry for trying to back out. We have a deal and I have gone too far to stop now. My associates and I invested too much time and money in this. I need to study the walking sticks and mask more closely. Hand them over. Consider that an order, not a request."*

Peaches turned to him. "Was that in an email?"

Sydney Preston-Baron gazed at the coffee table. "That was delivered by hand in the form of a letter. My employer used email only sporadically and preferred to communicate through the time-honored method of paper and pen. The Russian and Lord Hopkins agreed to use such for their correspondence and to destroy the letters afterwards. I, however, chose to keep those I deemed important. I am in the possession of one such note where the Russian assures my employer that the vault in his basement is the safest place in the world in which to secure my employer's African treasures. It goes into some detail describing the security measures employed."

"That might come in handy," Peaches said hopefully, looking in my direction.

"It's the perfect place," Rory went on. "Dad told me about that safe room which he saw himself or thought he did—sometimes with Dad you couldn't be too sure—and said it was a repository of treasures, most he believed stolen. There couldn't be a more perfect spot for storing contraband goods: nick them from this house next door and deposit them in your own nearby. How damn convenient. No risk of the police pulling you over, either, if you tried to make a run for it, not that the police knew about the theft." He shot the secretary another barbed glance. "No, those pieces are next door where nobody can get to them."

"Actually, they're not," I said, "Or at least one of them isn't, perhaps even two. The mask is now in our custody and the shredded diary pages may even be in the hands of the person who contacted us."

"Who is?" Rory demanded.

"Sofonisba Baldi. Her father was the late Alesso Baldi, a renown arms dealer," I told him.

"There we have it!" Rory snapped his fingers. "The bastard Semenov probably had arms dealers in his back pocket along with a host of other criminal organizations. This Baldi character must have been involved somehow but how did his daughter get a hold of the diary and mask and can you retrieve them?"

Peaches, Rupert, and I exchanged glances. "That's what we need to find out," said I. Damn it all to hell. The last thing I wanted was to be drawn deeper into Sonny's little game but the woman had set the trap with expert precision. "Perhaps the walking sticks are in her possession, too."

"Have no fear," Rupert assured him. "If Ms. Baldi has these items, I am certain we can retrieve them for your father's collection rather quickly. I have found the woman to be most reasonable when approached in the correct manner. We shall make contact at our earliest convenience."

I stared at him, hoping my expression screamed *We need to discuss this first* but Rupert had a way of studiously avoiding eye contact if he thought it might counter his plans.

"In any case," I said, "let's leave that for a moment and focus on whatever Baldi and Semenov may have been after in the first place. What about this lost civilization, is there anything to that? I've heard of ancient structures found in East Africa, on the edges of the Sahara, and the Mapungubwe civilization in South Africa, to name a few, but never anything in southern Africa."

"Louise wrote that she believed there was such a civilization that arose around the gold mines in what is now Zimbabwe, South Africa, and Zambia," Rory said. "She was convinced that a league of African kings had formed around gold mining in order to protect their trade routes. This league, according to Louise, amassed a trove of gold and precious gems and hid them somewhere in the region. Her hypothesis was and still is startling, especially the part where she claimed that these kings hid the location of the hoard in a series of codes and clues embedded into the local mythology."

"Cool," Peaches said.

"She claimed that the local mythology encoded into traditional art such as masks and the walking sticks would lead searchers to a stash of African gold and the remains of this ancient civilization. Her drawings and research were extensive as well as impressive," Rory continued.

"Surely you have a copy of the diary other than the original book?" I asked.

"Certainly," Preston-Baron replied, seeming to rouse himself from his thoughts. "We have both photocopies and pictorial representations of each page. However, it was Semenov's contention that Lady Hopkins had added additional notations in some kind of code of her own and it was on that point that he wished to remove the pages to apply them to a light table for further scrutiny. Lord Hopkins could not bear the thought of harming so much as a single sheaf and so forbid the diary's removal."

And look how that turned out? seemed to hover in the air unspoken.

"Provide us with a copy of diary pages, old boy, and we shall begin work immediately," Rupert announced with more energy than I'd heard in his voice for many months.

"You are going to help us, then?" Rory said, his face alight.

"Most certainly," Rupert assured him, getting to his feet. "Our mission is to assist with the repatriation of lost objects and the first thing we must assess is whether Ms. Baldi also has these walking sticks, at which point we can return your father's property as soon as possible."

"Once we assess who exactly they originally belong to, that is," Peaches said under her breath, sending a sidelong glance at Rupert.

"Excellent. I shall fetch the diary photocopies," Preston-Baron said, dashing from the room.

Several minutes later, after we had made our way into the foyer, the secretary was waiting with a leather folder tucked under his arm. Though I held out my hands, Preston-Baron placed the item into Rupert's grasp.

"This will no doubt provide much fascinating reading," Rupert remarked, patting the folio's leather cover. To Rory, he added: "We will take a great deal of pleasure retrieving your dear father's stolen items so that you may rest comfortably in the knowledge that your family's prized collection is once again where it belongs."

Sydney Preston-Baron actually gave him a slight bow. "Lord Hopkins was wise to have put his faith in you."

"Here, let me give you my card," Rory said, handing us each one. "Please contact me directly if you need anything, anything at all. I can't tell you how relieved we are to hear that you will help," Rory told him.

"I am so delighted that you will assist," Preston-Barron remarked, staring at some point on the wall.

I didn't want to hang around to overhear more barbs between the two men so ushered my colleagues out the door as quickly as possible.

"We'll be in touch," I assured Rory before bolting down the walk.

CHAPTER 7

"Rupert!" I hissed, catching up to him. "Why are you promising our services before discussing it with the rest of us? Whatever happened to your usual caution?"

He raised an eyebrow at me. "Why would I use caution to assist a neighbor who is also an earl with the repatriation of his stolen artifacts? Why, Phoebe, retrieving stolen art is both my modus operandi and, indeed, the very mission of The Agency of the Ancient Lost and Found."

I hated it when he did that. "Not when it involves a Russian oligarch and the daughter of an arm's dealer," I pointed out.

"All we need do is request that Ms. Baldi return the items that her father doubtless absconded with and the matter will be settled. My, it's so blasted hot still! I cannot believe I am saying this aloud but England needs a spot of rain!" We were growing closer to his house and Rupert was huffing along at more than his usual speed while wiping his brow with a handkerchief.

"You're missing an important point, aren't you, Rupe?" Peaches said, striding on his opposite side. "Baldi isn't going to just pass over the diary pages and conveniently put the walking sticks into our hands. She wants something in return."

"Yeah, me," I said. "Specifically, my lost-art sniffer-dog capabilities."

We were on the way up Rupert's walk when the front door opened and Evan stepped into view wearing a certain sternness in his expression.

"You were listening in to the whole meeting, weren't you?" I whispered as I passed him into the foyer, my fingers brushing his.

"Definitely," he said loudly enough for the others to hear. "This being agency business, of course I need to remain informed," he said. "Though I wasn't officially invited, I have your phones set on eavesdrop mode."

"Not mine," Peaches said with a grin. "I keep that feature switched off following the instructions you provided in the manual that nobody reads."

"What do you say, my boy?" Rupert addressed his son as we stood in the foyer moments later. Sloane was busy offering us tall glasses of lemonade plus rolls of cool damp hand towels. "Thank you, Sloane, dear chap. Isn't this the most exciting thing—African gold, secrets buried in artifacts, an explorer missing since the nineteenth century?" he asked, turning to us. "I haven't been so excited for a very long time. Why, we must contact Ms. Baldi at once and request her assistance."

"No, we must not contact Ms. Baldi at once," said Evan between his teeth. "She's setting a trap, Dad, and you're leading Phoebe and the team right into its jaws. Stop and reflect for a moment."

"I am reflecting, dear boy," said Rupert, his enthusiasm clearly undiminished. "I am suggesting nothing untoward but to request the missing artifacts from Ms. Baldi, a request to which I am certain she may readily agree since she has already delivered one item to Penelope unbidden. Our relations, if you recall, have been most cordial. She was so very gracious when she saved your life in Capri."

"Would that be after you arrived on the island just in time to miss all the action such as when she threatened Phoebe, Rupe?" Peaches enquired. "Fact is, you have no idea as to the true nature of this woman. Would you risk Phoebe's health and safety to appease some deceased hoity-toity earl next door?"

"Certainly not!" Rupert glared at her as if trying decide whether or not to be offended or apologetic. "Of course, I would do nothing to endanger dear Phoebe. What a thought! I merely suggest that we approach Ms Baldi reasonably in the spirit of cooperation."

There are none so blind...

We began strolling down the hall, as much to break the tension as to find some place more comfortable. Evan slipped an arm over my shoulders and pulled me close. "What did you think of the players in the Hopkins family drama?" he whispered into my ear.

I smiled up at him and tried to answer as fully as possible despite the man's distracting closeness. "A few bad actors. I can't speak for the deceased earl obviously, but his son Rory is pretty frustrated by his father's relationship with Ivan Semenov, a liaison that Sydney Preston-Baron—don't get me started on him—appears to have encouraged. I liked Rory, though. I think he's genuine. What's yours?"

"The Interpol version is more fact-based, of course, but my assessment aligns with yours. I'll disclose more once we're settled." He kissed me briefly on the cheek before releasing me.

We had reached the back garden where tall plane trees cast shady patterns onto the flagstones amid the surrounding topiaries and potted ornamentals. Beyond an opening in the box hedge, the southern fountain featuring a reproduction—or, at least, I hoped it was a reproduction—of a classical Venus could be seen sprinkling cooling spray into a marble basin while all around wafted the scent of Rupert's prized roses. Tall stone walls further enclosed the space creating a deceptively country feel to Rupert's slice of urban London that was seductively relaxing, almost magical.

Sloane led us to a table set under an awning on the main patio. Before the butler retreated, he extended an invitation for us to join Rupert for an early supper which it appeared that his employer had planned beforehand, to which we agreed.

The moment the man retreated and we were all seated in the cushioned wrought-iron chairs, Evan offered his research, one hand tapping the table top as he spoke. "While listening in on your recent conversation with Rory Hopkins and his father's secretary, I was simultaneously investigating Ivan Semenov through the Interpol database. It appears that the man has remained active despite the Western governments' freeze on his assets. Semenov is one of the few in Putin's circle that has yet to succumb to poisoning, some strange suicide, or an unfortunate defenestration."

"Defenestration?" Peaches asked.

"That's when somebody is murdered by being pushed from a window," I explained. "It's a popular technique among Russian hitmen."

"It is a word derived from the French root 'fenestra' or window," Rupert further clarified.

"Oh, that's helpful," Peaches muttered.

"In any case, these oligarchs have long tentacles that can remained well-greased by financial infusions despite sanctions, especially if they have investments in countries like Africa."

"So is Semenov in Africa?" Peaches asked.

"Nothing to confirm that either way but he does have interests there, including a safari lodge on the banks of the Zambezi River, an investment which appears to have included several financial backers over the past two years, including both Sir Hanley Hopkins and Alesso Baldi, to name but two. Hopkins withdrew his funds following the Ukrainian invasion but there's indication that Baldi only increased his involvement before his death. Perhaps Sofonisba has a foot in that operation since she's inherited her father's empire."

I turned to catch his eye. "Which is what brought her to our door in the first place, damn it. Okay, so now we know where she's coming from. Does this mean is that Alesso Baldi, Ivan Semenov, and Hanley Hopkins may have gone ahead in some way with plans to find this lost civilization?"

"So we believe," Evan said. "They are at least making the attempt."

"Then they must be using this safari lodge as a front," I said.

"A front and a launching pad for their explorations, is our thinking," Evan said, his tone measured but his eyes communicating something quite different. "Interpol was aware of the attack on Hopkins and thought it suspicious on all counts. Had the man not died of a heart attack, it would have been a clear case of murder. Lord Hopkins has been on our radar since he began dealings with Semenov and we are unconvinced that Sydney Preston-Baron has not been involved somehow but have no evidence. In any case, the picture is beginning to become clear."

Peaches jumped to her feet. "What's becoming clear is that these bastards are trying to steal a treasure from Africa to fund arms and weapons. Oh, my God, I could just scream! They're in there right now trying to find Louise Hanley's lost civilization for the sole purpose of stealing that heritage from the African people for their own foul purposes! Holy shit, will it never end? Are we just going to stand by and let that happen? The people of Africa are starving! They need their own resources and not have it ripped out from under their feet by these underhanded, despicable murdering bastards!"

Everything fell briefly silent but for the tinkle of the fountain, a siren wailing from somewhere nearby, and Peaches's sandals scuffing back and forth across the pavers.

"Dear Penelope," Rupert began after a moment, "Nobody disagrees with you on any of these statements and you must know that we share your concerns."

"Of course we do," I agreed.

"We certainly understand your fury," Evan continued, "but please calm down and help us approach this with a cooler mind. You know that nothing is simple, especially where the agency is concerned, and when you begin mixing in politics with Phoebe plus arms dealers and oligarchs in Africa, it becomes a toxic stew that we can't simply leap into."

"But if we don't do something about this, evil keeps on winning," she countered. "And Africa keeps losing. Are we going to let that happen?" It was a demand, a call to arms, a surge of rage and fury.

"Nobody said we weren't going to do something, Peach, but we must be just as strategic as the criminals involved in this mess," I cautioned. "Besides, I'm terrified of being dragged down into some traumatic timewalking event again—don't want to go there. What if I can't drag myself back?"

"Yeah, I know, Phoeb. We can't let that happen." She was standing in front of me now, her eyes blazing both hope and a promise. She badly wanted to dive right into this deadly tangle.

I gazed up at her from where I sat rigid in my chair, hunching in on myself as if I was locked in a snowstorm. "Remember that Sonny's prime goal from day one has been to use my sniffer-dog capabilities to find lost treasure and take half of whatever I—we—find. Do you really want to go there? You know that anything she does comes at a cost and with consequences, especially for me." I knew where this was going and I was on a train barreling down the tracks with no way to jump off. Damn Sonny.

"Yeah, I know," she said softly, her eyes fixed on mine, her rage simmering down into that cool resolution I knew too well. "There's no way I would agree to letting her steal half of anything ever again let alone jeopardize you—not if I have anything to do with it. But what if we could stay one step ahead of her and make damn sure that we find whatever she's looking for before anyone else?"

Here it comes.

"It's Interpol's belief that Semenov's African initiative has hit a roadblock over the past few months," Evan continued, his hand reaching for mine, squeezing tight. "Sofonisba Baldi didn't appear to be actively involved until now but it seems that she's decided to step out from the shadows."

"More like slither," Peaches muttered.

Evan grimaced, fixing his gaze towards the sun sinking behind the trees while he kept holding my hand. "Slither like a pit viper is the perfect analogy. Since the woman had the mask in her possession and perhaps the diary pages, too, I'm guessing she knows exactly where the walking sticks are located, if she doesn't have them already. She needs all of those components to locate the lost civilization—with Phoebe's help, of course. That must be her end goal, one which we must prevent at all costs."

"And our end goal is, dear boy?" Rupert had been silent up until then, as if the luster had diminished from his glee. "Surely we must not let these walking sticks fall into the wrong hands any more than we can permit that fate to befall our Phoebe."

"You know Sofonisba wants both." Evan's hazel eyes met mine, tender, protective. "Phoebe, you decide where this goes next and how far you want the agency involved."

His support fortified me, gave me a surge of courage which I admit I'd been lacking up until then. What he didn't say and didn't need to say is that without my involvement, efforts to find this civilization, if it even existed, might not get very far. Maybe Interpol would stop the infiltrators in Africa and maybe not. More likely another travesty was already unfolding.

"We need to retrieve those walking sticks and decipher the location of that lost civilization, of course we do," I said. "We need to do it for Africa, if nothing else, because it is the mythology, the stories of the people, that I'm convinced will provide the most crucial clues, as Louise said. And we'll need to engage further with Sonny and find out what she knows, damn it. Let's start there. But I'm putting it out there that I don't want to touch anything that belonged to Louise Hopkins, just in case. No timewalking, in other words."

"Have you felt a tug or whatever it is?" Peaches asked, still standing nearby.

"I have and it came early this time, far too soon, compared with previous events. With the mask it was more like a tremor of recognition but when we were in Hopkins's African collection today near Louise's tent, I felt a sense that time was reaching out to me. It was like having a powerful dream from the night before affecting me the morning after. It's like an overlay of emotions and sensations that don't belong to you superimposed over your current consciousness. You can see the present through it but briefly both times seem to exist simultaneously. I swear, I could smell the savannah."

"Seriously?" Peaches asked.

"That mural around the campsite diorama, it was as if I could catch the scent of burning grass mixed with something powerful and evocative—moods, feelings. It's almost as if I was feeling what Louise had experienced—fear, maybe. Does that make sense? Anyway, I won't touch anything of Louise's in case I'm sucked into her existence. She's that close."

"We'll have to prevent that at all costs." Peaches nodded. "Luckily, we have the diary in photocopy form so you won't have to touch the actual pages. Let's start there."

Which we did after devouring bowls of vichyssoise, a prawn salad so succulent that I stuffed myself, telling my stomach that it was light enough that second helping didn't count. Okay, so maybe a third wouldn't, either. Then came the peach melba, a dessert I'm convinced was in honor of Peaches, for which she rewarded both Sloane and the cook with a smile and a hug in that order.

When we finally settled down to read the diary, it was around seven o'clock and the sun was hanging low in the sky with a cooling breeze blowing through the open garden doors into the library. Around us, Rupert's collection of maidenhair ferns cast filigreed puzzle shadows onto the wall.

I had just finished scanning each page into my phone and posting the file off to the team. Now we each had the diary on our phones. There was plenty of reading there and each of us were to take a number of pages for closer study but, in the meantime, we were all just scrolling through the entries.

"Rory informed me that this is the only relevant journal of Louise's that the family has, or had, since the others went missing years ago," I explained, leaning back in Rupert's leather couch, Evan beside me. "This account describes Louise's last days in Africa before she disappeared. Seems that there are plenty of observations and illustrations throughout. Listen to this."

"August 1, 1840.

Now I understand that belief is more powerful than anything. Belief is religion. Call it what you will, but I have witnessed such that I would have never have thought possible. One incident involved the sick child of our trusted helper, Makwa, who believed that a curse had been placed on his child in punishment for some feud between families. The girl was very ill for I visited her myself and knew not what afflicted the child, only that she raged with fever and seemed unable to walk. A witch doctor, a nanga as they are called locally, was brought in and he instructed Makwa to perform a ceremony according to his instructions, one that both Terrence and I witnessed with our own eyes.

The child was to be placed in a hut away from the village according to the nanga and was to remain there alone while a special magic potion was prepared. Terrence and I watched with great interest as the father and witch doctor performed a ritual that included the entire village and involved throwing a potion over a bush some distance away from the child's hut. The moment that liquid hit the bush, we heard a blood-curdling scream from the child's bier. When we arrived by her side many minutes later, the girl's legs had been scalded from the knees down but the child in all other ways appeared cured. The very next day she was outside playing, a salve having been applied to her burns that appeared to be healing her wounds amazingly well.

So I ask myself, is another's god as powerful as our own or is every god, in truth, the same god? It is as if the entire village is bounded by the force of ritual and their version of prayer cured that child the way prayer in any church might be said to do the same, at least among those whose belief is pure and not driven by words and suppositions posed by the intellect. Here belief is unfettered and its power equally so, for good or evil.

Terrence claims the child's cure is the work of the devil but if that is true, why does this devil do good? What makes us believe that we know so much more than these people who live more simply and closer to the earth than ourselves? Is our judgement a fair assessment of our superiority? I think not! No, to me Africa is still the land of miracles and wherever there are miracles, there is God, by whatever name we choose to call Him, and the opposing force as well."

I LOOKED up to find my companions listening intently. The breeze had intensified, rustling the pages on a book Rupert had left open on the desk, threatening to topple the line of greeting cards on the mantel that had accumulated from his birthday days before.

Peaches leaned forward as if planning to close the doors but changed her mind. "Okay, so Louise was a thinker and a helluva lot wiser than many of the Victorian missionaries that plunged into the 'dark continent' to convert the 'heathen savages'," she said, adding air quotes as she spoke.

"So it appears," said Rupert, rousing himself. "Many explorers and missionaries speak of the power of African superstition and I—"

"Superstition? Our beliefs are considered superstition by others," Peaches countered. "Why do we think we're so damned superior, like Louise says? Religions are all based on events not considered possible by the scientific world. Religion is the language of faith and miracles."

"That is not at all what I was about to say, had I been permitted to speak my sentiments unaccosted," Rupert protested, growing annoyed. "I was about to say that the missionaries and Victorian explorers called these beliefs superstition, not that I agreed with that assessment."

"Oh, look at this," I interjected. "The illustrations Louise included are just spectacular. She sketched all kinds of things including the flora and fauna. It looks like anything Terrence found, his sister illustrated, except for her own interests. And, wait: there's the Nyami Nyami stick. Take a look at page 45."

I caught Evan's eye as Rupert and Peaches hastily scrolled through their phones. He smiled, holding my gaze while the others located the page, everyone pinching out the illustration on the screen for closer scrutiny.

My breath caught as I studied the drawing myself. An ink sketch of a tall intricately carved wooden walking stick maybe four feet tall had been vividly rendered under Louise's pen across two journal pages. The

JANE THORNLEY

curved head of a fanged snake formed the handle while just below that frightening sight, trees had been carved out in such three dimensional detail that the leaves and branches formed a canopy under which a man and a woman crouched beside a collection of ornamental pots. Below that, the carved coiled stick curved deeply in to make a more slender staff around which one wooden ring hung loosely resting over what looked to be a ball shape that a hand held aloft. The last foot or so of staff was smooth but for a carved eye that appeared to both warn and protect.

"Listen to Louise's notations," Peaches read, catching my excitement.

"The first Nyami Nyami stick we acquired was fashioned from the deepest, darkest mahogany depicting the king and his wife guarding a treasure that would protect the people forever more. This staff reportedly belonged to a king of the Tonga tribe and I believe is the first of the three kings' coded staffs. The snake curving down the stave is the god Nyami with eyes of ruby and fangs of ivory. It is indeed a most beautiful piece of art!

This fills me with hope and excitement! Should I locate the staves of all three kings, it will further strengthen my position with Terrence that these do, indeed, lead to the remains of an ancient settlement!"

I scrolled through my phone looking for the second illustration. "Rory said there had been two stolen but that Louise never found the third."

Evan located the second illustration near the end of the diary. "Page 103," he said, which sent us scrolling through our phones again.

"Found it, too," I said, gazing down at another walking stick, similar and yet unique. This one also had a snake's head for a cane handle but the snake coiled a forked tongue between its fangs and its eyes appeared to be emerald since Louise had carefully painted the slits a deep green.

Along its length, more three dimensional carvings rested on a platform depicting men and women in what looked to be a procession around the circumference carrying baskets upon their heads. This time a hand held a smooth orb above which two wooden rings rested. Below that, a half-closed eye was inset with another precious stone—aquamarine, topaz?

I read aloud:

"We have located the second of the three kings staves!" I read aloud. *"Though we have no idea which stave belongs to which king since the tribes have been nomadic over the years. Since this one is fashioned from what the locals call muhvumira wood or 'bastard*

marula' which resembles walnut and is grown locally, perhaps this king lived in the area of the great Mosi-oa-Tunya?

"Joseph tells me that this one was once in the possession of the king who resided farther down the Zambezi, a very powerful ruler. Still, he says that there is another, secret tribe which holds the third."

I looked up. "What is the Mosi-oa-Tunya?"

"It translates into the "Smoke that Thunders," Evan said, studying his translation app.

"What is that, a bush fire or what?" Peaches asked.

"No, it his a name the locals gave to Victoria Falls,": he remarked.

"Anyway," I said, "these *Nyami Nyami* sticks are incredibly beautiful and as detailed as any wood carvings I've seen anywhere at any age. They should be highly prized as art for themselves, even if there wasn't a story about an ancient secret supposedly encoded into each. They should be in a museum or an art gallery, preferably somewhere in southern Africa, the country of their origin, where they can be appreciated by all."

"Or, alternatively placed in the origin country's hands to permit them to decide their fate accordingly," Evan added.

"But where does the mask fit in? Any mention of that?"

"We'll have to study of the full diary to locate a mention of the mask, but until then, flip ahead to her final entry. It's very brief," Evan said, "and telling."

September 28, 1840

It is night. I write hastily without the benefit of illumination for unaccountably my lantern has gone dark and my tallows refuse to light! Something is afoot beyond my tent —there are noises and cries that are most alarming! I am to remain inside as Makwa implores, telling me that I am safer here than about the camp this night—"

"THEN A FEW PARAGRAPHS LATER, she abruptly stops," Peaches said, looking up, "right in the middle of a sentence:

In the middle of the night something roused me—the sound of crying, a howl of pain beyond the tent. I bounded out of bed and ran towards the opening afraid that they had come for me at last. I would not attempt to shoot nor wound them in any way though I gripped my knife by habit. My heart thundered in my ears and the words of the witch doctor repeated over and over again in my memory: 'When they come for you, go in joy for the story is about to begin!' But I was not prepared and even to my own ears, all I heard was panic..."

"Something happened," I said, gazing across the room at my companions. The last of the sun had leached from the sky leaving Rupert's usually cosy room alive with shifting shadows. Our phones glowed in the dusk with a kind of weird alien light. Usually, Sloane or one of the other staff would come in long before now to see if we needed anything and would switch on the lights at the same time.

"So what next?" Peaches asked after a moment.

"We contact Sonny using the number she gave me and arrange a meeting," I stated, sounding slightly more enthusiastic than I felt. My immediate concern was actually to turn on a lamp, a task which had taken on a sudden critical importance.

Rupert was fumbling with a desk light near the door without much success while Evan had suddenly jumped to his feet as if sensing something.

I was halfway across the room heading for one of Rupert's Tiffany stand lamps when Evan sounded the alarm. "Phoebe, stay—"

I heard a cry from somewhere near the front of the house, the sound of something metallic rolling across the floor followed by a hissing at the same time that the air became consumed by a thick black smoke.

Coughing and choking, I swung around in time to see a dark shadowy form reach out for me, heard a sharp cry of pain before stumbling down into the dark.

CHAPTER 8

When I came to later, I was lying on my back on the lawn near Rupert's Venus fountain. Though I sensed activity all around, I seemed unable to cobble together a coherent thought. My scrambled brain believed that maybe the smoke was caused by an electrical fire—something natural, in any event—but there was nothing natural about this, not that I understood that at first. Meanwhile, every time I took a breath, my lungs burned and my eyes watered so badly I could barely see.

By then the house was teeming with paramedics, firemen, and the police. I learned later that Sloane had managed to ring the alarm before being bound and blindfolded by Margaret Thatcher. The smoke detectors automatically called through to the nearest fire station.

When the emergency crews arrived, they had found the household in shambles, several of Rupert's employees having been either chloroformed or blindfolded and restrained. Meanwhile, all of us in the library had been accosted by a form of tear gas that turned Rupert and me into tearing, coughing, choking zombies as we stumbled around struggling to breathe. We both passed out soon after. Evan and Peaches were farther away from the initial attack and had covered their noses and mouths to stave off the worst effects.

They had managed to drag Rupert and me into the garden where Evan administered CPR on his father until the paramedics arrived. Evan had feared that his dad had suffered a heart attack but it turned out that shock had caused Rupert to hyperventilate and experience chest pains.

I learned all these details only later.

"Phoebe, are you all right?" Evan was crouching beside me touching my face, one arm around my shoulders, concern vivid in his eyes. All around I could see flashing lights and hear people calling but I really couldn't distinguish anything clearly yet.

"Yes," I whispered, leaning into him. "How's Rupert?" That could be him I saw on a stretcher a few yards away.

"He'll be fine," Evan said stroking my back, his relief palatable. "He's currently demanding tea." He passed me a glass of water which I consumed gratefully.

"A herd of buffalo are stampeding in my head. What happened?" I asked after I'd gulped down half the glass along with a couple of pain pills, and pressed the wet cloth he provided onto my eyes.

"We were attacked!" Peaches had arrived, landing on the grass beside me crosslegged. "Can you believe the nerve? Bastards used some kind of super tear gas that baffles the brain as well as burns the lungs and eyes. The medics say they've seen nothing like it. They're taking the canister to be investigated." She wiped her eyes with a cloth and swore. "My mucus membranes feel like they've been torched."

"Yeah, mine too," I rasped. "But why did Rupert and I pass out but not you two?" I asked.

"Because both of you were nearest to the door. They threw the canister inside and attempted to snatch you," Evan said. "Had kidnapping not been the intent, we might be dead by now. We're damn lucky they wanted you unharmed."

"But they miscalculated," Peaches added with a wicked grin.

"You were holding your phone at the time and the felon who attempted the kidnapping must have reached for it, thus searing his palm." Evan held up my super phone which revealed a vivid palm print emblazoned in red. Something like satisfaction blazed in his eyes. "I've sent the image off to headquarters for investigation. With a little luck we may identify the perpetrator."

"But nobody saw anything?" I whispered.

"Shadows," Evan stated grimly. "By the time I reached the bastards, they were gone."

"Think it was the same people who broke into Hopkin's house?" I asked.

"Possibly," Evan told me, "but to break in *here*."

"But what were they after?" I asked, knowing the answer before Peaches spoke it.

"You," they said in unison.

"Damn! But how did this happen?" I mumbled, pressing one hand to my head.

"There's the question." Peaches swore again. "All of our defenses were down, the house unalarmed, the servants cleaning up after a leisurely family meal. The doors and windows were open. None of us even had our phones' perimeter alerts activated."

Evan got to his feet and raked one hand through his hair. "I can't believe I permitted this to happen in my own house on my watch—attacked here!" He clenched his fists by his side. "If you're feeling better, Phoebe, I must get back to work. Things are chaos in there and the last thing we want is the Metropolitan Police or New Scotland Yard assuming control."

Peaches and I watched him storm across the lawn towards the house. It appeared as if every light was blazing inside and that the emergency folks had brought spotlights of their own. Now that I could see more clearly, I picked out police officers along with other emergency personnel and unidentified people in suits.

"He blames himself," I whispered.

"Yeah," Peaches said, "and I blame myself equally. Hell, I'm your bodyguard and I let this happen? Shit!"

"You're not to blame—neither of you. The bastards who attacked us were clever enough to strike when our defenses were down. They must have been watching us. Semenov is still a dangerous bastard despite the sanctions."

"Hopefully that palm print will give something away but nobody saw anything. The servants who are able to speak—there are no casualties requiring hospitalization, thank God—say that they were suddenly overcome by bad guys wearing Halloween-type masks of famous people. Sloane swears that Thatcher was his attacker and the cook glimpsed Donald Trump just before falling unconscious with chloroform. They broke in through the kitchen and constrained the staff while gassing us up in the library."

"And nothing was taken?"

"Not that we can see."

"Then they *were* after me." I wasn't surprised. Every criminal in the world seemed to be after me at one time or another but I couldn't figure out how Sonny fit into all of this.

"Yeah, but we don't know what else they wanted besides you. Ev thought they might be after the diary photocopies. I had left them on the ottoman and after the smoke cleared, they were spread all over the floor."

"That could have been from the breeze."

JANE THORNLEY

"Maybe, but I don't think so. Anyway, whoever they were, they didn't know about our super phones."

I looked up, my eyes finally clearing enough to see the blond woman in the navy suit and low heeled pumps rapidly approaching. "Shit."

"You know her?" Peaches asked.

"Chief Inspector Drury of the Metropolitan Police Department," I whispered. "She flash-grilled me crispy over that Bentley Broadhurst museum incident a few months ago and would like nothing better than to see me rot in jail."

"For what?" Peaches demanded, turning to me aghast.

"Anything, wouldn't matter what. My very existence offends her. She knows about the agency and believes we've been given too much power and too many toys with which to break the rules."

"She's a shit-face, in other words."

By the time Drury reached me, I was still sitting on the grass, but Peaches was on her feet looking down at her. Peach knew how to use her height.

"Chief Inspector, what a pleasant surprise," I lied. "This is my colleague Penelope Williams."

The inspector nodded briefly toward Peaches but fixed her chill blue gaze on me. "I see you experienced a serious incident here today. Several employees we interviewed are suffering from various injuries and yet it seems that none are able to shed any light upon the events. Maybe you can be of more assistance?"

"Sorry, I was out cold—gassed, apparently."

"And you have no idea what they may have been after?" Drury pressed.

"No, but since Sir Rupert has a sizable collection of rare art, I can only assume that they were after something there," I offered. Yes, I had learned to lie with the best of them.

"And yet they took nothing and apparently bypassed multiple priceless objects. Amazing how these thieves also didn't realize that this was the abode of a former Interpol operative and his band of merry art repatriation experts? How very odd," she stated. "And careless."

I tried to smile. "Yes, isn't it?"

"No accounting for thieves these days," Peaches remarked with a shrug. "They hear that somebody's got loot and think they can just launch a quick break-and-snatch job."

"With tear gas, chloroform, and at least five hands on deck?" Drury kept her eyes averted from Peaches, presumably because looking up might put her at a strategic disadvantage. "This operation seems too organized and methodical to be a snatch-and-run job. So, are you going to disclose what's really going on here or shall I march you down to the station where we can speak in privacy and more thoroughly?"

Could she do that? Maybe she'd try. The woman was eyeing my phone sitting on the grass beside me before I whipped it up and shoved it into my pocket. How she'd love to get her hands on that if she could figure out how to do it without maiming herself.

"You can't take us anywhere," Peaches protested. "We're still under the effects of tear gas so why don't you just bugger off and bully somebody else?"

Double shit. Drury looked ready to explode. Visions of the gray Metro interrogation room danced in my head.

"Get to your feet, Ms. McCabe," Drury said between her teeth. "You and Ms. Williams will accompany me to headquarters for a little chat."

"But we're the victims here, not the perpetrators," Peaches complained.

"And unless you're arresting us, we're not going anywhere." I got unsteadily to my feet, hanging on to Peaches for support. My confusion had dissipated. "I know how it works, Chief Inspector. We are not legally obliged to go anywhere with you unless you have reason to suggest that we are somehow responsible for teargassing ourselves or breaking into our own house." I had more to say since my legal training had kindly kicked in, but at that moment I caught sight of Evan marching towards us, head down, his expression chiseled into signs of suppressed rage.

But Drury's back was to him. "I know that there's more going on here than any of you choose to divulge but may I remind you that we are the Metropolitan Police and what goes on within London falls within our jurisdiction," she was saying. "I invite you to the station for an interview, if you prefer that language better, so that I can truly understand the depths of the illegal activity in which your agency is involved."

Really, that was going too far but Peaches and I fell silent watching Evan approach. He was briefly stopped by a suited man asking a question, and Evan curtly dispatched him with a wave of the hand. Evan Barrows was in full command here, no doubt about that.

May I just say that a man in full command affects a woman at nearly a cellular level. Call it biological conditioning, I don't care, and don't get me started on the feminist position—I get that, too—but just then, I was loving the alpha male thing, especially this particular male doing his thing at this particular moment.

Meanwhile Drury was awaiting our response and appeared just about to launch her next attack when Evan arrived.

"Inspector Drury, may we have a word?" he asked coolly.

Drury looked up at him, annoyed. "It's Chief Inspector Drury and you are?"

He held out his ID, something I'd rarely seen him do, and I took pleasure (shameful pleasure, I admit) in seeing the inspector blanch before reddening. It's a fair-skinned thing. I had the same issue and should have felt more sympathy. Within moments, she had stepped away with him, never to return to harass us again that night.

Peaches turned to me and grinned. "Shall we check on Rupe?"

"Yes, let's."

Rupert was now comfortably ensconced in an armchair on the patio, Sloane beside him, with the cook, housekeeper and groundsman all sitting nearby in various states of recovery. Somebody had made tea accompanied by a box of digestive biscuits slid somewhat indecorously onto a plate. The police had commandeered the house and as best as I could discern and Evan appeared to have commandeered them.

Drury had apparently been called away at the last minute.

"Are you feeling fortified?" I asked Rupert, squeezing his hand.

"I am, indeed, and you? After all, it was you the unscrupulous bastards were after, don't you think?"

"I feel much better, too," I admitted, "but we don't really know what these guys were after. I'm just stunned that such a thing even happened in the first place."

"We will keep the security system engaged at all times from now on, even the tedious electronic tripwires that bedevil the staff during the daytime hours. Blasted inconvenience! Who do you believe is responsible?" Rupert asked.

"Maybe Semenov, maybe not," I replied.

"But why would he make such a move if he and Sonny are somehow in cahoots?" Peaches asked.

"Good question. Let's see if I can find out. Excuse me for a sec." I left the patio and strolled out under the trees. The breeze had picked up, cooling down the city after the searing afternoon heat and a single star pricked the sky directly overhead. About one hundred feet away, two officers were inspecting the perimeter wall, their flashlights raking the shadows.

Pulling out the card that Sonny had passed me, I tapped in the number provided and waited while it dialed, keeping my eyes fixed on the star. I had no fear of hacker's breaking into my call: Evan had made our communications completely secure.

Sonny answered in four rings. "Ciao, Phoebe. I wondered when you would call."

"Did you wonder if I would call so close to the attack?" I posed.

"What attack? What are you talking about?"

There was alarm in her tone, genuine surprise. "I'm taking about the break-in at Rupert's place tonight, the tear gas attack, the possible attempt to kidnap me."

She swore in Italian including a few juicy words that I figured I might add to my lexicon if I could ever translate them. "Who did this?" she demanded.

"That's what we want to know and thought you might have some idea. Your father was involved with Semenov, correct?"

She sighed gustily. "Yes, I told you."

"Only it would have been so much easier if you would have just told us everything in the beginning."

"You would not have understood the full history if you had not visited the Hopkins house yourself."

She was right about that. "So now we know what you're after and why, but what we don't understand is where the oligarch fits in with your plans. Care to explain?"

She swore again, adding a few more inventive and biologically impossible suggestions relating to the Russian, in particular. "That Semenov! Why are you speaking these things by phone? Phones are not safe!"

"Mine is, remember? But still, I get your point. We need to meet soon."

"Tonight, then. I will find you" And she hung up.

* * *

IT WAS close to twelve o'clock before Evan pulled up to the curb of the gallery above which I still lived. The place was thoroughly secured and alarmed enough for even Evan to declare it safe.

Usually, we would have taken the back entrance through the loading bay but today only front entrances would do. Peaches was going to stay in my spare room where she kept an overnight bag but Evan had decided to return home to Belgravia to further secure the mansion and keep an eye on his dad. The police had finally exited the premises, leaving everyone frayed and exhausted.

"It's okay, Evan," I told him as I disengaged the alarm and stepped into the gallery showroom, Peaches moving ahead on security patrol. "We're good now. Go home to your dad."

Discreet lighting illuminated the jeweled colors of my godfather's prized carpets. Baker and Mermaid had become one of England's foremost purveyors of fine rugs and I still loved living above all that splendor. Besides, with the agency headquarters in the basement level, I didn't need to travel far to get to work.

"I'm just going to do a parameter search with Peaches and then I'll say good night properly." He touched my face in passing. The poor man had to be beat. Actually, we all were.

"I'll take the bottom level, you take the apartment," Peaches called as she headed for the elevator.

The moment, they had both disappeared, I stifled a yawn and went to doublecheck the front door. It was there that I realized a figure stood outside. She began knocking sharply on the glass. Unbelievable! I quickly unlocked the door and let her in.

"Are you crazy coming here?" I exclaimed.

Sonny pushed past me. "What better place for a private chat? Besides, they know where we are no matter where we go."

I resecured the lock. "Who does?" I demanded, turning to face her.

"Semenov's boys. They knew you went to Hopkins's and know that you and I are working together."

"We are not working together!" I nearly screamed.

"Of course we are, Phoebe. Now that you know what's at stake, how can you refuse?"

"You planned this, set a trap for me that you knew I couldn't refuse. Was it Semenov who attacked us at Rupert's place tonight?"

"Of course, but that I did not expect or I would have warned you. He must know that I was playing a double game and now plans to move on his own. This puts us in a very dangerous position."

"*Us?* Argh!" I covered my face with my hands to keep myself from shaking her teeth out. "*You* put us in a dangerous position!" But I had no one to blame but myself. Curiosity had gotten the better of me and I had taken the first step, after all. "Damn it!" I cried. I actually said much worse but you get the gist.

"You want to find out what happened to Louise—she speaks to you, yes?—and find the gold for the people of Africa. Do not deny it. I know you that well. But you cannot proceed without information that only I possess. My father was friends with Semenov, I am ashamed to say. I know things no one else does. We must make certain that the African gold does not fall into Russian hands."

"Or yours!" I swung away to pace a big circle before a Chinese key carpet.

"You are making me dizzy! Do you have someplace where we cannot be watched? Somebody followed me here and probably you, too." She paused for a moment to read her phone. "My man just texted to say that there are two black cars parked nearby."

Footsteps on the stairs alerted me to Evan's approach and the elevator just dinged telling me that Peaches was on her way, too.

"In here." I headed toward the back storeroom cum staff lounge, Evan arriving seconds after Sonny and me.

"You," Evan said as he strode into the room. "You're behind all of this, Baldi," he said the moment he strode through the door. "Tonight's attack could have put Phoebe in Semenov's hands and caused a great deal of harm to all the people I care about!"

I'd never seen him unleash his anger like that. It was a powerful force and even Sonny cringed. Her mascaraed eyes seemed consumed with remorse, or something like it. "For this I am sorry. I should have alerted Phoebe much sooner to Semenov's involvement but I did not expect him to launch an attack like this! The idiot is an impatient bully who always wants his way—now, now, always now. I played a double game promising him that I would get Phoebe on my side. Somehow he discovered my duplication—"

"Duplicity," I corrected.

"Yes, that. I am very upset so I mix up my English, okay?"

"Goddamn it! I knew you were behind all this shit!" Peaches had entered the room and appeared ready to physically accost the woman before Evan held her back. "What do you want?"

"I want us to work together, of course," Sonny explained. "Together we get the African gold and we find out what happened to Louise. We do this together so we can beat Semenov and keep him from taking the gold to fund war in Ukraine. We do this soon or it will be too late."

"And why do we need you to do any of that?" I demanded.

She turned to me, her eyes searching, drilling deep into my head. "Because I have other diary pages Semenov does not, including maps and Louise's theories. My father kept those from Semenov. Also, I visited Semenov's place with my father once and know my way around. You will need me to help you break into his mansion to retrieve the walking sticks."

CHAPTER 9

"We are not breaking into Semenov's mansion!" That was more an explosion of frustration than a statement of truth on my part. I already knew that our options were limited. If my conscience didn't haunt me, Peaches would.

As we sat over breakfast at Rupert's the next morning chewing over what may lie ahead, my appetite had evaporated long before I had plucked up the second piece of toast.

Rupert was much improved given his condition the night before. The doctor had declared that he'd had "a bit of a shock" but had suffered no lasting effects other than the lingering headache that plagued us all. I also felt strangely emotional but was attempting to stifle that. Mostly we were infuriated while feeling both helpless and violated simultaneously. There's something about a home invasion that sets ones sense of safety spiraling down. But then, mine had hardly been on stable ground in the first place.

I stared glumly at my plate. Across from me, Rupert gazed down at his kippers while Evan stared into space with a grim expression grooved into his face. Peaches kept her eyes fixed firmly on me.

"How else do we get the Nyami Nyami sticks?" she asked. "Sonny—curse her pointed little head—told us that only by seeing the three-dimensional power of the sticks in person could we ever hope to unlock their mysteries. Sorry—could *you* ever hope to unlock their mysteries. For once I actually believe her because it makes sense. African art is only understood by seeing and feeling the powers of the artistry of their makers. Why are we even hesitating? Of course we must break into Semenov's mansion and retrieve what doesn't belong to him in the first place. And besides, are we really going to let the bastard get away with this?"

Rupert dabbed his mouth. "If he is aware of Phoebe's powers, he will undoubtedly attempt to kidnap her again. However, in terms of breaking into the Russian's estate, it would be much more acceptable if we were to do so under the legal auspices of the British government and to that end, I propose that I approach my contact—a very elevated contact, I assure you—and attempt to speed things along."

"And how long would that take," Peaches asked, "the speeding along part, I mean—weeks?"

"More like months if it is to be done properly," Evan said. "Approximately eighteen billion pounds of Russian assets have been seized in Britain, but the terms of those holdings require that they be held intact until further decisions are made by parliament, at which point they are either to be returned to the original owners or liquidated to assist the Ukraine to rebuild their infrastructure."

Rupert stirred his tea. "In other words, not even cleaners are permitted to cross the threshold of Ivan Semenov's abode until such time as the next steps are resolved. Should the government decide to confiscate and liquidate the assets, it would be damnably difficult for anyone to make a case for the ownership of any individual pieces that may remain in this man's premises."

"So are you saying that we shouldn't go in there and retrieve those staves, that we just leave them?" Peaches demanded.

"Absolutely not," said Rupert as calmly as if he were discussing a speck of dust on his sleeve. "I believe it only right that we go forth and retrieve those items that do not belong to Semenov in the first place, especially if doing so will assist us in locating the African treasure as well as possibly repatriating the Hopkins estate art in the process. It appears that the property has been secured by an elite private guard whose sole mission it is to prevent anyone from entering the premises."

"Well, that makes it easier," Peaches remarked sourly.

I met Evan's eyes. "Evan, where do you stand on this?" He had been unaccountably silent on the matter after Sonny had left my place the night before.

His expression remained serious, his voice measured, but the eyes touching my face burned with emotion. "Of course, it would be against regulations for me to do anything to counter a government decree nor would I want to suggest that the agency engage in such activities."

"So is that a no?" Peaches challenged.

"That is not a no," I said quietly. "That's a question—to me, actually. That's your official answer, Evan, but what's your personal one?"

His features hardened. "I'd like to annihilate the bastards who dared violate my home, attempted to kidnap the woman I love, and harm my father in the process, not to mention the efforts of their leader to rape a country of its heritage to assist with the murder of innocent people living in another."

"Okay, so you're ambivalent about the whole thing. I get it." Peaches grinned.

"But only you, Phoebe, can decide next steps" he added softly, "not because I desire to put you on the spot but because you are at the very crux of it all."

"I know it," said I.

"And what do you say, Phoebe?" Peaches pressed.

"All of you know my answer because you know me: of course, the Agency of the Ancient Lost and Found must retrieve those items from Semenov's estate, just not under any official auspices that involve Evan."

"Officially," Evan added.

"Officially," I acknowledged. "However, as you have all reminded me, this falls clearly in the agency's mission and I've known from the beginning that I can't let my own fears hold us back. We'll do whatever it takes to secure Africa's cultural heritage and not let any power-hungry, unscrupulous, brutal regime abscond with it to fuel their own ends." I stood up. "We are going to break into Ivan Semenov's estate and retrieve those walking sticks, and if it means going to Africa, we'll do that, too!"

And damn it all to hell if I didn't just issue a battle cry.

"Oh, my God, I love it when you do this 'I am Phoebe, hear me roar' stuff!" Peaches exclaimed. "To Africa!" She was on her feet, too, and soon we were all clinking juice glasses across the table.

Evan was gazing at me, a little smile playing on his lips. His eyes met mine, questioning as if probing my thoughts. He knew me well enough to know that I couldn't resist a challenge like this and I knew him well enough to know how badly he wanted to bring these bastards to their knees.

So I had started it and now I would finish it, the hell with the consequences. I would not touch anything that might draw me in or under a time-walking event, though I knew that might not always be in my control. And as for working with Sonny, hell, I'd allowed myself to be outmaneuvered, so who was to blame there? Whether we liked it or not, she was part of the team to an extent. She had yet to put her terms on the table, which meant she planned to outmaneuver me again. Until further notice, I'd just proceed as if there weren't actual terms and stay one step ahead of her.

"When?" Peaches asked.

"Tonight," I replied, my stomach clenching.

Her eyes widened with excitement or maybe that was alarm. "Tonight, really?"

"We have to strike while they think we're still regrouping after the attack. and besides, they don't know about our phones, or do they?" That was addressed to Evan.

"Maybe not," he said, "but one would think that after a phone severely burned one member's palm last night, the gang might now have some notion of the phone's capabilities."

"If the Metropolitan Police know, it can't be that big a secret," I suggested.

"However," Rupert pointed out, "even if the perpetrators of last night's offensive maneuver are now somewhat aware of these superphones, they may not realize the full extent of the their capabilities. I daresay that I do not even know my device's full capacity since—"

"Try reading the manual, Rupe," Peaches chided.

Rupert frowned in her direction. "As I was saying, Evan is constantly improving and enhancing the devices making it damnably difficult to assess exactly what they are capable of at any given time."

"Unless you read his regular update emails, that is. Did I mention that? Anything new, Ev?" Peaches gazed over at Evan. "Like maybe the *sleep tight* feature?"

"Sleep tight, what the devil is *sleep tight?*" Rupert demanded, looking affronted.

Evan gazed down at his hands. "It's still in development stage but the intent is to create a version of the stun app that is so finely-tuned, one need only point the device in the direction of a chosen target to plunge them into a deep sleep. Rather than jolting their nervous system with potentially damaging electrical currents as does the stun app, this is far milder and stimulates part of the brain that induces a profound sense of relaxation. Early trials have been very promising."

Peaches raised her hand and grinned. "I've been having the best sleeps in ages, just saying."

"You've never used that on me," I said accusingly as I turned to Evan, my eyes locking with his.

"When I'm with you, sleep is not on my mind," Evan replied softly.

"Okay, too much information." Peaches slapped her hands over her ears while Rupert actually blushed.

"Anyway," I said quickly, "a sleep feature could be useful, seeing as we don't want to harm the guards minding the Semenov fort but merely to disable them. Since they are not part of the gang that attacked us, they shouldn't be harmed."

"But they sure as hell may try to hurt us if they catch us breaking into the mansion," Peaches pointed out. "We can sever the security grid and put those dudes to sleep but that's no guarantee that Semenov isn't having the place watched or that somebody somewhere won't clue in to what's going on and bring in the police."

The thought of the police being alerted while I and the team were on the Semenov premises was almost as bad as being snared by Simonov's men. Not rational, I know.

Evan continued to hold my gaze. "Entering the facility will not be the challenging part. My preliminary research indicates that there are multiple security systems each working independently. A further challenge will be getting in and out without drawing attention to ourselves, which means that our actions must be accomplished quickly."

"Perhaps it's time to inform young Lord Hopkins of our intentions. He could be most helpful," suggested Rupert. "I would be pleased to contact him."

"No need, Rupert," I said smoothly. "Let me do that. I'll invite him to the gallery to look at a few fine carpets and fill him in on the details. We want to ensure that no one else in the household knows what's up, including that secretary."

Rupert appeared about to protest until his son stepped in. "Excellent idea," Evan agreed, which, of course, settled the matter.

"And then there's Sonny Baldi," I said.

"And then there's Sonny Baldi." Peaches shook her head. "Another wild card in what promises to be a wild operation."

Nevertheless, we devised a plan that sent Rupert off to design his control southern grid on his laptop and put in a call into what he referred to as his "sartorial wizard," who would quickly spin out replica guard uniforms matching our measurements. I invited Rory to meet me that afternoon with the intent to request that he briefly lend us his property and ensure that his father's secretary was off the premises.

Evan, Peaches and I retreated to Evan's office upstairs to scope out a plan that would involve keeping Sonny in touch by earpiece only as everyone agreed that having her actually enter with us could spell disaster.

"This will not work," Sonny complained on my speakerphone hours later. "How can I tell you where to go unless I am there with you?"

"You'll see what we're seeing as Peaches, Evan, and I will be wearing head cams that will send back images into a southern system operated by Rupert. The fewer people we have tripping over one another in there, the better. Three of us is too many as it is. Besides, Rupert has located the original blueprints for the mansion which will be available on our devices."

"What good are original blueprints when this house has been renovated multiple times?"

"We'll manage. On what level is this vault of Semenov's?"

"The basement but it is like a big bank vault—you know, steel, very big, very impenetrable, a whole wing."

Peaches mouthed beside me: *We have an app for that.*

"We'll manage, Sonny. In the meantime, we need you to stand by on your phone using a link we'll send you."

"Maybe I come to be with Rupert, you know, watch his back?"

"His back will be well-protected, thanks."

"What if I provide men to help you out, like extra brawn?" she suggested.

Now that interested me. I knew of Evan's reluctance to bring in his extended network given the sensitivity of this operation so involving five men from a known arms cartel might be useful in multiple ways. Yes, that statement might be considered counter-intuitive. I checked with Evan who reluctantly gave the nod. "Brawn is not needed but we would appreciate a few men whose only role will be to wear the guard's clothes and walk back and forth outside the estate. None of them can utter a word and promise me that they won't know the details of this operation or who is involved."

"I give you my word. Team Baldi operates on what you English call 'the need to know' basis."

Peaches rolled her eyes.

"Great. I'll send you instructions. Be someplace private at 11 p.m. and on your phone. We expect to be in and out of there within thirty minutes, tops."

CHAPTER 10

*A*t 10:45 p.m. a man was seen strolling down the street beside one of the gated gardens of Belgravia, head down, apparently intent on reaching his destination as quickly as possible. Nothing about him stood out in anyone's memory except that he was tall, bearded, wore a black short-sleeved shirt, and might have spoken Russian because he had greeted a fellow passerby earlier with what that person believed was a strong Russian accent. Other than him and the five drunken tourists that were seen exiting a chic little pub in Chelsea and laughing down the sidewalk, the neighborhood retained its usual quiet demeanor.

Whatever the case, several minutes later, one of the elite guard watching the impounded estate of one Ivan Semenov reported feeling unaccountably tired. He asked one of the standby guards waiting in the van to take over while he climbed inside and dosed himself with coffee. No sooner had he entered the van when he slumped into a deep slumber.

His colleagues immediately thought of poison, but before he could sound the alarm, he, too, was fast asleep. Within the next fifteen minutes, each of the five men guarding the exterior of the Semenov estate were sleeping in the van. Nobody saw a thing, nor would a casual viewer have cause to wonder since shortly later the five men were back at their posts outside the van, their attention fixed on business, or so it seemed.

"We just deactivated the perimeter security tripwires," Peaches whispered into her microphone. "The cameras should be transmitting that all's quiet in Semenovland."

I was standing next to her, both of us safely tucked away in the shadows around the back of the mansion waiting for Evan. We had turned off the security lighting since each of us wore night vision glasses, which at that moment I had shoved onto my forehead so I could better peer down at my phone.

"That is precisely how matters look on my end," Rupert told us. "The power in the manse has been turned off since the day the assets were frozen. However, I have detected that the system securing the premises is operated by a generator and that, should the generator be tampered with, a silent alarm will be sent to New Scotland Yard and the Metropolitan Police simultaneously."

"Damn!" Peaches exclaimed.

"Don't worry," came Evan's calm voice. "I have the location of the control panel in my virtual sights and can rig it to appear as though all is well. I'm heading in your direction now."

"Sonny, are you there?" I whispered.

"I am here," she said, "and my men are outside pretending to be guards as arranged."

Evan suddenly slipped up beside us dressed as one of the guards as was Peaches and I. He quickly donned the night glasses and headset that we all wore."Hurry," he said heading towards the back door. "No time to spare. We have fifteen minutes before the police do their nightly rounds. I will proceed to the control panel while you head for the vault."

Peaches and I stood watching him thumb into his tablet, bringing up multiple schematics of the mansion. "There," Peaches said, pointing to the screen. "Down the back staircase to the basement."

I brought the blueprint up onto my phone, too.

"But the back staircase is hidden," Sonny said into our ears. "I see this blueprint you use. It is old. Semenov made many renovations, I said. I remember a sliding wall. Ivan pushed a button or something."

"That's no help unless you can tell us exactly where that wall is located and how to open the thing," I whispered.

"If I was with you, maybe yes but perhaps not by memory alone. It was many years ago."

"Let's move!" Evan urged.

"Maybe, Baldi, *maybe*? Are you kidding me?" Peaches growled.

Within seconds we had the doors unlocked and the local security system disengaged while Evan headed in the opposite direction towards the basement control panel. Unless he could successfully override generator external security system, we had maybe five minutes before multiple forces stormed down on top of our heads.

We ran through the back hallway into the kitchen and through the pantry, a clock clicking away in our minds.

"Sonny, you must remember whether this hidden staircase was at the front of the building or the rear?"

"At least that much," Peaches hissed.

All around the strange green and black shapes of our night vision environment opened up like we were inhabiting some kind of foreign planet. The air hitting our noses smelled stale and musty, forcing me to stifle a sneeze. A sense of impending doom was hitting me that didn't seem solely due to the countdown. I was particularly interested in what looked to be symbols framed on the walls, some of which I recognized, others I didn't.

"Put your mask on, Peach," I said suddenly.

"Dust doesn't bother me like it does you," she replied.

"Just do it," I ordered. Wearing our gloves at all times was a given but the powerful need to wear the oxygenated masks we carried at best as an emergency measure was overwhelming.

"Good idea," Evan said into my ear.

Peaches reluctantly complied as we stepped carefully down the hall, turning frequently to run our footprint sweeper app across the dusty tiles behind us. "Rupert, Semenov didn't anticipate having his assets seized when he left on that skiing trip months ago, did he?"

"I doubt it," he said. "He was launching a heist against Sir Hopkins and no doubt fully expected to return to London at his earliest convenience. Nevertheless, I would be most careful to ensure that you do not encounter any booby traps as you progress."

"Everything looks like he intended to come home at any minute," I remarked, "only dustier."

"His staff was sent off the premises when his assets were seized," Rupert said. "I am certain that even a speck of dust would not be permitted otherwise."

"But they might have had instructions to secure his belongings," Sonny added. Those close to Putin have their tricks."

"Sonny, is Semenov into the occult, that you know of?'

"Like magic? Yes, I remember Papa saying that he studied the ancient alchemists."

"Why?" Peaches asked.

"Just trying to understand the man."

"He believed that Hitler was onto something when he studied the ancient arts," Sonny added.

We had reached the front of the building where we stood staring at numerous doors opening up from the main corridor and at the modern art pieces that appeared contrary to the man's reported collecting tastes, including metallic sculptures of balloon animals and large abstract art installations.

"Sonny, we need help here," I said.

"It was near the front, I remember now. My father and Semenov had just had a drink and then Ivan led us through to a den or a study, perhaps—many books."

"Let's try the library," I said, gazing at the door to our right where I had glimpsed walls of books. "Evan, how are you doing with the generator?"

"Almost there," he replied, "but we are still running out of time."

Peaches dashed through one door and swept her phone around 360 degrees while I did the same on the other side. "Do you recognize anything, Baldi?"

"Nada. Try the next," she said.

We ran into two more rooms, spacious well-appointed living spaces each, and performed the same maneuver with still no luck. I began thinking that we'd have to exit the mansion empty-handed.

"Wait, go back to the last room," Sonny said.

"Peaches or me?" I asked.

"The gladiator."

I ran across the hall to join Peaches inside what looked to be an office overlooking the garden. The room appeared to have been designed like a nineteenth century gentleman's study with traditional padded leather seats, carved book cases, and an enormous carved wooden Tudor desk anchoring the space. Framed at least two decks of framed tarot cards by different illustrators hung on the walls.

"See the brass monkey lamp on the desk? I remember that!" Sonny exclaimed into our ears. "Bring the phone closer," she ordered.

Peaches did as instructed while I stared down at a brass sculpture of the three wise monkeys variety that served here as a lamp base. It was old, perhaps even a seventeenth century Japanese original with impressive detailing. Every hair on the monkeys' bodies had been articulated with amazing precision, in fact; every detail was expertly rendered.

"I remember Semenov whispered something and my father laughed. I saw them touch that monkey lamp and then the wall opened!" Sonny was saying.

"Well, I'll be damned," Peaches mused, peering as close to the sculpture as her head paraphernalia would allow. "The Semenov bastard has a sense of humor. The center monkey's genitals move. Let's see what happens if I twist his knob like this…"

Peaches tweaked and the wall behind us creaked. We turned to watch a case of books slide away.

"Evan, we're in!" I cried.

"I'm on my way and the generator alarm has been over-ridden!"

Our jubilant glee soon dampened when, seconds later after a taking three flights of stairs down, the three of us stood shoulder to shoulder staring at a steel vaulted safe the size of a wall.

Evan wasted no time bringing onto his screen the X-ray schematics of the safe mechanism while checking with Rupert as to the status of the street outside.

"All quite still," Rupert said. "Seven minutes remaining."

The vault was secured by separate systems. They appeared on our screens as three interlocking circles indicated by red, blue and yellow.

"Primary colors," I mused.

"The bastard has a thing for threes," Peaches commented while she studied the schematics on her screen.

"The number three was the first true number according to the Pythagoreans," Evan stated, "and is also believed to denote harmony, wisdom, and understanding—all close to an oligarch's heart, as you can imagine."

"It's also a magic number in fairytales, as in three wishes. Three is also the number of time: past, present and future," I said.

"Birth, life, death; beginning, middle, and end—okay, I get it," Peaches said.

"Three is believed to hold potent magic," I added.

"These systems have to be disengaged in order," Evan told us, deep in concentration. I sensed that only a small part of him was currently in our presence but luckily there were no bad parts. "As in a Borromeam ring."

Borromeam ring? "Wait!" I said. "As with a Borromeam ring, if you unlock one without the others, the whole thing collapses. They must be disengaged simultaneously."

Evan shot me a grin. Yes, that alone was enough to fuel my jets for what was to come. "So we will focus on one system each: Phoebe, you take red, Peaches blue, and I'll do yellow. Wait for my signal before you unlock."

Evan's powerful safe-unlocking apps did the heavy lifting by overlaying the safe schematics over the x-ray images and cueing us on what to tap where. In less than thirty seconds we had the three systems ready to unlock with a single remaining tap on our screens and we waited for Evan's signal.

But something held him back. Though I couldn't make out his expression behind the mask and glasses, I sensed he was scanning the external mechanism one more time, running his phone along the online of the door.

"Evan, wait," Rupert said into our earpieces. "Observe the clear-cased box affixed to the external door to the left; it is barely visible and possibly not observable with your night vision devices. If I'm not mistaken, that is some form of boobytrap mechanism."

Evan swore under his breath. "You're right, Dad," Leaning forward, he aimed his phone towards the object. "It's a package of what appears to be some kind of white powder—"

"Poison!" Rupert croaked. "Should that door open without the addition of some final step, the case breaks ,releasing the—"

"The neurotoxin," Peaches cried. "Nasty bastards! The Russian government is famous for using poison and toxins as weapons of choice."

We followed Evan's finger to where a clear-cased little box appeared fixed to the side of the door.

"Five minutes left," came Rupert's ominous announcement.

Evan aimed a stream of white light from his phone to the object causing the thing to fall to the floor in a ball of melted plastic. "Applying intense heat fuses the toxin into the plastic compound rendering it harmless as long as it is not touched with ungloved hands. Ready? On the count of three, unlock your safes."

Moments later, we tapped our open buttons at the same time and Evan heaved open the vault door. We were in.

It took several seconds to adjust to what we were seeing—a huge space of closely-packed objects, many encased in glass, row upon row of the most amazing items carved, engraved, embedded in ivory and jewels. A quick sweep of our lights across the walls revealed a collection of leering masks with startling expressions rendered in amazing artistry.

"Will you look at this!" Peaches was crying. "It's like one of the best collections of African art I've seen anywhere! Oh, my God! Bet you most of it is stolen!"

"Straight ahead. southern cases!" Sonny said.

We saw them immediately rising up in the green darkness—two sacred walking sticks standing side-by-side—and within seconds Evan had sliced the surrounding glass. Gently, he and Peaches lifted the carved sticks and carefully lowered them into the two purpose-built quiver-like backpacks.

Rupert's voice interrupted our concentration. "A Metro police car just pulled up to the guards and asked one chap how things are going and the man replied in Italian."

"Shit!" Peaches exploded.

"My men know English!" Sonny exclaimed.

"Tell them that!" Peaches swore.

"We're coming out," Evan said. And to us, he added, "Run!"

CHAPTER 11

The next morning Peaches and I stood in the agency lab below the gallery waiting for Rupert, Evan, and Sonny to patch in by Zoom. Our full attention was entranced by the presence of the two Nyami Nyami sticks, their magnificence completely surpassing our expectations.

The night before had been as close to a precision maneuver as I'd ever come. We had only seconds to bound across the lawn, past Semenov's glass orangery, and up to the tall stone wall bordering the two properties while eradicating our resulting footprints as we went. From there, Peaches had rigged a pulley and sling contraption to lift the walking stick backpacks up and over the wall followed by a collapsible ladder that enabled us to climb to safety onto the Hopkins estate. Rupert sent a drone over the wall just long enough to check for any telltale signs of our presence.

While Peaches and I slipped from a back garage onto a side street in a Mercedes driven by a jubilant Rory Hopkins, Evan bolted over the wall and around the corner to climb into his own car and disappear into the night.

"I can't believe you pulled this off and retrieved our walking sticks!" our driver had exclaimed. He appeared thrilled to be included in our retribution efforts.

"We're not home-free yet, Rory," I warned him, "not until we're all safely back into our nests with no clues left behind."

"Besides, the ownership of these sticks is still under investigation so until further notice, stop calling them *your* walking sticks," Peaches pointed out.

83

"I understand that. As I've said, I'm behind your efforts regardless and just want to see the larger matter resolved and my father's attacker's dealt with. We'll wrangle ownership issues some other time but until then, count me in."

"Just keep that double-barrel named secretary of your dad's out of the loop," Peaches warned. "Nobody can know anything."

"I completely understand, I assure you. The man is infuriating. Rest assured that I'll follow all your instructions to the last letter."

Meanwhile, I prayed that the vault door closed as it should, that the back door relocked, that the security system reengaged smoothly, and that we had eradicated all telltale signs of our presence.

The other remaining issue was the guards. According to plan, the Baldinos were to vacate the premises leaving the real guards slumbering in the van, but it appeared that may have already been compromised. According to Rupert's report, the police drove away only to return minutes later with three more squad cars. Sonny assured us that by the time the they had arrived, her men had already vacated the area, but that had yet to be confirmed.

And then there was Semenov. We had no doubt that we were being watched but whether spies witnessed any of our activities that night—let alone saw us transferring from Rory's car into the panel van parked in the Heathrow parking lot—was also a definite unknown.

But all that was temporarily forgotten late the next morning when we studied the Nyami Nyami sticks fully for the first time. Peaches had them propped in a pair of makeshift stands where they sat in the agency lab bathed in light, completely mesmerizing. The carvings were remarkable, the pieces worked in such detail that even Louise's illustrating skills couldn't capture.

Each stick told a moving story carved three dimensionally around the circumference. At first glance, we could decipher very little—a gathering of people and a procession with a snake coiling around and through the background of both scenes. Trees and coils, curves and sinuous motion, loose wooden rings that slipped and slid around the upper stave—all emanated a powerful energy when witnessed complete even with one stick missing.

"The people along the Zambezi River saw the river god Nyami Nyami as southern to their existence," Peaches said. "The shape of the river aligns with the shape of the twisting, winding staves and they believed that anything the river gave, the river could rip away."

"They lived and breathed by the river that they worshipped," I added, "but how does one stick relate to the other? What other messages are they trying to tell us?"

"To us, maybe nothing," Peaches stated, "but to the communities that once lived and breathed magic, they are speaking of secrets that hold great power."

"Yet we don't grasp the symbolic language."

"How could we when we live here in modern London removed from their language and their land?" Peaches asked. Her gaze never left the walking sticks nor had mine.

"Yes, really, how could we? But at least we recognize a gathering of the people in the one stick and a man and a woman who seem to be stooping or crouching over pots in the other," I said. "And if those are people moving somewhere, they appear to be in a kind of procession."

"Maybe they're migrating? And those people are carrying something important. Look at the warriors in the second holding spears and arrows as if guarding the cargo."

"Something precious, maybe. Those rubies in the eye of the snake and the large blue aquamarine are pretty impressive," I mused aloud. The aquamarine in particular was the size of an egg, roughly cut and so luminous that it seemed to capture the essence of water in its depths. "If these sticks somehow unlock a mystery, then not only is the third stick needed to complete the story but we require the full panorama of the land plus a deeper understanding of the culture to comprehend. What story of three kings are locked in the mythology and campfire tales of these communities?"

"One thing is for certain, the nations of Africa were on the move in those days, sometimes even becoming nomadic, depending on circumstances like drought and political upheaval. Everybody was at war then much as we are everywhere now," Peaches continued. "All the languages—Bantu, Shona, Zulu—to name only a few—currently mingle in southern Africa today. There's something like thirty-three dialects so how are we going to trace the third stave to the third king at a time when there was no recorded history, if it even still exists?"

"Especially since we really don't know who these two once belonged to," I said. "Louise claimed that the first belonged to the king of the Tonga and suspected that this one—" I was pointing to the stave with the carved procession, "—might have once belonged to the king of the Makololo people."

"In other words, it's all boggling. I've been spending every night researching these peoples trying to keep them all straight but one thing is obvious," Peaches said with a look of profound joy. "We need to go to Africa."

Evan and Rupert patched in at that moment, their faces appearing on our large wall-mounted screen.

"Good morning Phoebe and Peaches. I am delighted to announce that we appear to have pulled off our operation relatively smoothly, at least as far as we know," Evan announced.

"With a few minor and confounding hitches," Rupert added, "such as the Metro Police and New Scotland Yard being alerted as to something unusual afoot around the Semenov premises. The Italian chaps had vacated the van and the surrounding area at the appointed time as Ms. Baldi assured us they would but not without leaving unanswered questions to plague the authorities, which is to be expected."

"What kind of unanswered questions, beside the one pseudo guard speaking Italian, that is?" I inquired.

"Cigarette butts probably containing the Baldi men's DNA. Let us hope that they will not or cannot be traced," Evan replied.

"We knew that the real guards awakened in complete befuddlement and must certainly realize that they had succumbed to some kind of sleeping aid but, of course, would fail to find any sign of such in their coffees. Unable to identify anything that caused them to collapse, the guard team, and I dare say the security company itself, are faced with the difficult choice as to whether to formally announce to the authorities that the entire elite squad had fallen asleep on the job." Rupert steepled his fingers under his chin. "I'd say that such an admission would best not be disclosed should the company wish to retain such lucrative employment, wouldn't you say?"

"And," Evan added, "neither New Scotland Yard nor the Metro Police are permitted to enter the premises unless by order of parliament which I can guarantee is not forthcoming."

"So, we did it!" Peaches clapped her hands.

I spun the camera towards the Nyami Nyami sticks. "But these staves, as beautiful and wondrous as they are, will not give up their secrets alone. We'll take panoramic pictures of both and rake through Louise's diary applying whatever we currently know to begin decoding the secret to this lost civilization."

"But that won't be enough," added Peaches firmly.

Sonny had joined our virtual gathering by then. "No, it will not but the remaining pages of Louise's diary I have already digitized—that is the right word, yes? I like that word—tells the location where she believed the first king lived."

"Which is where exactly?" Evan posed.

"On the banks of the Zambezi near where she and her brother set up camp," she said. "Shall we start packing?"

"No," Evan said in a tone that prevented argument. "If we go, and there's no decision made yet either way, you can not be in our party, Sofonisba. Semenov already suspects you so it's best that you head for Italy and keep your head down."

Sonny swore in Italian, at which point, Peaches hit her mute button.

"Whatever we do next must be handled with the utmost secrecy," Evan was saying. "Alternative passports must be issued to assure that we travel under assumed names; vaccines must be arranged that fit travel to a continent known for tropical diseases. Myself, Phoebe and Peaches are to go for certain but we we can't all travel at the same time and, additionally, we must each ensure that it appears as if we are living our lives normally up until we depart."

"We hardly live a normal life, Ev," Peaches pointed out.

"Not so," he countered. "When not on a job, Phoebe, for instance, remains mostly at home—in the lab to be precise—but external observers don't know that. In any case, I'll take care of the details and will email you the particulars and courier the necessary travel documents."

"I shall begin selecting my wardrobe," Rupert said.

"Dad, I regret to say that you cannot be included in this mission," Evan stated quietly but firmly. "Both the environment and the circumstances make it far too dangerous."

Rupert immediately launched his protest which Evan aborted by giving us a quick goodbye-and-talk-later followed by disconnecting them both from the system. I waved goodbye to Sonny, who was busy scribbling furious messages onto random pieces of paper and holding them up to the screen, and ended the session, too.

Peaches turned to me. "So, who's going to win that argument in the end, Evan or Rupe?"

"Rupert, hands down," I said.

"Seriously?"

"Oh, yes. Just watch."

"By the way," my friend said. "When you arrive in Africa you'll be in for a bit of a shock."

"I'm expecting it, maybe from multiple angles. Which one are you referring to?"

She wore a wry grin. "I'm referring to you experiencing for the first time what it's like to be a minority and I won't be there to help you through it at first. Just remember that anytime you feel like one in a million, you'll still be one in a million."

Good advice for any human.

CHAPTER 12

Our preparation for Africa was not only a matter of aliases and vaccinations but an investigative mission that must be enacted in a land that had suffered multiple setbacks including political upheaval, famine, and drought. The additional presence of Semenov's team infiltrating the continent looking for a cache of treasure would further complicate things since we would have no idea how to identify friend from foe.

Zimbabwe was desperately attempting to resuscitate its tourist industry and to that end the various game lodges and facilities we researched near the Zambezi River were surprisingly luxurious and mostly foreign-backed. Evan selected the Zambezi Expedition Lodge positioned halfway between Victoria Falls and the Teak Guest Lodge, the latter reportedly owned and operated by Ivan Semenov and his investors. Additionally, we were to be part of an elite private safari group that would deliver us to our lodge.

Evan left for Africa two days later while Sonny dispatched herself to Italy convinced that Semenov's men were already on her heels. Peaches refused to leave until I was safely on the plane. We were to meet up a week later at the Zambezi Expedition Lodge under assumed aliases. Only Evan and I would rendezvous at the Harare Airport in advanced since we would be continuing on to Victoria Falls, our first stop, as a married couple—Julie and Harold Thorne. Since Evan had already left before I read the particulars of the assignment, I didn't have a chance to comment. Or respond. Or anything.

Typical of the man, detailed descriptions of how we were to behave according to our cover identities were suggested to us in advance. I was to play a tentative and easily frightened wife of an overbearing husband traveling to Africa on our third wedding anniversary.

He texted me later:

> Do you approve of your assignment?
>
> Me: Are you kidding? I've grown over the years into a kick-a** woman and you want me to play a snowflake??
>
> Evan: As long as you melt into my arms. This will make an excellent cover.

He sent his usual array of animated gifs including chiming wedding bells, which I assume referred to our pseudo anniversary celebrations. Still, it puzzled me. Why wedding bells? Was this some kind of hint or just a joke? It's true that he had alluded to the two of us formalizing our relationship in the recent past but I had always shut that conversation down. I wasn't ready, was I? What did pushing forty years old have to do with anything?

"I'm nervous about this one," I confessed to Peaches by video call the day before the two of us were to leave separately on different flights. Peaches was to take the Eurostar to Paris and fly from there.

"Yes, me, too, only for other reasons. Anyway, tomorrow we fly and today I have to head for the doc's. Will you be okay while I'm gone? I'll come right over the minute I'm out. His office is just off Church Street."

"Of course I will!" I said, directing a look of mock outrage in her direction. "All I do is hang around the lab all day, anyway. Besides, I have to pack, though I've been told that a new wardrobe awaits me in Africa."

"Don't tell me any details." She grinned. My friend was obviously enjoying this—the pending voyage to Africa, Evan's insistence on false identities, the whole thing. "Anyway, don't budge until I arrive. Besides, you need to rest. You haven't been yourself since the attack. See you later." She clicked off.

Meanwhile, I had printed out a sectional panoramic photo of each of the two staves and laid them on the light table in the lab along with an enlarged version of Louise's illustrations.

Rory had mentioned that Louise had added codes to her drawings but the only thing I could distinguish was a tiny figure inscribed over the illustrations above each of the staves' southern figures. One appeared to have a man and a woman stooped over a set of decorated pots and above the head of the female, she had jotted the letter "P". Beside the lead figure in the processional carving, a man wearing what looked to be a crown of feathers with armbands decorating his muscled biceps, a tiny "K" had been added. What did those mean?

And then there was the mask. No distinguishing features that we could see. It appeared to be a ceremonial mask as most were but how this one related to the staves was lost on me. Frustrated by my lack of progress, I began to stare into space, my head still foggy from the gas attack. I was not my usual productive self.

That left me to ruminate over my minimal packing efforts. Evan had suggested that I bring a medium-size suitcase but to leave it mostly empty. Curiouser and curiouser. Since I didn't have a case of my own fitting that description, I had borrowed Max's, which smelled faintly of his Bay Rum aftershave. August is the wind-down of winter in the southern hemisphere. It would be warm in the daylight hours and chilly at night so I needed layers, but warmth could not come by way of my art knit wraps. I gazed down into my nearly empty suitcase thinking of its owner.

Thoughts of Max sent me downstairs into the gallery to where my godfather stood, head bent over an auction catalogue for rare carpets and textiles. The gallery didn't open until 1:00 p.m. that day so we had all that glory of color and pattern to ourselves.

"Phoebe, darlin'," he said, looking up. Today dressed in a silk shirt and pinstriped trousers, he looked every inch the energetic seventy-four-year-old man he was. "Did the luggage work?"

"Perfectly, thanks." It had been hard going between us while I had been focused on bringing Noel to his knees but ever since the episode in Capri, Max had finally resigned himself to the true nature of his son. Now all had been forgiven between us including the early days when he had played a role in deceiving me. We were moving on in the truest sense of the word. It felt good, it felt right, and I hadn't realized how much I had missed our early camaraderie.

"You look a mite out of sorts today, Phoebe," he said turning to gaze at me, his blue eyes searching my face. "Is everything all right or are you still recovering from whatever it was that you won't tell me about?"

We had agreed that agency business must be kept secret and that Max not be brought into the loop unless completely necessary. Now that we had drawn a clear line between the gallery and the agency, that made sense—mostly. When I dragged myself home the morning after the attack, no questions were asked. Well, that's not true: they were asked, just not answered.

"I'm fine," I assured him, "maybe just a bit distracted."

"Look, darlin', I don't know what's going on or where you're off to this time but I know that it's likely dangerous and that some bastard is chasing you. Every criminal out there seems bent on using those super searching skills of yours for his or her own dark purposes, like I did with Toby all those years ago." He looked away, his expression pained.

"That's all in the past now," I said. Finally.

"How long are you planning to go on like this, how long can you—until every last thieving bastard is gone from this earth or until you get hurt badly?"

"I know, Max, but I just can't let go. Having this ability is both a gift and a curse but it's also a responsibility. In my own small way, I feel that by preserving art for everybody that maybe I'm helping to make the world a better place. Is that naive or just foolish? Anyway, the Agency of the Ancient Lost and Found is my life's work. I'm in it for the long term. Even Toby's supporting me now." In fact, we had been in regular contact since my visit, possible now that he had been given limited internet access for good behavior.

Max placed his hands on my shoulders and gazed down at me with an earnest expression. "I understand, Phoebe, but remember that any time that you want to come home—anytime at all—the gallery will be waiting for you. I'd love nothing more than to be have you by my side when I go off searching for the finest textiles like we used to, remember?"

I stepped away, smiling. "Of course, I remember Max, and I'll always be grateful to you for giving me half of this business, but there's no going back now, only forward. Actually, I have something to ask and I just hope it's not too big an ask."

"Bigger than requesting to borrow my luggage?" He grinned.

"Much bigger, just not too much, I hope."

He spread his hands. "Just ask me anything, darlin', you know that."

I smiled, hoping that was true. "Could you and Serena just go on another carpet hunting trip for a couple of weeks, please?"

That surprised him. "Go away? But we just got back, honey, why would we go again?"

Because I had this terrible foreboding, because suddenly I felt consumed with worry for absolutely everyone I cared for. "Please, Max, just for a couple of weeks."

"I don't know whether I can find somebody reliable to work here, Phoebe. Jenn's a hotshot designer now and Marco is a star of stage and screen. Who can I train at the drop of a hat?"

"Close the gallery, Max, please. I'll only be for a couple of weeks. You do so much work online, anyway." I picked up the catalogue he'd been leafing through, an advanced book of the offerings soon to be auctioned by a prestigious house in Brussels. These auction houses produced high-end pictorials of especially magnificent collections to provide a lasting record. "Belgium—perfect! Don't you love Brugge? You could show Serena the sights. I'd bet she'd adore that."

He stared at me. "What the hell are you into now, Phoebe? Is it that big that you're afraid that I might be in danger?"

I tried to smile and failed. "Yes, Max, and I'm sorry that I can't tell you more than that." I turned and strode towards the elevator before turning and asking: "So, do you need your suitcase back?"

His expression was as grim as if he'd been chewing nails. "No thanks. I have plenty."

That left the rest of the afternoon to try to appease my fractured mind. Maybe my mood was an aftereffect of the gassing, maybe pending death around every corner was enough, but I could not settle down.

I decided against Peaches orders and vowed to pay an impulsive flash-visit to Rupert. To avoid attracting attention, I sneaked out from the loading bay door onto a back street and hailed a cab.

I knew that Rupert was sulking, which was further confirmed by the glowering expression that greeted me when I arrived at his abode twenty minutes later. To appease the savage beast, I brought the sock kit he had compiled for me as a gift years ago, thinking that me agreeing to knit socks might put him in a better mood.

"Rupert, it's important that you remain here in England where you'll safe and healthy," I said over tea as I attempted to follow his instructions long enough to get my stitches on the three fiddly cable needles. Up until the point, I had refused to even try to knit socks as if sock avoidance was some kind of badge of honor. After several attempts to cast on, I despised sock knitting even more. "Africa is risky even if we weren't racing an oligarch to find a lost civilization."

"Risky?" Rupert humphed, his nimble fingers racing around the circumference of his green argyle-style sock while mine couldn't successfully lay the first row. "Do you think that I am not accustomed to risk, Phoebe? I daresay risk has been the very fiber of my existence over the past two decades and here I suffer the ultimate humiliation of having my own son *forbid me*—forbid me, I say— to participate in what I can only describe as the adventure of a lifetime."

"He's only worried about you," I pointed out. "Your health has not been as robust as it once was and this is hardly an adventure but a dangerous mission against a powerful and deadly adversary, not to mention a continent roaming with predators, human and otherwise. Of course, he wants to protect his dad. He loves you."

Rupert lowered his knitting, his bushy brows colliding above his nose. "Speaking of love, Phoebe, let us have a little chat about your relationship with Evan for a moment, shall we?"

I had expected this a long time ago but his timing puzzled me. I set my own aborted sock down for a moment and tried to do a cheeky grin. "Is this where you ask if I have honorable intentions for your son?"

"Do not make light of the matter, Phoebe. The lad has strong feelings for you and though I believe you do return those feelings, I can not help but remember a time when you declared an undying devotion to Noel."

That hit me like a sucker punch. "Rupert, how could you bring his name up in the same discussion as Evan? Noel was—*is*—a gaslighting bastard who tricked and used me! Mentioning his name in this context feels like a kick in the gut." And that's exactly how it hit me, and to my shock, I found the pain great enough to bring tears into my eyes. I was in danger of breaking down completely. What was wrong with me?

I got to my feet. "I have to leave, Rupert. Coming here today obviously wasn't a good idea."

"Wait, Phoebe, forgive my careless words. That was most unfair of me and merely a reflection of my disgruntled mood. I do believe it's that dreadful gassing we suffered. I haven't felt quite the same since. Please do stay. You know that I love you like a daughter and that nothing would please me more than for you and Evan to formalized your attachment with a wedding."

A wedding now! But for whatever reason, I had reverted to adolescent inability to control my emotions, as if I had been jettisoned to junior high. Dashing from the room, I passed a startled Sloane arriving with a tray of biscuits, snatched my bag from the chair in the hall, and exited the house, leaving everything else—including my aborted sock and possibly my good sense—behind.

I needed to walk and think. The gallery wasn't that far from Rupert's mansion. I'd just stride past Eaton Square onto Cliveden Road, cross Sloane Square, onto King's Road and home. Besides, the temps were cooler than they had been all summer and I could use the exercise to get my roiling emotions in line. What was wrong with me?

Maybe I'd cut through the side streets past the town houses where roses and hollyhocks pushed through the iron gates to brush pedestrians with color and fragrance. Yes, that's what I'd do. I needed flowers just then. I certainly needed something, though I wasn't certain what exactly.

It had been a long time since a stray comment had sent me stirring some emotional stew. This was something that needed sorting. At times, we all have to pause and pick around the tumble of our life events to make sense of them, to see if there was some emotional knot that required untangling. I was certain that my roiling emotions must have to do from the gassing attack, as Rupert suggested. Maybe I needed detox.

Obviously, Noel was a trigger still as was my relationship to Evan. One had ended, the other blossomed, but where did I fit into the mix? And why did I feel like a lonely orphan instead of an adult nearing forty? Wasn't it about time I grew up?

And then somewhere between stopping to sniff a mass of pink roses climbing up the side of a wrought iron railing and taking stock of my location, I sensed I was being followed—nothing new, I know, but this one felt different. I cursed myself for being such an idiot.

My nervous system jolted me into action. In seconds, I was bounding down the sidewalk, excruciatingly aware of the two men behind me who had also quickened their pace. I was in a busy city in broad daylight, I kept telling myself, while simultaneously thinking how little setting mattered to professional snatchers. There'd be a car somewhere nearby waiting for the men to get close enough to do something—stun me, most likely—and then throw me into the vehicle.

I had my phone, of course, but perimeter alerts didn't work in cities, for obvious reasons. I pulled the device from my pocket and engaged the stun app while swinging around looking for the chance to nail the bastards. By now I was on Clivedon Road and at least ten people walked between me and them. At least I got a good look at my stalkers—in their early thirties wearing standard-issue streetwear of jeans and T-shirts.

Damn! I had a feeling that they'd run me to ground if they could. I was still a good fifteen minutes away from home and I couldn't risk the chance that, if I headed there now, my stalkers would follow and try to use whatever weapons they had to kill everyone inside. Or use something or someone for blackmail. The gallery usually only had a few by-appointment-only clients on site so the venue would be perfect. After the attack at Rupert's house, nothing would surprise me.

I had to try another tack. Working on a flash decision and keeping my phone clutched in my hand, I bounded down the street to Sloane Square toward the Sloane Square Hotel. Below the hotel, sat one of my favorite restaurants—the Côte. I'd just duck in there and lay a trap of my own. Restaurants were perfect. These guys wouldn't want to bring undue attention to themselves and it was still too public a place to launch a full-scale attack. They'd prefer a more private venue like a residence or a quiet carpet gallery.

The maître d', a guy I'd befriended over the years, was just about to welcome me with his usual merry grin when he caught my look of alarm.

"A seat please, Cuba, quickly." I pointed to the one I wanted, in a corner against a wall on the padded bench beside an older couple enjoying a glass of wine. I needed someplace where my stalkers could not sit too close but where they could still observe me.

Cuba sat me down where I'd requested and took off to order my croque monsieur while my two followers sauntered into the restaurant choosing the table right across mine according to plan. Their demeanor was self-satisfied, though neither looked like the typical clientele. One was sporting a day-old beard that looked more scruffy than fashionable and the other was fidgety, as if he badly needed a cigarette. Both cast me furtive glances every few seconds and one even had the gall to cast me a feral smile.

Bastards thought they had me; they thought they'd wait and then follow me out. There'd probably be a car waiting at the curb. Usually the curb was congested with black cabs this time of day but I expected something like a panel van to pull up at some point.

Meanwhile, I texted Peaches:

> Don't throttle me but I'm having a late lunch at the Côte. Want to join me? I have company who have followed me from Rupert's. Look out for a car or a van outside that shouldn't be there and refuses to move along. See you soon.
>
> She got back to me in seconds. Why didn't you stay put???

Thirty minutes later, I saw Peaches slip past the restaurant towards the hotel, and seconds after that, a flower delivery van pulled up to the curb. I had paid my bill by then and my new friends were waiting for theirs. I got up to head for the bathroom, smiling at the two guys as I approached. One man half rose in his seat while I laid a hand on his shoulder. "Felix, is that you?"

The phone had been set to *sleep tight* mode and it took no time to buzz both men in passing with enough brain waves to make one fall back in his chair in a deep snore and the other shake his head as if suddenly dizzy. I didn't want their affliction to be mistaken for food poisoning and suggested to the management on my way out that I had noticed both men yawning like crazy. Maybe they needed coffee and lots of it?

When I left the restaurant minutes later, the flower van had two flat tires and the driver was arguing with a taxi driver.

CHAPTER 13

If there ever was an entry to another world, my flight to Africa fit the description. I was traveling by the United Emirates airline with one stop in Dubai and for the first time in a long time, I managed to relax. With Louise's diary on my tablet, a comfortable console with a bed in which to rest, and very edible food provided, I actually slept. Evan, who was already in Africa, texted to say that he was awaiting to take me in his arms. I realized only later that the message came from a Harold Thorne with no accompanying animated gifs.

There was one point during the Dubai to Harare leg when I gazed out the window at an inky storm cloud rearing its fearsome anvil into the sunrise against the horizon and felt a tingle of excitement—or maybe that was foreboding. I knew from my flight map that the storm glowered somewhere over Chad thousands of miles to the west but to me but it felt far closer.

Whatever the case, the flight gave me a long margin of musing and study in which to prepare Mrs. Julie Thorne for her anniversary travels. She was born and raised in Ontario, Canada, and had attended the University of Waterloo as a history major but had never completed her degree. Though she had only worked at a few museums part-time before marriage, she was an enthusiastic follower of anything historical. Not uninformed, then, but perhaps a bit unfocused. Most of the details of her personality, Evan left to me to color in, as was my decision to stuff my red hair into a chignon at the back of my neck. No curls for Julie.

On the other hand, her husband, Harold (Harold, why Harold? Evan did not look like a Harold to me. Did that mean that I had to call him "Harry"?) Thorne was a successful insurance man with his own company in Sussex. The two met in London at a party and married shortly afterward, and me, who always read hidden meanings into everything, wondered whether Evan was making a plug for love at first sight. He always claimed that he fell head-over-heels for me the moment we met. Still, the married part gave me something to chew on. As a topic, it kept coming up a little too frequently.

Despite my preparation for the role of Julie Thorne, by far my most absorbing homework was reading Louise Hopkins's diary from start to finish, including the new pages Sonny had provided. Every time I learned something new, caught another nuance in her turn of phrase.

We would follow her steps beginning with Victoria Falls, which though named by the famous Scottish explorer, had roared in the heart of Africa for eons as "Mosi-oaTunya", the Smoke that Thunders, a term that none of us had comprehended when first we read the words. It was there that she would locate her first walking stick, meet her mysterious witch doctor, and deepen her conviction that the African bush or *bundu* held a deep lasting secret.

Evan and I would spend just two days there before traveling upriver to the lodge that would become our home base, which happened to be less than a quarter mile downstream from Semenov's. But long before I arrived, I needed to climb into the head of my intrepid explorer Louise while remaining anchored to myself—challenging. Once, I had wanted to cross that line but no more.

Louise was intrepid as well as undaunted. Even on the ocean crossing when her brother was so seasick that he could barely leave his cabin for weeks on end, Louise was striding on deck every day she could, her gaze fixed on the horizon eager for the first glimpse of Africa. I gathered from his sister's description that Terrence was a studious, intellectual man who craved adventure trapped in a body that was given to frequent bouts of illness. She noted that it took a great act of courage on his part to even embark on such a voyage and she remained steadfastly by his side.

Eventually, their boat was to arrive on the coast of Zanzibar. Louise treated every sight with intense curiosity and an intelligent, questing mind. While Terrence the botanist sought out rare plants, his sister dutifully illustrated each specimen until she launched her own search for the secret civilization.

I read all about her travels, the research that lead to her conviction that three African kings had formed a triad for some mysterious purpose hundreds of years prior, the details of which had eluded everyone then or since. She had first reached this conclusion after years of studying the letters and journals of primarily missionaries and slavers, including David Livingstone for whom she had a profound respect. He had explored the area she and her brother were to travel not long after the famed explorer and Louise had half-hoped that she might even encounter the man himself, though he had already moved on by then.

Somewhere in the mass of accounts she studied, she had become convinced that a lost civilization lay hidden somewhere in southern Africa. The other explorers and missionaries, fixed as they were on either finding routes to oceans or seeking to convert everyone in their path, failed to recognize the clues that lay before them.

She came across the first Nyami Nyami stick among a collection of what she referred to as "curios" for sale at a local market near Victoria Falls. The piece which she found to be exquisitely carved and quite old-looking, was vastly different from any of the carvings she had seen previously. The seller when pressed admitted that he had not carved it himself but that it had been given to him, and had supposedly once belonged to a great king. Though he claimed to be reluctant to sell it, the man soon capitulated since he badly needed to take care of his family, he said. They struck a bargain and the deal was sealed. With no idea as to its meaning, Louise carried the stick almost like a talisman at first.

As she conducted research in the areas around her brother's various camps sites, she met a witch doctor or *nganga* who was to play a crucial role in her days in Africa. It was this witch doctor who warned her that possessing such a stave would draw intense magic to her door. To say that they became friends might be overstating their relationship but they definitely formed a strong bond.

It was through him that she learned of the story of the staves of the three kings, a tale that he claimed had existed in one form or another among all the southern African peoples. The witch doctor had warned her that she needed all three staves to find the lost civilization but that the path she must follow would awaken the river god and would be very dangerous. Along her travels and with the witch doctor's assistance, she located the second stave and heard that the third lay safe with a mysterious tribe that had been guarding it for centuries.

It all sounded so fantastical the way the story of Troy appeared too strange to be true until the actual site was uncovered. As I read, I wondered whether the power of the number three was universal since it seemed to exist in one form or another almost everywhere. Even Louise had mentioned it as being somehow significant. And the three kings mythology certainly had echoes throughout time.

Somewhere near the last quarter of Louise's diary, the dreams began and from my perspective as a twenty-first century observer, indicated the early signs of fever. Louise appeared to be both hearing and seeing strange things. But then, when one is camping out surrounded by some of the most dangerous predators on the planet with a probable case of malaria, a cry in the night isn't totally expected:. :Louise wrote:

> *In the middle of the night something roused me—the sound of crying, a howl of pain beyond the tent. I bounded out of bed and ran towards the opening afraid that they had come for me at last. I would not attempt to shoot nor wound them in any way though I gripped my knife by habit. My heart thundered in my ears and the words of the witch doctor repeated over and over again in my memory: speak to the bearers with respect, say that you are part of the Great Story! But I was not prepared and even to my own ears, all I heard was panic...*

IT WAS at this point that the journal entries stopped because the intrepid explorer illustrator disappeared. I leaned back against my seat with my eyes closed. What had happened to her and what was "the Great Story" and whose story?

Terrence had launched a rescue for his sister but by that time was so ill himself, he could only send forth a team of men who had returned with nothing but a mask, presumably the mask we now held in our lab. Soon he was to gather everything he and his sister had accumulated and made the long trek home where he died soon after his arrival in the arms of his heartbroken father.

Finally, my own long voyage ended when the jet set down at the Robert Gabriel Mugabe International Airport in Harare, Africa. *Africa.* My first step on the tarmac for the short guided walk to the terminal affected me in unexpected ways.

This was an airport with all the trappings of any hub—aircrafts, a terminal, the faint scent of fuel and heat rising from the concrete—but there was something else, too, something impossible to explain. It was as if the land itself emanated a power beneath my feet, a sensation that was both disorienting and energizing.

I joined the other passengers filing from the plane towards the terminal while searching the horizon for signs that this was truly Africa. The air felt hazy though the sun was bright and I could detect the faint scent of burning grass. This was another hemisphere, I reminded myself. Everything would hit my senses in strange new ways.

Peaches's comment about being a minority hit home when I walked into to the building, answered the customs questions, tried to adjust to the fact that I was only one of a handful of Caucasians. Besides jet lag in another hemisphere and a potentially deadly situation around every corner, I had also assumed another identity and was eager to find a man disguised as someone else. To say that I was disorientated was an understatement. Somehow, I managed to grab my single bag and make my way out into the arrivals section.

I saw friends and families greeting one another bustling everywhere along with porters and taxi drivers calling out their services but no Evan. Though a tall suited businessman was waiting for someone, he was not Harold Thorne unless Evan had managed to shrink two inches as part of his new identity.

Swaying with phone in hand, I waited for the device to locate his signal thinking how ironic it was that our phones might greet one another before we did. I had been warned that cell service would be spotty here but since we used satellite hopefully that would not be an issue.

And then arms wrapped around me from behind. "Don't scream or kick me, darling. That would be such an unfortunate way in which to begin our anniversary excursion," he whispered.

I swung around and embraced him, murmuring "Darling!" along with "I'm never going to call you 'Harry'!" fiercely in his ear.

"He is definably one hundred percent a Harold," he whispered back. "Just wait until you spend some time with him. Meanwhile, here we are on our anniversary trip."

Before I could say another word, he held my left hand in his long enough to slip a plain gold band on my ring finger.

For a moment, I just stared at it transfixed. "Don't tell me that this belonged to your mother or great grandmother or something?" I asked.

"Sadly not. I picked this up in a pawn shop but, believe me, Phoebe, the day you finally agree to marry me, the ring I slip on your finger will be as unique as you are, my love."

Had he just proposed? I needed more time to unpack that remark so I only flashed him a smile while gazing up at him. Evan/Harold now sported excruciatingly short hair along with black wire-rimmed glasses. Everything about his outfit was buttoned-down including the polo shirt he wore under the windbreaker.

"We have to be careful," he was saying in a low voice. "If we're not under observation now, we soon will be. Use your phone to communicate anything sensitive and avoid speaking as ourselves unless someplace private or open, even inside bedrooms unless I give the signal. I have our devices locked-down and ultra impenetrable."

Okay, so romantic moment aborted.

He pulled abruptly away. "Come, my dear, we must hurry. Our car is waiting outside. Here, I've brought your hat and I trust you have your sunglasses?"

Got it: wear the hat and put on sunglasses. I retreated under the wide brimmed hat and donned my sunnies. I was now Mrs. Harold Thorne, apparently quite old-school and not averse to being called a missus without the addition of my given name.

With that, Harold picked up my single suitcase and led me by the arm out of the terminal into a blast of bright sunlight while I pondered playing the role of submissive female to his domineering male.

Everything was hitting me on fast-forward—the green double-decker Range Rover awaiting us, the smiling man named Jarvis in the safari suit emblazoned with *Elite Adventure Safaris* across the pocket, the streets of Harare whizzing by in eucalyptus trees, hibiscus, pitted roads badly in need of repair—the entire swirl of a city far removed from London.

People were selling fruit and vegetables from blankets spread on the sidewalks, uniformed children strolled home from school, men and women in business clothes darted along as much in a rush as at home only with a more relaxed loping gate and less of that newly-laundered freshness. Every second person seemed to be hitchhiking and many clung to the back of old-model cars just happy to have a lift. Pockets of what we might consider slums were everywhere.

"We have only two hours, darling, before we catch our private plane to Victoria Falls. Until then, I've arranged a lunch for us in an excellent restaurant nearby. I do hope you're enjoying yourself so far?"

So this was how it was going to be, was it? I grinned. "Oh, Harold, I'm just so excited!"

We did have a lovely lunch in a gated hibiscus-festooned dining room where plate glass and electric fences effectively sealed away the fractious city. I had a strong sense of a tiny wealthy minority desperately clinging to what they had while millions of others were just trying to survive. But the hermetically-sealed world in which we dined helped sustain the illusion that we were safely entitled. There were plenty of Africans of all faces out there who weren't.

I played the game, enjoying Evan's proximity even though his behavior was definitely not what I would normally anticipate from the man I knew and loved. Harold attempted to order for me, and made several suggestions as to acceptable apparel for a female tourist on safari while alluding to the careful wardrobe selections he had made on my behalf. I sensed he was secretly enjoying teasing me.

"You will just love the places we're going, Julie. All have pools and I know how much you love to swim. However, it is best that ladies not bring too much attention to themselves in these places so avoid the bright colors and skimpy swimwear, right, darling?" he remarked by dabbing his lips with the napkin.

"Oh, of course, Harold. I left my Hawaiian patterned bikini at home", I assured him with a bright smile. That would be the Hawaiian patterned bikini I didn't own.

A flash of amusement quirked his lips. *Too bad*, I sensed him thinking. "Relieved to hear it," he remarked.

I needed to read between the lines for everything. He was telling me that he'd brought clothes to fit my role and many of his lectures I endured were also designed to provide background information. Otherwise, Harold seemed pleasant enough company despite being generally rather dull.

While lingering over coffee, I pulled out my phone. "Just going to text Mom to tell her that I've arrived."

"Good idea," Harold acknowledged. "I'd best do the same for the team back in the office."

I immediately sent him a message:

> Do you think they know we're here?

> Evan: Word is that S has every suspicious entry into the country scrutinized and that there are people on his payroll throughout Zimbabwe. He also knows his house was broken into.

> Me: But not that the staves were stolen?

> Evan: I doubt that he knows anything that specific. If he discovered the loss somehow, he'll probably blame Sofonisba initially but we may be implicated eventually.

I looked up at him seeing his gaze still fixed on his phone.

> Me: In the meantime, do you think our disguises will hold?
>
> Evan: Hopefully long enough to find what we're looking for. I've screened the staff at our safari lodge upstream to ensure that all are who they seem and we will have two other operatives besides Peaches arriving. One is an experienced tracker, the other also a tracker but also an expert in local folklore, a doctor educated in anthropology in South Africa. We must be careful. Our first stop at Victoria Falls is wide open.

Wide open meant that our fellow guests for the first few days were unknown.

> Me: And our driver?
>
> Evan: He thinks we're tourists on an anniversary trip, darling.
>
> Me: Here we are only three years married and we're already on our phones ignoring one another.

That provoked a flash grin. He finished with: Let the games begin.

Begin? We were already deep into it, only now the setting had changed dramatically. Soon, our ride arrived to return us to the airport.

I knew from my research that few people were thriving in Zimbabwe. Political unrest, drought, and famine were bad enough but then came a pandemic. The expressions on the faces glimpsed through our car window as we made our way to our private plane ran the gamut from curious, angry, bleak, to welcoming.

Jarvis, our go-to man for the elite safari company with whom we would travel to the lodge, assured us that many of his countrymen were totally delighted to have visitors with deep pockets arrive. So many people fed their families by working in and around the tourism industry through game lodges and sites like Victoria Falls, he assured us, though the numbers had dropped off dramatically over the years.

I liked Jarvis at once. Though he seemed ageless in spirit, I estimated him to be in his early forties with close-cropped hair, a wide bright grin which he flashed often, and a determination to show us just how wonderful his country truly was. He had trained in Johannesburg, to which he referred to as "Jo'burg", as a veterinarian and sometimes did vet work still.

"You will see when we arrive in Victoria Falls how happy people are to see you," he told us with a big smile as he gathered our luggage for our short flight. His accent held the British colonial lilt that I would grow accustomed to and which I heard all around me along with mixes of the Shona language and other dialects.

As thrilling as it was to be in Africa at last, the exhaustion that hit straight after lunch sent me deep into a doze while leaning on my husband's shoulder throughout the short flight. We bounced and glided through the clouds until finally touching down in the town of Victoria Falls. I completely missed the aerial view of the largest falls in the world when finally Harold nudged me awake.

"Julie, darling. Wake up now. We're almost here."

Here was yet another world away from Harare; here were glimpses of bushland divided by a broad backed river, here was the towering mist roaring in plumes overhead. Somewhere from the time I climbed out of the Rover and strode into the hotel and into our suite with the sweeping views, it finally hit me that, yes, I was in Africa. I could actually sit on the balcony and watch wild animals arrive at the watering hole, apparently, yet I could hardly keep my eyes open. It was thrilling, or soon would be once I had the energy to feel thrilled.

After a light meal and a long bath in a clawfoot tub on a wide balcony overlooking the game reserve, Evan remaining in the character of Harold Thorne, I was ready for bed. With little conversation between us, I soon dropped into a deep ten-hour sleep. I could sense Evan—the real Evan—watching over me as I slept but I did not feel comfortable interacting with him in my normal manner. Someone might be watching.

I would have expected to remain in that state until well into the morning but in the middle of the night something roused me—the sound of crying, a howl of pain beyond the tent.

I bounded out of bed and ran towards the opening afraid that they had come for me at last. I would not attempt to shoot nor wound them in any way, though I gripped my knife by habit. My heart thundered in my ears and the words of the witch doctor repeated over and over again in my memory: *say you are part of the Great Story*. But I was not prepared, and even to my own ears, all I heard was the roar of panic.

"I will come willingly! I am part of the Great Story!" I cried.

I felt myself being gently shaken. "Julie, Julie, wake up! You are dreaming!"

I tried to pull myself away from the strong arms that held me. "Leave me. I must go with them. They await me!"

"It is just an animal crying out in the night," I heard the man say. "There's a pool just beyond our balcony that they drink from. You heard the hyenas."

I stopped and swung around shivering in the cool night air. "Hyenas? Terrence, is that you?"

CHAPTER 14

The events of the night before had left me shaken. Dream, alternate reality, a cross time-walking episode—what did it matter? It wasn't me who had run out of our room the night before. If there hadn't been a balcony suspended three stories up, who knows what I would have done?

Evan was alarmed enough to insist that I wear a tracker fixed onto my watch that, other than to charge an hour each day, I never removed. He didn't say anything, only fixed the button onto the strap before passing it back to me. I understood. He was afraid I might wander someplace without my phone and he wasn't taking any risks.

We had spent most of breakfast texting each other while Harold and Julie remained fixed on their phones. To a casual observer, the third anniversary was not getting off to a great start.

> Evan: Are you certain it was Louise you experienced?
>
> Me: Who else could it be anyone else? She talked about taking part in a great story.
>
> Evan: Perhaps it was a dream, then. Even without your incredible gifts, after all the trauma of the past week plus jet lag, not to mention the gassing episode, is it too much to believe that your unconscious mind became entangled?

I lowered my phone and cast him a look. It was the kind of nonverbal communication that makes its point more vividly than words. Instantly, we both saw the humor in it and tried not to laugh.

Evan lowered his gaze and wrote:

> Of course you know when you're not in your right mind.

I stifled a smile.

Besides texting me, Evan was also running scans on the various guests for signs of surveillance devices. Finally, he appeared satisfied that the array of international fellow tourists were exactly who they seemed, which was more than could be said about us.

"Let's put away our devices, darling, and enjoy this beautiful day," Harold remarked, a tiny bit of Evan still at play on his lips. "Today we visit Victoria Falls. I cannot wait to see it."

"Of course, Harold. Let me just finish my message to Mom first." I ended my text by adding: *Victoria Falls was where Louise first met the witch doctor.*

His eyes met mine across the fruit plate but we said nothing.

Following that, I put away my phone and returned to breakfast, trying to focus on the panorama beyond the balcony and the fresh sliced fruits on my plate instead of the maelstrom churning in my head.

From this vantage, a sweeping view of the bushland stretched far into the distance, a purple ridge of mountains smudging the horizon. A tall electric fence separated the game park from the lodge since the only way to travel into the actual reserve was by vehicle and armed guides. We'd save that part of our experience for our upriver lodge.

The falls were located on the other side of our hotel close enough for a perpetual roar to be always present. Our true reason for being here was because Victoria Falls had featured in Louise's diary. She and Terrence had spent nearly a week camping in the area studying the flora and fauna.

No animals were visible at the moment though several people peered over the balcony with binoculars hungering for a glimpse. I detected mostly African accents from our fellow guests though a few British and Americans were in the mix.

"I saw an elephant yesterday," one young woman told me in passing. "It's just thrilling to be so close to nature!"

However, as Jarvis explained when he came to get us an hour later, "close" in this context was still a matter of safety. As we would learn when we carried on to the game lodge later, there was a serious rule book on what one does and does not do while on safari in Africa. Never leave the camp without the presence of an armed guide was only the beginning. Of course, we added a few caveats of our own since we had more than a few wild animals to worry about.

Julie kept her hair tucked under her straw hat, though a few locks escaped no matter what. Otherwise, her crisp little beige Bermuda shorts outfit was about as far away from my normal duds as I could get. I almost enjoyed striding about in somebody else's persona and resolved to enjoy it while it lasted.

The Falls were about a mile away from the lodge along a paved path that separated the game reserve from the area bordering the river. We decided to walk that morning since fresh air might be an ideal antidote to all my inner turmoil. Jarvis kept up a detailed commentary of historical and general facts about the area but by that time, I'd crammed quite a bit into my frazzled brain.

Glimpsing Victoria Falls soon shoved all else from my mind. From the moment I approached the broad plume of spray rising far into the sky, I knew Louise had experienced the same sensations—wonder, awe, fear. Though we could see the 'mist that thunders' from the hotel, the closer we came, the more incredible it seemed.

It was impossible to think or feel anything but wonder at the largest waterfall in the world plunging deep into a massive chasm in a furious boil so intense that at certain locations it was as though it rained vertically. Twice the height of Niagara Falls as well as twice its width, Victoria Falls was both terrifying and awe-inspiring all at once, a breathless fury of water with brilliant rainbows hovering above. This wasn't the rainy season and yet still the volume of water plunging over the falls struck me speechless and three rainbows at a time was amazing in itself.

"On the Zambia side," Jarvis was saying while pointing across the back of the magnificent Zambezi River towards the neighboring nation. "They call it *Chongwe*, or "Place of the Rainbow." On nights when the moon is full like tonight, you will see moonbows. Moonbows!" he exclaimed with visible glee.

Louise had mentioned first seeing a dual moonbow at Victoria Falls. She and Terrence had been camping on what was the other side of the very road we now followed. I had memorized the map she'd sketched and knew there could be no other location but the area in which we currently trod.

On that side, the earth was dry and peppered with the typical bushland, while closer to the falls it was pure rainforest, a rainforest as thick and tropical as any jungle. It was also home to a myriad of unusual flora that Terrence had recorded and Louise had illustrated. Louise and Terrance had stood together on the edge of the river and viewed the phenomena. *The local tribes believe that moonbows hold great magic*, she had written.

I gripped Evan's hand as I'm sure Julie would have Harold's as we traveled along the path to gaze down at the churning boil. Here, everyone had to shout in order to be heard.

"Be careful!" Jarvis called. "Path very slippery!"

I carried a foldable plastic rain cape for the spray but this felt more like an intense mist only far fiercer. Still, the cape helped Julie's curly hair stay trapped in its chignon as we grabbed the wooden railing and climbed through the wet jungle towards the Knife Edge viewing bridge.

Jarvis was shouting facts and figures. "The gorges are numbered as the occur—First Gorge to Fifth Gorge with the Songwe Gorge the last and longest at 3.3 kilometers and named after the small river coming from the north-east. We can just see the Second George over there, only reached by very steep path on Zambian side."

But where he pointed was shrouded in thundering mist. "That is where the Boiling Pot is," he called. "The Boiling Pot very fearsome. Usually the bodies are found floating there."

"Bodies, what bodies?" Julie asked quickly.

"Crocodile, hippo, sometimes human. In 1910, Mrs. Moss and Mr. Orchard canoes capsized by hippos and over they went. Badly chewed up by crocodiles. There have been many others before and since."

Hell, like I needed to hear that. "Where did their canoes capsize?" I asked while Evan squeezed my hand, probably in warning that Julie might not ask such details. I disagreed: Julie was curious.

"At Long Island above the falls," Jarvis told me. "The Zambezi has many islands, big and small. At this time of year, you will see the little outcrops all the way to the edge of the falls. People swim in them."

"They swim in pools at the edge of Victoria Falls?" I gasped. Actually, that sounded like fun though I doubt Julie would agree.

"Yes," Jarvis laughed. "All very almost safe. The rocks protect your from falling over the edge. They even bungee jump off the edge."

"Good Lord!" Harold exclaimed. "Imagine that, my dear. I can't bear to think of it!"

But I could see the tiny rocky island myself and could almost picture going for a dip.

"Your next lodge is located on a much bigger island, you will see. Come, I will show you more."

Terrence and Louise had traveled by canoe upstream on the Zambezi and supposedly set up camp somewhere near where our next lodge was located so we were following their tracks as closely as possible.

Though there were visitors all around, their voices were quickly consumed by the raging mist, leaving the three of us to pick our way along as if in caught in a roaring cloud. It was strangely disorientating, almost as if we were disembodied spirits floating in the ether.

Crossing a small footbridge, we were finally suspended over one of the gorges in the midst of the vertical rain. I gripped the wet railing and gazed down at a gorge's boiling throat.

"Wow!" I exclaimed, thinking what this sight must have been like over a hundred years ago when Louise and her brother first ventured into this territory. There would have been no bridges so any viewing would have to have been managed from the edge. Livingstone and others had claimed a perfect vista by canoeing to what was now named Livingston Island where one could stare down at the tumultuous gorge in relative safety, providing one didn't capsize getting there.

Jarvis lead us across the bridge and back up onto dry land. Here red-hot poker flowers grew in abundance amid tall grasses and palms. I inhaled the damp air, savoring the spicy scents, the cry of strange birds, and the overall sense of being somewhere far away. We continued along the path, enjoying the falls and the river from a variety of views before returning to the main road

Craftspeople set up shop all along the pathways, selling everything from beaded jewelry to wood and soapstone carvings, and I couldn't help but linger. We were warned to watch out for scammers but one look in a man's eyes told me whether he was desperate enough to cheat and one look at Evan probably convinced him not to try.

Women knitting and crocheting drew me the most. I crouched beside them asking Jarvis to translate as I asked about their craft. They smiled shyly, their nimble fingers never faltering for a second as I explained that I knit, too, but not with their skill. I ended up buying several tablecloths and doilies to support their incredible art.

"Julie, we don't need another tablecloth, surely?" Harold complained.

"Of course we do, darling." That darling thing was getting old but I was sure Julie would use it whenever she needed to wheedle her husband. Besides, it had become a kind of joke between the two of us. "Harold, darling, why don't you buy me one of those carved elephants over there? You know elephants are supposed to bring you good luck." And we could use all the luck we could get.

While my supposed husband haggled, I studied the carvings. I had heard that walking sticks once were offered to the tourist trade but nothing I saw that day was anything near to Louise's Nyami sticks. I understood from my reading that carving masks and sculptures were part of the curio trade begun by David Livingstone and would later morph into the British South Africa Company established by Cecil Rhodes in 1889, though that company's intent was to capitalize on diamonds and gold. Nowhere in any of those accounts had there been more than a passing reference to an earlier great African nation.

That afternoon we toured Livingstone Island and the Devil's Pool after which Jarvis drove us out to a rural village to meet the locals. Julie had expressed an interest in hearing local African stories and Jarvis assured her that every village had storytellers who would be happy to oblige.

Though the village with its brightly patterned mud and thatch rondavel huts had benefited from an infusion of tourist dollars and probably was better outfitted than most, I still felt slightly closer to the real African by just being there. They were genuinely welcoming and we dined on their *sudsa*, or corn meal mash, along with a tasty vegetarian stew. Everywhere, the scent of woodsmoke infused the air as we sat inside their round houses beside their cook fires. Many knew enough English for us all to get by but nobody seemed able to tell the stories of the local mythology that I craved, though Jarvis translated several for Julie's benefit.

I was so busy playing tourist and enjoying this transfusion of another culture that for awhile I forgot what had brought me here in the first place. This must be what it was like to travel with an open heart and mind, I thought, and not to be always looking over my shoulder or checking under the bed. Even Evan was enjoying himself deep in conversation with a village elder while Jarvis translated. The older villagers did not grasp English as well as the younger generations many of whom worked in the town.

It was in this relaxed state of mind that I wandered around the village, smiling and nodding at all the villagers who stepped out to greet me. It was while I was admiring a small boy's pet goat that I noticed an older man watching me from behind a rondavel. He was small and very dark and wore a peculiar headdress that appeared to be fashioned from the feathers of some kind of colorful bird. The little boy was tugging at my hand wanting to show me something else while the strange man began beckoning for me to follow him.

I released the child's hand and told him I'd find him later and followed the man around the corner. There, under the shade of a giant acacia tree, the man had spread a multitude of tiny earthenware pots on a trestle table. At first I thought he was attempting to sell me something but instead he stood there with his hands spread looking deeply into my eyes. It was clear that he didn't understand my language any more than I did his but was attempting to communicate on a deeper level.

"I'm sorry but I don't understand Ndebele or Shona," I said, shrugging.

The man nodded, pushing a pot of something that looked like a dark goo toward me. I inspected it with interest but still had no idea what he was trying to say. He didn't frighten me. In fact, I found myself drawn to him the way you would any interesting stranger. There was just something about him that inspired curiosity and even respect.

When he picked up a knife from the table, I instinctively took a step back, clutching my phone in my pocket, but he made no threatening actions. Instead, he pointed to my head and made a sawing motion in the air beside his own. Then I got it: he wanted a lock of my hair in exchange for the pot of black goo. I was baffled. *Why?*

I had no idea what he was trying to tell me but thought, really, it was only a lock of hair. I nodded and fished a curl out from under my hat.

Smiling and nodding, he sliced off the curl and held it between his fingers. Then he was beckoning me back to the table where he took a pencil and sketched something into the sand. I stared, uncomprehending. It looked like a claw or maybe a three-stemmed leaf but I knew it to be a gift so I nodded. I understood at a level so deep, I couldn't put it into words.

I stood gazing at him and he at me when Evan and Jarvis rounded the corner, alarm in their faces.

Jarvis explained something to the man with a great deal of smiling and nodding but seemed determined that nothing transactional pass between us. I caught the man's gaze and held it. He was trying to tell me something. I waved at him as the men lead me away.

"That was a witch doctor," Jarvis told me on the way back to the hotel. "He wanted a lock of your hair in exchange for some of his medicines—very bad idea."

I sat back in the Rover watching the bushland whiz by. "Bad idea, why?" I asked, fingering the lock of hair now missing its curl.

"If a witch doctor has a lock of your hair, he can find you anywhere, anytime, and red hair is believed to have very powerful magic or mooti, as it is called here. You have no idea if this is good witch doctor or bad witch doctor. Mooti men very powerful. Some trade in both good and evil and this man is not a local but has been moving from village to village. The villagers allow him to remain for as long as he wants in exchange for medicines but he does not belong. Best to stay away."

Interesting. Jarvis clearly believed in the power of witch doctors, though every inch a modern guy, presumably.

I hastily texted Evan. *He was a good mooti man.*

His fine brows raised. He caught my gaze and I knew he believed me. Hell, I believed me.

The rest of that afternoon was spent relaxing at the hotel, which had a large outdoor pool where a few people where attempting to roast themselves in the recliners. I preferred to actually swim. The time I did spend drip-drying on the chairs in my modest swimsuit, I was actually riveted to my phone.

Everybody's tracking dot had gone dark. Startled, I texted Evan who was lounging next to me, the picture of a relaxed Harold allowing his insurance business woes to melt away. He responded by telling me that he had darkened the the agency's location map briefly as an additional safety feature but it would return to visible one we reached the lodge. I didn't have the chance to ask why because at that moment Jarvis texted to announce that our Zambezi dinner cruise would launch in a little over an hour.

After a hasty shower and change of clothes, our guide led us to the banks of the river and to a wooden dock where we boarded an open tour boat to cruise the mighty Zambezi. I had seen the river as we had wandered by its banks earlier, experienced the might of its falls, but sailing on its back at sunset rated right up there as one of my most memorable moments, of the pleasurable kind, that is.

Forget the pods of hippos close to the shore, the tall grasses that harbored wildfowl and other creatures too numerous to mention. Forget that this boat sailed on one of the most amazing rivers in Africa, one that could lead me to the Indian Ocean if our journey was so headed. Every gilded moment was simply magnificent with or without the occasional crocodile for special effects.

Standing on deck watching that riverscape slide by, it was all I could do to remind myself that this was not some National Geographic special or a wild Africa theme park ride. I was actually there, in Africa, and that six-foot crocodile I'd spotted was not remotely operated and could kill me with a snap of its jaws.

"Darling, would you like me to fetch you a drink?" Harold asked at my elbow. Always attentive, I gazed up at him, his hazel eyes partially shrouded under the Tilley sunhat, his fine mouth caught in a tight little smile. The man was a great actor, whether from years in MI6 or natural aptitude, I didn't know. He still managed to communicate that the real Evan was still there, watching, protecting.

"Oh, that would be lovely, thank you. White wine, please."

He touched my hand and strode to the bar towards the prow of the tour boat, leaving me to enjoy the river bathed in molten sun with the other guests, all of whom were staying at the many hotels in the area. A man stood nearby. He must be have been a guest at one of the other hotels because I didn't recognize him.

"Enjoying the sites?" the man asked, sliding closer. Shorts, tee-shirt, and white linen dinner jacket, nothing about either his clothes or his accent said North American. He was deeply tanned, blonde, and good-looking in that tall, Nordic way.

"Oh, yes, thank you, and you?"

"Yes, brilliant." He slid closer to me. "First time in Africa, darling?"

Darling? Maybe the term was contagious. "Very first and you?"

"No, I live in Jo'burg but I'm from these parts originally. In my real life, I take people on hunting trips." He grinned, all white teeth and confidence.

"As in a big game hunter?" I turned to look at him. "Do people still hunt wild animals on a continent where the animal numbers have been decimated?"

He laughed. "Ah, a bleeding heart, I see, but yes, they do and they pay big greenbacks for the honor, too." He rubbed his fingers together. "Countries like Zim and Zambia, South Africa, too, badly need the dollars these wannabe great white hunters bring in. Don't worry, though: it's all controlled, in a manner of speaking. They call it 'culling' in these parts, say it's to keep the numbers down. Name's Justin, by the way."

I was shocked, not because there were still big game hunters paying to prey on a rapidly shrinking animal kingdom—I knew that already—but because this guy felt the need to tell this little tourist that. I didn't introduce myself in return but he didn't seem to notice.

"Visitors believe that lions and leopards are the most dangerous of African beasts here but in fact, when you're on a river like the Zambezi," he continued, "hippos are the ones to watch out for. They'll come up under your boat and tip you into the drink." He grinned, leaning back against the railing.

"Not likely a boat of this size, though," Julie remarked. "Still, I would have thought that the crocodiles were the deadliest."

"Oh, they are bad, too. They finish off what the hippos leave behind." He laughed at his own little joke, not that I could find the humor in it.

Harold returned with a drink in each hand at which point the man strode away. "What was that about?" he asked.

"That's what I wondered. Why would a supposed big game hunter take a river cruise? Isn't it a bit too tame for him?" I took the wine and clinked my glass with his.

"Here's to all the dangerous creatures, no matter what the breed," Harold remarked.

CHAPTER 15

The next morning was a long but exhilarating drive by Rover towards our lodge, and after we had left the highway behind, most of it was through bushland that wove toward the river and back again.

By then we had picked up another guide, Akatendeka, "Deek" for short, who arrived with a rifle, a rucksack, and a grin. I learned along the way that Deek worked with Jarvis when the Zambezi Expedition Lodge swelled with guests and that he'd be on hand to help us enjoy our adventure excursion.

Since it was technically not high season in Zimbabwe being their winter, the lodge was not filled to capacity. I had asked Evan days before whether we had commandeered the entire lodge and he had told me no, but since there were so few bookings at that time of year, we should have the place more or less to ourselves. Besides, he had added, booking an entire luxury lodge for a handful of people would attract too much attention unless one was a millionaire or an oligarch. There would be the two trained operatives he had mentioned, one of whom he was certain Peaches would approve. That piqued my curiosity but I had little time to question him further.

Apparently, we would be experiencing game rides and guided walks, river rafting and canoe trips, among other adventure delights. Privately, of course, our intent was something quite different and far more dangerous.

At one point, we climbed outside of the cab to take a seat on the Rover's top viewing bench so that we might glimpse game en route, but unfortunately glimpsed nothing wild and dangerous. Deek explained that the best times for game sightings were mornings and evenings and since this was midafternoon, not to expect to see much. Harold, however, always peering everywhere with his binoculars, spotted the top of giraffe far in the distance at which point Julie let out a squeal of delight. Otherwise, we bumped and jostled along a dirt track for many miles, until I thought my teeth might loosen.

Finally, we arrived on the banks of the Zambezi by late afternoon. I strolled to the end of the wooden dock which was high enough off the water's surface to feel reasonably safe. Across the river straight ahead I could see a pod of hippos basking in the shallows. By now, I'd been cued to look for danger everywhere.

Shielding my eyes with my hand, I searched up and down the river for for our new home but could see nothing but a fringe of pampas grass along the banks.

"We take boat," Deek told me, bringing along our luggage and lowering them over the edge. The boat moored to the post was smaller than the diner cruise variety but large enough to carry at least ten people. We all piled in for the next leg of our journey.

The Zambezi Expedition Lodge was on a string of islands in the middle of the river rather than on its edge, I was told. Described as a "designer destination," meaning that it was exclusive and so upscale to apparently put it off the charts.

Though I had seen photos, nothing prepared me for the multilevel spread of tree houses, cottages, dining rooms, private and communal pools—all clustered amid riverine ebony and other trees and interlinked by wooden walkways and mini suspension bridges. The one southern island was connected by a series of bridges to smaller islets, some of which had cottages. Apparently, the last guest had been a big-name Hollywood producer who had brought his entire family.

The objective of the lodge, I learned, was to ensure that the guests' maximum safety and privacy while immersing them as much as possible in the African experience. Common areas were covered in thatched roofs while being exposed to the open air on at least three sides and many of the buildings were on stilts to give the treehouse illusion.

I stepped onto the jetty completely enchanted. Wooden walkways linked the chalets over and above the river, all lit with lanterns for maximum ambience, with a large stilted dining patio commanding the most stunning view above where I stood. Everywhere the lodge brewed a sense of exotic mysterious luxury. Though it was still daylight, the lights were lit early to enhance the sense of welcome.

I strode the walkways guided by Jarvis past the common spaces that included tiny tropical gardens, plunge pools, a bar, and multiple viewing balconies. At last, we were lead to our private accommodations, a massive three-room open-space treehouse directly over the river. Though open to the air but for mosquito netting, I was assured that it wasn't mosquito season and that sliding glass doors existed for our comfort.

Wild animals could not access our accommodations due to the height and all predators had been removed from the series of islands. To add to the luxury, I was assured, our private accommodations came with a soaker tub in a sheltered open area and an outdoor shower, a personal dining patio, and a valet, which Harold instantly dismissed saying that we required privacy.

I texted Evan immediately:

> Is he one of ours?

> No. That's why I've instructed him to take care of room service only—no valet needed. Two qualified operatives arrive tomorrow. The rest are all employees that we need to convince that we are who we claim. The subterfuge had stilted more than just our conversation.

Another message popped up on my screen. Peaches!

> It's about time you arrived!

Leaving Evan to scan the accommodations looking for surveillance devices and installing our personal security system, I slipped out to find my friend.

I followed the lodge map along walkways, past a plunge pool, and up to the main deck. She was waiting for me at the end of a spacious curved mahogany patio under a thatched roof that sheltered comfy couches. Nearby was an open-air bar and a spread of wicker seats pulled around candlelit tables.

A text popped onto my screen:

> Look at this place! I arrived yesterday. What took you so long?

The moment I spied her standing in a white jersey shift dress, it was all I could do not to run up and hug her. She strode towards me, hand outstretched.

"Hiya," she said with a smile. "Glad to meet another female Londoner. The manager said you'd be coming. Until the others arrive, it's just you and me, kid. I'm Kenyatta, by the way, and you?"

"Julie," I said, "Julie Thorne. My husband and I are on our third-anniversary trip."

"Wow." Kenyatta nodded, her eyes spread wide with unspoken commentary. "Great choice for an anniversary. Can't imagine a place more romantic than this. Just think, the moment you nearly get eaten by a lion, you can fall into your husband's big strong arms."

Damn. She was going to have fun with this. "Harold's an insurance salesman and, though he does have big strong arms, those muscles come by working at the gym on weekends. I doubt he'd know what to do with a wild animal if one attacked me. Are there lions on the island, really?"

She laughed. "There are on both sides of the river—Zimbabwe there and Zambia on the other side—so I'm sure we'll be seeing some soon. There are certainly hippos and crocs, too. Hell, you have to be careful where you walk around here, especially at night when the hippos come up from the river to graze. Talk about ferocious vegetarians. You can hear them chomping from our cottages."

"So you're here on vacation?" I asked.

"Sort of. Want a drink?"

A server dressed in crisp white shorts and shirt with white gloves which turned out to be the lodge's standard uniform had arrived to ask our pleasure. Julie ordered a glass of white wine and Kenyatta ordered up another martini. She had already downed one by the looks of the empty glass the server whisked away.

"I'm an anthropologist," she told me as we each took a seat, not even attempting to hide her satisfaction at that pronouncement. Evan would get kudos for that. "Yeah, that's me. I'm studying the indigenous cultures for my doctoral thesis and Daddy gave me this sojourn as a gift." She beamed, spreading one hand.

Nice daddy. "Lucky you," Julie enthused.

My companion leaned over and whispered.,"I scanned this place for bugs. I really think it's safe to be ourselves outside around here."

"Okay, so fill me in quickly: who else is here?" Relieved, I readily agreed.

"So far, no one but us. I was the only guest here last night, which is a weird experience, I can tell you—talk about cries in the night. One of the staff,

Randall, tells me to expect more arriving tomorrow. Beats me who they are but those numbers don't add up to the agency crew. Did Evan ensure that only our people were guests here?"

"He said he tried but could only do so much without booking the whole place out, which is the cost of a London townhouse and suspicious for an insurance salesman. We will have two African operatives joining us, though."

"Anyway, I've been doing some snooping." She paused to take her martini and flash the server, whose name was Eniko, a smile. "Cute guy," she whispered as the man strode away. "So, the staff talk about the next game lodge upriver and think it's kind of strange that they only bring in a very limited amount of patronage even in high season. They don't hire the locals, either. We need to canoe up there and snoop around."

I shot her a look and said while Eniko was in earshot. "So, what else can you tell me? Harold dismissed both Jarvis and our valet when they tried to explain the lay of the land, saying that he had a headache."

"A headache, seriously?" Peaches rolled her eyes and lowered her voice as the server walked away. "Anyway, I can tell you that this place may be luxurious but they rely heavily on foreign tourists to stay afloat, of which there have been pitifully few of late. They see our arrival as a sign of good things to come and I hope they're right. The staff sleep at the other end of the island in round huts, by the way."

"Rondavels," I told her. "That's where I met my witch doctor, in a village of rondavels."

"You met a witch doctor already?"

"As weird as it sounds, my meeting him feels like fate. Louise had a witch doctor figure prominently, too."

"And you think that's fate? With you it probably is. It's only when we live too deeply in the modern world that we lose our gifts. You, of course, are our favorite anomaly."

"Thanks."

"Anyway, I can tell you that nobody knows about the legend of three kings among this lot. Every night presumably we'll be gathering around an open fire for story hour. I got a taste of one last night but they're not telling traditional tales here. It's all made-for-tourist junk."

"What about the staff?"

"From all over, a melding of various African dialects—the scatterings of Africa, a topic of which Kenyatta is intensely interested along with local mythology, her being an anthropologist."

I recognized the title of the song *Scatterings of Africa* by the British born

South African anthropologist turned musician Johnny Clegg and toasted a music hero. "To Johnny Clegg and the Scatterings of Africa."

"To Johnny Clegg," Peaches agreed, "the man who fought apartheid with music. May he be singing up a storm wherever he is today, with the angels, maybe."

On my second glass of wine, I filled her in on my experiences with my dream.

Peaches snapped her fingers. "Damn, so soon?"

"Powerful magic on this continent," I murmured, "and what's worse is that I can't speak freely with Evan since he's always playing Harold Thorne, even in private. It's all been texting so far but that should change once he get's everything debugged."

"Hard on the love life," she acknowledged. "Meanwhile, to texting!" Peaches exclaimed, on her third martini by then.

We clinked our glasses together again.

Later, when Julie finally decided to weave back to her quarters to shower and change before supper, she required a bit of help from her new friend. Apparently, she had developed a bit of a list. We traveled up wavering rope and planking suspension bridges and along the interconnecting tree house walkways before reaching our upper level aerie.

"Think I'd better lay off the vino," I whispered. A man in a white suit stepped off a walkway and paused just before our door.

"This is Mr. Watu, the manager," Peaches informed me. "Oh, Watty, look. I just found a new friend," she said to the manager as she linked her arm with mine.

Mr. Watu, very lean with black short-cropped hair and spectacles, delivered a little bow. "I am delighted to hear this. Our establishment is designed to encourage congenial discourse. Mrs. Thorne, Ms. Jones, how are you finding the lodge?" he asked with a brilliant smile. "And Mrs. Thorne, welcome on behalf of all the staff. It is a true pleasure to have you as guests at our lodge. Rest assured that we will tend to your every need. Are you settling in well?"

"Wonderfully, thank you. It's just so, ah, wow, and look, Kenyatta here's been telling me how rich in myth and magic this area is."

"Oh, yes," he agreed. "That is true for all Africa."

"We wondered if you could find us a real witch doctor to talk to."

"A witch doctor, ma'am?"

"A witch doctor. We're hoping that one could really spiff up story hour, what do you think?" Kenyatta pressed.

Mr. Watu hesitated but quickly rallied. "Yes, Ms. Jones, of course, but we do not wish to expose our guests to…"

"Vermin, unwashed bodies?" she suggested.

"If we should successfully locate such a person, I assure you we would ask him to, ah, bathe first. Now, please enjoy your stay and I am here have you any questions." At which point, he slipped away down the polished wooden walkway and through a door that lead to the lodge's offices.

"Oh," I said, remembering something, "about the two men arriving tomorrow, both are trackers and both trained operatives but one is a doctor with a specialty in African mythology."

"A real anthropologist?"

"Maybe."

"And trackers as in finders of footprints?" she hissed.

"Footprints, paw prints, spoor—that sort of thing." I opened the door to our room.

Evan was nowhere to be seen. I checked my phone. He had messaged me saying:

> Off on reconnaissance.

I replied:

> I found Peaches, A.K.A. Kenyatta. Off to shower and change. See you at dinner.

He shot back an answer:

> I'll arrive in time to escort you to our table as any doting husband should.

"Swanky," Peaches commented on our tree house. "I mean, mine is grand but this is just beyond."

"The Honeymoon Suite. Harold promised me nothing but the best."

"I just bet," she said with a mischievous grin. "Nobody does it better, I bet. I'm going to stick around while you wash up. I am your bodyguard, after all."

"No need. This place must be well-secured by now. I think I'm safe enough."

"Yeah, right." Peaches laughed while I floated off to shower. "Wait until you see your first crocodile up close or maybe a puff adder emerging from hibernation in your toilet," she called after me. "That happened to me yesterday—I flushed and out he came. Always check every dark corner."

So, I did. An enclosed outdoor cubicle just off the toilet offered complete privacy while providing the illusion of showering under the ebony tree that grew up through the deck. I leaned back, peering up into the branches where a bird flitted from branch to branch high up in the canopy. Then I began looking for snakes.

When I emerged later, Peaches was nowhere to be seen. I stood on the deck watching the sun sinking into the river as I dried my hair remembering how Louisa had described her occasional showers. By employing a contraption that used boiled water from the river, she had pulled a cord to release a stream from a tin barrel overhead. How things change. This island had its own generator, used solar power, and spared guests no comfort even though the surrounding environment teamed with the wild and the dangerous.

Something shrieked from behind me. I swung around to see what looked to be a white bird sweeping from one side of the room to the other and out through the open walls. When Evan entered seconds later, it was to find me clutching my phone doing a perimeter sweep.

"How do our devices detect non-human interlopers?" I whispered as Evan gazed at me, questioningly.

"I've sensitized it to the lowest possible degree, but during the daytime I didn't want the alarm to sound for every bug or bird."

He was obviously confident that we could now speak freely in our room, too. "Fabulous," I said. "And you look so handsome tonight, darling."

Holding out his arms, I was just about to collect an anniversary kiss when Peaches burst into our quarters. "Okay, guys, I just chased somebody I heard sneaking around down there." She was pointing underneath our stilted room.

"Peach, you didn't go down there close to the water unarmed, did you?" But one look at her dirt-splotched shift made me know otherwise.

"Of course I did but I had my phone, okay? If I can stun a human, I can stun a croc."

"Not if it grabs you before you see it coming," Evan pointed out, his face stern.

"Forget about that for a moment. What I saw scrambling around down there was of the two-legged variety in a canoe." She held out her phone which framed the back of a man dressed in a dark shirt paddling a canoe into the tall grasses that lined the river. "He took off before I could catch him."

"This islet isn't as secure as our hosts would like us to believe," Evan stated. "I've been from one end to the other and discovered that interlopers can approach by water from both the Zambian and the Zimbabwe sides; much requires us to be prepared for the possibility of thieves as well as our usual assortment of criminals."

"And wildlife," I added.

"And wildlife," he agreed. "There are supposedly guards on patrol all the time here but this place won't make any kind of surveillance easy or even possible which is why we have extra hands arriving."

"Fascinating, but now I have to go change, damn it!" And with that Peaches dashed away.

Once she had gone, Evan filled me in on next steps. "Later tonight, we're sending a drone upriver to check out Semenov's lodge. We need to know exactly what they're up to."

"Meanwhile, Peach and I are trying to untangle the local mythologies, too, or as much of the traditional stories that may still exist. Peaches tells me that so far, she hasn't heard much of what she considers authentic storytelling, maybe because there has been so much migration among the peoples that it's difficult to pluck out a clear thread. But, since there are no recorded histories, how else can we follow the trail of this lost civilization or the three kings?"

"We'll have to approach this from multiple angles. What about Louise?" he asked. "I've studied her diaries but so far have I've gleaned nothing new except her conviction that the third stave may be in the keeping of a secret tribe."

"Which is just boggling—a secret tribe in this day and age? Maybe they existed a century ago but now? Anyway, I haven't felt Louise's presence since we left Victoria Falls."

"You may tomorrow when we go for our first game drive. According to the map, they camped upriver in the bush. Tomorrow, I will ensure that we get to the exact spot. Now, let's go off to dinner, darling. You look ravishing, by the way."

I took his arm and smiled, caught in a microsecond of pure happiness.

But it didn't last. Even as we strolled through the walkways towards the dining area, I was pondering the challenges of unlocking secrets of a lost civilization without the existence of recorded histories. And yet I remained convinced, as was Louise, that clues did exist somewhere in the verbal and visual stories left behind.

Soon, the three of us sat down to dine on the lodge's main dinner deck. Lit as it was by lanterns and candlelight, it was beautifully evocative with a feast of stars pricking the sky above and the moon melting over the river. Relaxed and languid, it was challenging to keep my mind fixed on danger while it was simultaneously so full of wonder.

Harold reminded his wife to forgo the wine and I saw the wisdom in that advice and sipped lemonade, instead.

Kenyatta played her role as anthropologist by regaling the Thornes with all she had learned about the indigenous peoples of the area while the servers assured our every comfort and delight with a three course dinner of bream, a local fish, and roasted vegetables.

Later, we took our seats on the lower lounge deck around an inset fire pit for story hour, a nightly lodge event designed to entertain the guests in the manner in which people used to enthrall one another for time immemorial. Across the river, we could see a wood fire and hear singing in an evocative harmony, singing a song as old as time. That village, Jarvis explained, housed many of the workers who served our lodge.

Everybody took turns telling a story but since we were with Jarvis, we really couldn't tell our best tales—the agency accounts—though we were urged to make them as exciting as possible. Julie made up something about the day she fell off a horse and her husband had a charming tale about the Jack the Ripper, which entertained Jarvis, at least.

Jarvis, on the other hand, told how he had once gone tiger fishing on the Zambezi with another man who, refusing to listen to his advice, waded to shore to untangle his line from the pampas grass. Jarvis attempted to guard his back but a hippo sneaked up under the boat, capsized the canoe, and chomped off the butt cheek of the fisherman. Plastic surgery was needed there.

Despite Kenyatta's story of fending off robbers in Jamaica, Jarvis won the story award hands-down.

"Anybody except staff and guests here?" Kenyatta asked. "I saw a guy in a canoe earlier."

Jarvis frowned, peering around the deck. Nobody but the barman was visible behind us. "There is nobody but we will check."

"Do you think it could be somebody from the other lodge checking us out?" I asked.

"Possibly. We should learn more tonight," Evan said.

When Jarvis arrived a few minutes later, it was to say that the property had been thoroughly checked and that we had nothing to fear.

In our room later, Evan waited only until he was certain that the lodge had settled in for the night before sending our drone upriver. I was fascinated by the whole process and, of course, didn't realize that he had brought such a thing along in those massive suitcases he had dragged with him.

The drone was dispatched straight down the center of the river where,

Evan informed me, it would be least likely to encounter any flying encumbrances—his word, not mine.

A few minutes later, we were receiving a live video feed of a lodge not unlike our own but much smaller and far less grand. This one was on the Zambia side and though lit with solar walk lights, appeared to be deserted. The drone could detect no signs of life other than the heat sensor picking up a single person presumed sleeping in one of the buildings.

"They've temporarily abandoned the lodge," Evan whispered as if we could be heard upstairs. "That's probably a guard's heat signature it's picking up. We'll go up tomorrow night and check it out once our operatives arrive."

He fed the live stream from the drone into his laptop which began mapping out the enclosure. Unlike our lodge, this one was not on an island but on the mainland with the complex was enclosed behind a barbed wire fence presumably to keep away wild animals and thieves. At the back of the lodge was a parking area that must have sheltered vehicles, though now vacant.

"Wherever they went, they obviously drove," I remarked.

"Which could mean that they rode to the nearest airstrip or to a helicopter. My intel informs me that Semenov's operation has access to both."

"Great, and do we?"

"We will. I have arranged both a plane and a helicopter and one of the men arriving tomorrow is a pilot, though I can fly a helicopter, too, if necessary," he assured me, his hands occupied with the drone's remote.

"Of course you can," I smiled. "I've already realized that there isn't much you can't do except maybe knit."

"And that's only because you refuse to teach me," he complained, his lips quirking in such a way I badly wanted to kiss them but not at the risk of crashing the drone.

"Because you'd trump me and I couldn't bear that. Anyway, these new guys have specific skill sets for African encounters. Sounds good so far," I murmured.

"Everything we need," he told me. "Additionally, they are more knowledgable about the Zambezi River in southern Africa than most of their ilk. The two men have worked together previously."

"Sounds better and better. How much do they know?"

"Only what I've told them, which is very little. Initially, just enough to be of assistance."

"So we're going to sail up the Zambezi river at night?" I said, not realizing that my tone came out with a bit of a gasp.

"Yes, darling," Evan said in pure Harold mode, pulling me close. "But don't worry your pretty little head about it."

I swiped him with a pillow.

Despite my concerns, I slept deeply that night, caught in a lullaby of images of rivers and sunsets, moonbows and tall grasses swaying in the breeze. No memories of Louise made an appearance and yet, at 3:35 a.m., I shot upright in bed, wide awake.

The room was still, the folding doors closed against night breezes and flying creatures. Evan was gone. Maddeningly, his dot was not showing on our agency locator app, either, and he had not left a message. Yet, my phone's parameter alert remained calm. He had left our room and reengaged the security features behind him?

Bounding out of bed, I quickly dressed, activated my personal safety net, and kept the phone in hand when I opened the door, my feet shoved into sneakers. Outside, the solar lit walkway provided just enough illumination for me to see my way across the first little bridge that hung over a tiny tributary.

The breeze had picked up and the night was alive with sounds as the rope bridges swayed beneath me. I'd turn every few seconds to spin my light 360 degrees seeking signs of life, animal or human. A flash of amber eyes in the water below told me that I was far from alone out there.

Where was Evan? No signs of the staff were about this time of night though I understood that the premises were being patrolled.

I padded across the wooden floor of the main lounge and up to the dining room. The bar area remained lit as if inviting guests to help themselves day or night. I stepped up to the open viewing deck and gazed across the river to where we had heard singing earlier. All was quiet in that direction but I could just see a light away to the left somewhere in our mini archipelago.

Leaving the lounge, I took a back stairway down and across a bridge, past other accommodations, on past a plunge pool, and up onto another level.

By then, I was following my instinct, my feet leading me on, so when I realized that I had arrived someplace I had never been, I paused. Ahead, I could see six canoes moored on a tiny riverside beach and knew that the only way to cross to the huts on the other side was to walk along that shore. That had to be the staff quarters.

The hairs at the base of my neck bristled as my parameter alert began beeping. A dark shape was standing in the tall grasses next to the canoes but the sound of footsteps made me swing around to see that someone was also approaching from behind me.

CHAPTER 16

"Mrs. Thorne!"

Deek, damn. When I glanced back towards the beach, the other figure had disappeared.

"Madam, you should not be out at night," the young man explained. "It very dangerous."

Deactivating my intruder app and shoving my phone deep into my pocket, I shrugged. "I couldn't sleep—jet lag, I guess—so I thought I'd take a stroll. Is that where you moor all the canoes for the lodge?"

"Yes, and the staff quarters are there. Come, please. I walk you back to your quarters. It is safe to go to upper lounge areas only but not down here so close to the water. Do you hear that?"

I paused, listening. A snuffling sound was coming from the other side of the islet. Staring through the foliage, I could just make out the shape of something large moving over there.

"Hippos. Hippos run very fast on land despite size. Come."

I followed him, looking over my shoulder for the other man. I was positive that I had seen the nganga, my mooti man, but how was that even possible? And, if it was him, how could I get to him or he to me? Deek, Jarvis, and the others were there to protect me but in my business, it was a thin line between protection and obstruction.

Evan—Harold—was beside himself looking for his little wife, apparently.

He met us on the lounge deck. "Darling, why must you wander away like this? How many times must I warn you to stay by my side?"

"Sorry, Harold. I couldn't sleep."

"How much does Deek know?" I asked the moment we were alone again.

"Nothing. Neither he nor Jarvis are in the loop but there's someone moving around out here—of the human variety, that is—besides the staff. I've patched trackers on each of the men working here—the manager, Jarvis, and Deek plus the chef, the cook, two cleaning staff and the valet, and none of them were close to our quarters when our scanner picked up a signal at 2:35 a.m."

"The witch doctor? I'm sure I saw him tonight down by the canoes."

"But how would he have got here? Anyway, we need to exercise extreme caution just the same, especially you, Phoebe." He was holding me close. "Proceed on the assumption that we could have spies everywhere. I have every reason to believe that Semenov's crew will have the neighboring lodge watched while they're away and that the sudden influx of guests here might have set off a warning. We'll know more when we head up river tomorrow night."

"And why are we waiting until tomorrow again?" I asked. "Oh, wait, I remember: because we don't have a clue of how to maneuver a canoe on an African river at night."

He laughed while gazing over my head at some point across the room, deep in thought. "I have a few clues, Phoebe, but believe it's best to bring in expertise whenever needed. Remain vigilant, my love."

The next morning straight after breakfast, Kenyatta, the Thornes plus Deek and Jarvis set out for our first game ride. We were instructed not to wear red or anything striped so we all appeared properly outfitted in safari clothes, even Julie. Beige on beige ruled. Actually, beige was a Julie color and the outfits Harold had brought mostly followed that color code.

The first part of our excursion was by canoe—Kenyatta and Deek in one, Harold, Jarvis and myself in the other. Harold had urged the guides to paddle us upstream far enough to at least glimpse the other lodge, which Jarvis resisted at first. He claimed that the two lodges maintained an unspoken agreement to avoid one another's territory, presumably to ensure that guests had the illusion of being in the wilderness. In any case, he cheerfully agreed in the end, seeing as the other lodge was closed at the moment.

"Does it close often?" Harold asked.

"Frequently, yes." But Jarvis seemed reluctant to discuss his neighbors further.

The twenty-minute paddle upstream was hard going for the two guides because the Zambezi was a fast-flowing river, though the water appeared smooth and unhurried on the surface. Pampas grass islands sailed on the river's back and along its edges. At this point, the Zambezi wasn't more than one hundred feet across at its widest. Jarvis assured us that an opportunity for white river rafting could be experienced downstream. Any takers? Kenyatta held up her hand at which point Julie croaked: "No way!"

"Later, then." She grinned at me.

Harold and Julie were not outdoor enthusiasts, though Harold enjoyed a round of golf. For that reason, neither offered to help with the oaring though Kenyatta put her muscles into the act. Though I knew my way around canoes and kayaks, and if this were really my holiday, I'd do the white water rafting thing in a minute.—Julie, not likely.

Regardless, I was preoccupied with considering paddling back that way at night. Were the crocodiles more active at night or less? We glimpsed one enormous reptile at least six feet long basking on a rock and I all but shivered.

Pods of hippos bathed close to shore and we spotted one elephant on the Zambezi side pausing for a drink. I took photos enthusiastically and was genuinely thrilled, this being my first wild elephant sighting. Deek and Jarvis, both of whom were manning the paddles, kept a wide berth from the beast, explaining that it was best not to attract their attention.

Finally, we turned a bend in the river and spotted Semenov's lodge, a far less grand affair than ours but no less impressive. This one made liberal use of canvas sun shades and offered guests authentic rondavel cottages close to the river. The common space was a stilted open deck under the canvas tenting and chairs could be seen positioned to maximize river views.

Harold took numerous photos telling our hosts that maybe he'd book us in there some day just for a change. Very hard to get a booking there, Jarvis assured him, looking skeptical.

By early afternoon, we had paddled back down and pulled into shore on the Zimbabwe side where a barbed wire fence enclosed three green Rover tour-style vehicles emblazoned with *Elite Adventure Safaris.* One truck came pre-loaded with picnic provisions and the other with every creature comfort including a portable potty. It was safari time.

We plunged into the national game park in two of these vehicles and with a little luck, might actually glimpse more wild game. Chief on our goals, however, was not to spy a gazelle or a zebra, but to get as close as possible to the location of Louise and Terrence's last known camp. Luckily, Louise had kept a detailed map and Evan had instructed Jarvis to take us to that exact spot.

It was a long but exhilarating ride interrupted by giraffe sightings, a kudu, two wildebeests, and a glimpse of elephants ambling across the bushland, and enough baobab trees to excite Peaches who clung to the character of Kenyatta despite her enthusiasm for all things flora.

When we finally arrived at Louise and Terrence's camp site, I knew it at once. Little had changed over the century since the explorers had passed that way. The same thorn-and-bush studded savannah spread before us, the same smudge of purple blue hills far in the distance. Perhaps the grass was not quite as high as it had once been and certainly the wildlife wouldn't be nearly as abundant, but this was the spot.

"We'll stop for lunch here, Jarvis," Harold announced.

"We have a much nicer place on an escarpment not far away," the man explained, flashing his ready grin.

"Not necessary. My wife needs a spot of tea right now, don't you darling?"

"Yes, that's true. I cannot wait, in fact!"

Poor Jarvis and Deek—what a pain the Thornes were.

The moment the Rover pulled to a stop, we jumped out leaving the others to ensure that the area hadn't been commandeered by snakes and undesirable critters, a standard practice, I was to learn. Our guides would set up our picnic site and pitch a mini tent. Meanwhile Kenyatta and Julie strode away from the others letting them do the manly thing.

"Don't go too far, darling," Harold called.

"Stay within sight, ladies, " Jarvis added.

We waved at them once we had reached the desired location.

"Feel anything from Louise?," Peaches asked after a moment.

Shielding my eyes with my hand, I stifled my disappointment. "Nothing yet but this is the place, I know it."

"So, from her illustration, they must have pitched their tents right there—," Peaches pointed to slight rise in the terrain, "—and there. Those mountains over there were at this vantage and her painting put a large acacia tree between their two tents with thornbushes all around."

"That's how I remember the drawing, too. They formed a boma for added protection and yet she was still dragged away," I said. Terrence had recorded very little besides his botanical notations but he had written that drag marks were found emerging from his sister's tent.

"Snatched by wild animals, maybe?" Peaches mused.

"Only ostrich tracks were found."

"I haven't seen one of those yet. Do large birds drag their prey away in the middle of the night. I mean, aren't they too busy hiding their heads in the sand?"

I chuckled. "Since ostriches aren't carnivorous, I doubt they dragged her away."

"Human, then, but why would anybody kidnap Louise? I mean, it's not like there's somewhere close by where they could drag her off to, right? Those mountains over there have to be at least twenty miles away and why not take Terrence while they were at it?"

I shook my head. "They took Louise because she knew something they—whoever they were—didn't want her to disclose. Either that or she was part of something."

"Like what?"

"I have no idea." I pressed one finger between my temples.

"She was getting close, in other words," Peaches said.

"Maybe."

"Well, I suppose we should get back to being Julie and Kenyatta. Oh, wait. Look at that!" Peaches gazed down at the ground, something our guides had been encouraging us to do as part of the game sighting experience. "What the hell is that?" she whispered. "A theropod track?"

"A dinosaur?" I laughed but when I peered close to where she pointed, I was shocked to see a large bird-like print. "An emu or an ostrich, maybe?"

"Emus are Australian but an ostrich is a definite perhaps. Do, there are ostriches around here."

"It looks a bit like the something the witch doctor scribbled in the sand when I saw him yesterday."

"Weird."

We took pictures and scanned for similar prints but found nothing.

Soon we were being called to join the others for lunch set up on a trestle table not unlike those our Victorian explorers had used. I sipped my tea, nibbled my sandwiches, and took panoramic photos of the landscape, a terrain Jarvis and Deek called the *bundu* or bushland.

The whole time I struggled with a feeling of loss, of a profound sadness which made no sense to me at all. I had fully expected to be drawn into Louise's memories but nothing like that had yet occurred even while standing at the same place where she had disappeared. It left me baffled.

When our expedition sailed back across the Zambezi late that afternoon, we could see a larger tour boat docked on the lower jetty.

"Our new guests have arrived!" Jarvis exclaimed.

JANE THORNLEY

I strode up to the lounge deck where two of the new arrivals were being offered cool drinks. Though unsure who I'd meet among the new guests, the tall blond hunter and his tall dark companion were not in my viewfinder.

The man strode up to shake Evan's hand. "Justin VanHoute. You must be Harold Thorne and the missus. Saw you on the boat ride but didn't know who you were, of course. They told me there would be an insurance man from Britain among the guests and that must be you since you're the only bloke in residence."

"We spoke on the river tour," the missus said. "Who would have thought that you'd show up here at our game lodge?"

But VanHoute's attention was fixed on Harold, their hands grasped in some kind of understanding. Damn, if this insufferable hunter guy wasn't on the payroll.

"Delighted to meet you," Harold was saying.

"Likewise," Justin agreed.

The other man had slipped away, deep in conversation with Kenyatta.

Turning away, I accepted a cold lemonade from a server and escaped to our quarters, dreaming of a cool shower. On the way, I encountered Peaches-Kenyatta strolling along beside the tall, powerfully-built man who had arrived with VanHoute. This then must be our river guide and the other African operative.

"Julie, meet Dr. Kagisogani Abioye, a doctor of anthropology— known as Kagiso for short. He's *Zulu*." Her eyes widened when she spoke the word as if secretly describing a mythic race.

I returned Kagiso's engaging smile and shook his strong hand. "And you are a specialist in African mythology, I hear."

"I am, and happy to be of service." Dr. Abioye had the kind of expressive eyes that could smile without the man moving his lips, his personality communicating warmth, competency, and knowledge all at once. No wonder Peaches seemed besotted.

Okay then, with this expert Zambezi river expert anthropologist and the tracker-slash-hunter onboard, along with Peaches, Evan, and me, we were presumably outfitted for whatever lay ahead. Or, so I hoped, though preparing to a paddle a canoe up the Zambezi at night didn't inspire confidence.

I took a shower as soon as I returned to our room and moments after that had spread the panoramic images of the two staves across the floor, studying them closely. Now more than ever I was convinced that they told part of the story we needed to decipher. Still, a big piece remained missing.

The cultures we studied had used visual imagery combined with ritual traditions to infuse people with an understanding of their histories. Western explorers had attempted to provide their own versions, none of which were reliable since they were judged by a limited Western sensibility. Only Louise had started with their voices inscribed in their art, the first time such an approach had been taken, as far as I knew. She was a maverick.

I gazed down at the photo of the stave carvings which I had placed beside Louise's illustrations. It was then that I noticed how the pots featured in both depictions differed. One stave had decorative motives in a series of interconnecting triangles and the other used a distinctive wavy design. The triangles and geometric motifs were widely seen everywhere we'd been to date and the major decoration on the rondavels in Victoria Falls but the wavy design was something I had yet to see. They must represent a different tribe. I decided to ask Kagiso as soon as I had the chance.

Someone was knocking on the door. Seconds later, I opened it to face a jubilant Peaches.

"Did you see that gorgeous hunk of man who just arrived?" she said sweeping into my room. "Zulus are brilliant warriors, probably brilliant at everything. I mean, be still my beating heart."

I smiled. "I bet his chest roughly approximates those on the covers of those man-chest novels you read."

"I hope so." She grinned. "Maybe I'll get to check it out before we're done here."

"We can put those biceps to the test when we paddle upriver tonight to check out Semenov's lodge," I said, turning back to put away the photos and drawings.

"We're actually heading up river tonight?"

"Absolutely. Since Semenov's crew have abandoned—I presume temporarily—the lodge, it makes it a prime time to go snooping, not to mention place surveillance devices while we're at it. Evan's filling the men in on the details now."

"Damn, but that sounds like fun. Anyway, that's not why I dropped by this afternoon, Mrs. Thorne. I have something, I mean *someone*, to show you. While Evan is deep in conversation with Kagiso and Justin. This will be a surprise even to him but he'll find out soon enough. Come on, follow me. Might want to get dressed first, though. That robe is so not cool."

Baffled, I threw on my clothes, set the room alarm, locked the door, and followed her down the walkway. "Where are we going?" I asked as she took took a left-hand turn up a mini-ladder.

JANE THORNLEY

"Shortcut," she told me. "I found this back route the other day. By the way, you did win the bet."

"What bet?"

After crossing a mini suspension bridge, we arrived at a chalet positioned on the highest point on the islet commanding the best views by far. From here we could see the whole river panorama with Zimbabwe on one side, Zambia on the other. Peaches knocked sharply, the door opened, and we were ushered into another spacious and luxurious abode.

There stood Rupert in full safari regalia right down to the pith helmet held in one hand.

"I knew it!" I exclaimed, giving him a hug. "I was expecting you!"

"Does this mean that I am forgiven?" he asked, sounding a little breathless.

"Forgiven for what? I can't speak for your son who actually expects you to follow his directions, but I'm certainly glad to see you. I'm Julie Thorne, by the way."

Rupert beamed at me. "Are you? I am Sir Hillary Brown." Without addressing the matter directly, we had resolved to put the tea and meltdown incident behind us.

"Sir Hillary, really, Rupe?" Peaches chided. "Couldn't you drop the nose-tilting title at least for this game?"

"Never," he assured us. "And this—" he turned to sweep a hand towards a door through which Rory Hopkins suddenly strode, "—is my nephew, Adrian."

" I'll never keep all these false names straight," Peaches whispered.

"Rory!" I exclaimed.

"Adrian, please," he assured me with a grin. "When Uncle Hillary informed me what was afoot, I insisted on coming along. After all, this is my story you're seeking, Louise being my ancestor. I'm here on behalf of my dad. He always wanted to go on a safari to seek out his ancestors."

"And Sydney the secretary?" I asked.

"None the wiser," he assured me. "He believes I've returned to New York to tidy matters up there. He's really not such a bad chap, just infuriating."

"Evan's probably not going to be happy to see you two but I sure am." And I filled them in on what had transpired over the last few days.

"I'm convinced that if Rupert and I had remained in London, Semenov would have put a hit on us," Rory told me.

"You could be right," Peaches agreed. "They tried to nab Phoebe before she left."

"I urged my godfather, Max, to close up the gallery and take off for a few weeks and I'm relieved to say he did."

Rupert and Rory decided to make an appearance over supper, probably to delay private commentary from Evan for as long as possible.

After leaving them to settle in, I busied myself by doing Julie things like swimming in the plunge pool followed by conversation with Kenyatta at the bar. I didn't want to deliberately keep secrets from Evan but, in this case, I thought it best that he encounter his father without my alerting him in advance. To that end, I dashed back to the room to change, managing to miss Evan by minutes.

He texted me from the lounge.

> Phoebe, are you avoiding me?
>
> Me: See you at dinner, darling.

At 7:00 p.m., the guests convened. Now our numbers had swelled to fill several more tables on the lodge's dining deck and sent the staff scurrying to keep us all attended.

By this time, Evan had begun texting Peaches and me with instructions for the evening's operation, adding more than a few warnings. While I was changing, Peaches informed me that Evan had had his first encounter with his father acting as Sir Hillary and I missed the whole thing, damn it. It hadn't gone well, as I anticipated. Actually, it hadn't gone, period, seeing as Evan had still declined to acknowledge Sir Hillary and his supposed nephew but for a curt nod to both.

Over a long languorous candlelight dinner where kabobs were served with roasted vegetables, the company became better acquainted. Harold Thorne continued to more or less ignore Sir Hillary and his nephew, preferring instead to be entertained by his two new friends, Baron and Kagiso. Even his poor wife Julie had been trumped by the dudes but she didn't seem to mind since she was enjoying the company of her new friends, too.

The wine flowed for many while others such as myself remained with non-alcoholic drinks. Story hour was actually thrilling that night since both Baron and Kagiso had plenty of tales with which to regale us but the night's mission was never far from our minds.

Our new operatives were patched into a joint email group with the following instructions: at 11:15, we would all go off to our rooms. The idea was to allow the staff to settle into their nightly routines. At 12:15, Peaches, Evan, Kagiso, Baron, and I were to meet by the canoes for our trip upstream.

Luckily we knew our way around a canoe whereas Baron and Kagiso presumably knew their way around everything. Rupert was not patched into our email exchange.

Later in our room while readying for the evening's adventure, I grilled Evan about our two new operatives. By then we were both outfitted in our evening's black-on-black stealth gear, which differed from our usual wear because we added tall boots to avoid snakebites and possible waterborne diseases. I preferred Evan dressed in this manner rather than the shorts and polo shirts the Harold version sported.

"They know only that we're tracking something priceless while attempting to stay one step ahead of Semenov's team," he told me. "It's a delicate balance ensuring that they are well-informed without disclosing too much unnecessary information."

"Do you trust them?" I asked.

"Yes and no. I have every reason to believe that both men are reliable and trustworthy operatives but since I have never met them before today, I remain cautious. At least they've worked together before."

"Do they know about me?"

He turned around and cupped my face in his hands. "Do you mean did I disclose that my lady friend possesses what might be considered supernatural powers?" he said softly. "I doubt that they'd believe me. I'm not sure that I would if I were them. No, it's best that they learn what they need to through observation and work the details out for themselves. Those two men have no idea what to expect from either you or Peaches."

"And you're not going to tell them because you plan to enjoy their reactions," I accused playfully.

He shook his head, all serious man-on-task. "Thought that might bring a little entertainment to discover that the two women accompanying me are not quite what they seem, that is not my reason for keeping these men in the dark. In this business, it's always best to work on the-need-to-know basis."

I had been joking but he answered me earnestly. That reminded me that this man had spent most of his life tuned into serious missions and when he was focused, he was all-in. What would it be like to live with this man for real? Could we really fit all our habits together? Would he really tolerate all my eccentricities and my his?

Someone knocked sharply on our door. We both turned to where Evan's phone screen that he'd rigged into a makeshift security system revealed the caller.

"It's your dad. I wondered when he'd show."

Evan ran a hand through his hair as he open the door.

"Evan, dear boy, we must speak," Rupert announced.

Evan nudged him into the room and shut the door. "What is the idea of you coming here expressly against my wishes, Father?" he demanded.

I backed away, taking the seat on the deck and propping my feet on the stool. There, I proceeded to eavesdrop.

"Since when am I excluded from agency business, son?" Rupert inquired.

"Since you partially retired or possibly since your health began to falter—take your pick. Either way, coming to Africa while we're chasing down gold-hunting Russian thieves is foolhardy."

Evan always spoke like his dad when angry. *Foolhardy.*

"Nonsense. As usual you will find me exceedingly useful should you include me in your missions. I was a rowing champion at Oxford, I'll have you know, and, indeed, Rory assures me that he, too, was an oarsman at Cambridge."

"Have you seen the high-sided craft they use to keep the crocs away from paddlers here, Father? They are about as far removed from a racing scull on the Avon River as you can get!" Evan was truly angry, poor guy.

"Well, it is true that the only wild creatures we had to deal with back in those days were lovely young women and a few men who were eager for our attentions. In any event, give me a task to do, my good lad, and do stop being so pugnacious."

Even while eavesdropping, I was trying to provide them an illusion of privacy which meant that I missed facial expressions. I would have loved to see Evan's face when his dad called him pugnacious.

"Very well, here's a task for you that I know you to be very good at: tonight we'll be sailing upstream to Semenov's lodge on reconnaissance. Ensure that the staff here remain unaware of our absence. In other words, create a distraction, distractions being your specialty."

After Rupert had left, I slipped back into the room to find Evan gazing out towards the river, his jaw tight. Wrapping my arms around his waist, I murmured: *"Sons should know that fathers follow their example, not their advice.* Okay, so I reversed the order but it still works." He smiled, but his response was cut short by the wail of a siren.

"What the hell is that?" I gasped, pulling away.

"That is Dad's distraction occurring about twenty minutes too early."

CHAPTER 17

"Did you give him a set time to launch this distraction?" I whispered as we grabbed our backpacks and bolted for the door.

"He's to wait until I give the signal, that's the drill. Here, this way." Evan nudged me up the same wavering rope bridge that Peaches had led me across earlier. "Now we have to scramble."

Far up on one of the highest decks we paused long enough to see the panorama of explosions below—red, blue, green, including one starburst that belonged in a carnival rather than at a game lodge.

"Pyrotechnics," Evan muttered. "Dad's a master at creating explosions that do no harm other than to startle every living creature within a forty mile radius." We could see the staff running back and forth in their shorts trying to put out fires that didn't exist. They probably believed they were under attack. "Come on, let's get to the canoes."

By now Rupert could be heard loudly demanding that staff get this frightful disturbance under control pronto. Didn't they know who he was?

"He'll keel over in a faint next," I whispered as I slipped down to the water's edge to claim a canoe. "You have to admit that it's a pretty good distraction."

"I'm not going to admit anything," Evan clenched his teeth. "Semenov's guard would have had to have seen that display up river which might provoke him to alert his bosses that something's afoot. We may have even less time to get up there and back before the reinforcements arrive."

Good point. He had already texted the other three to meet us at the canoes as soon as possible, which left us counting the seconds waiting.

Peaches arrived first. "Rupert—I mean Hillary—has just clutched his ticker and fallen over backward in a faint. He's got the staff running circles around him while Rory acts as if he's really in charge. Did you arrange this, Ev? Brilliant if you did," she whispered.

"That was entirely his own invention," Evan assured him.

Then Kagiso appeared, a rifle slung over one shoulder. "What is happening?"

Evan filled him in while Kagiso pulled out a canoe. Peaches immediately climbed into the boat with him. "Four biceps are better than two." He flashed her a grin which she returned with glee.

When Justin arrived with his rifle seconds later, Evan told him to travel with me while he manned a canoe solo.

"Why?" I asked him as we pushed the boats into the river.

"In case I get held up, Justin will ensure your safety," he whispered. "He has instructions to protect you, no matter what."

"What instructions?" I demanded.

"Don't worry, I'll keep you safe," Justin assured me. "Here, wear this."

I stared at the black nylon stocking cap he passed me. That along with a life jacket completed my ensemble.

"Best disguise for we whities," he told me. I noted that Evan donned one but not Peaches and Kagiso. I pulled mine on, immediately getting how I melded in with the night.

"Natural blending," Kagiso added.

"Try not to be too jealous," Peaches said with a grin.

Conversation was soon aborted as we focused on maneuvering the river. Kagiso took the lead, guiding us to the side of the island closest to the Zambian shore in order to avoid scrutiny from the frazzled staff.

It was enough for me to keep concentrating on paddling. I hadn't manned oars for a couple of years so my muscles were rusty and rowing upstream on a fast-flowing current didn't help. Justin, obviously a skilled rower, did most of the heavy lifting. Evan had shared that the hunter had protested at having two women accompany the team upstream that night, but he didn't share those objections with me.

Of all the things I had imagined about paddling the Zambezi at night, the one thing I hadn't considered was the lack of artificial light. This being a stealth mission, we could hardly afford to fix a spotlight to our prows which meant that navigation had to be by the moon and stars alone. With the feast of timeless natural illumination from the sky, we could see every rivulet, every current below while a river of stars glowed above. If only I had time to savor the beauty.

Kagiso kept us more or less in the center of the river to avoid predators and it wasn't until we rounded the final bend that our canoes began moving toward shore again. Ahead, we could see the solar lights of Semenov's lodge but no sign of movement. We slipped up to the edge of the riverbank downstream from the lodge by about a hundred feet and dragged our canoes onto shore.

The first task was to locate and debilitate the lone guard. Evan's phone had detected his heat signature near the back of the facility and the three men spread out in that direction.

Peaches and I activated our explosives detectors in case of boobytraps, our main task being to get inside the buildings and snoop for relevant clues. We were to behave as thieves and brought a standard garbage bag for carrying away our supposed booty, something apparently local thieves did because they often couldn't afford expensive gear. We also wore plastic over our boots to disguise our footprints.

Evan gave us twenty minutes before we were to meet by the boats.

When Peaches and I reached the main lounge, we found the area furnished with wicker chairs and mostly open to the elements. The furniture was well-worn, even grubby in places.

Other than overflowing ashtrays and a well-used bar filled with half-empty and drained bottles of vodka and other liquor, the area showed no signs of recent occupation.

Peaches and I stole a few bottles of alcohol to make things look authentic. Meanwhile, we scanned for surveillance devices but found none. Next, we unlocked the kitchen and ran our lights over the shelves. By the supplies and the jugs of soured milk in the fridge, the lodge had been vacated for at least two weeks.

"Doesn't look like a tourist place," Peaches whispered. "More like a camp."

"Base camp," I agreed, shining my light along the shelves and tossing a few choice items like flour and canned goods into the bag.

We found the library shortly after that and not surprisingly, many of the books on African history and topography were in Russian. What interested us most was the corkboard propped on one wall. Paper upon paper had been tacked onto its surface.

My heart began thumping when I spied a photocopy of one of Louise's sketches. "Look!"

Peaches began photographing every note and page while I investigated closer. "The Nyami sticks! If we ever needed proof that Semenov is after the same thing, this is it."

"Yeah, but what does he know that we don't? That bastard has to have gone some place important but where?"

"Maybe there's a map around?" I shone my light up the walls and across every surface and almost missed the white paper edge sticking out of a folding table against the wall. Flipping it down, we hit paydirt. There, taped down on the tabletop, was exactly what we sought: a standard map of southern Africa so thick with tape, it may as well have been laminated.

Peaches and I studied the felt marker lines and circles beneath the tape. "All the places they must suspect the gold to be. Damn it, they are way ahead of us."

"Not necessarily. They could be going around in circles, no pun intended."

"Of course, the pun is intended. You never miss a pun." Peaches zoomed in to take shots of all the circled places before pulling out for several full-sized photos. "See anything else?"

"No, but we'll get these back to the lodge, enlarge them, and see what we can find out."

We tried not to touch anything. We used gloves and checked for any footprints left behind but still we worried that somehow they'd figure out our identities.

"Let's search the huts next."

Evan texted to say that they'd found and disabled the guard and the they had now separated to comb the rest of the property. *One surveillance device found, no explosives*, he wrote. *Be back to the canoes in ten minutes.* I updated him on our end as we kept going.

The rondavels were next. At one point, these huts would have been guest accommodations and were appointed with all the comforts of a budget motel room made thrilling by the very authenticity of their mud and thatch construction. Now, they had taken on the appearance of what Peaches referred to as "flop houses"—untidy, mostly in need of maintenance, and all desperate for a deep clean. In some, clothing lay strewn across rumpled sheets. In others, beds had been made, glasses washed out, and ashtrays emptied, obviously, according to the lodger's disposition. They all looked as if the roomers intended to return.

"Semenov doesn't hire room service, I guess," Peaches remarked.

"The best way to keep their activities secret. Let's go."

We dropped our garbage bags filled with supposed loot along the paths as if we had abandoned them on the run.

We were halfway on the path heading towards the main lodge when we saw lights rapidly approaching through the bush behind the lodge. Headlights! And then we heard a cry. Animal or human we didn't know but we took off in the direction of the canoes, arriving in time to see Justin apparently wrestling with something by the shore.

At first, I thought it could be a crocodile but soon realized he was struggling with a man. I zapped the assailant between the shoulder blades and watched him drop to his knees into the water. Justin looked at me, stunned: "What the hell?"

"Heart attack?" I said with a shrug.

He took aim with his rifle, ready to kill the man.

"Leave him," I said. "He's incapacitated. That's enough."

But Justin shot him in the leg. "There, now he's incapacitated, sweetheart."

"What's happening?" Peaches demanded as she ran up beside me.

"A truckload of these bastards have returned! Let's get out of here!" Justin began dragging a canoe towards the water.

Overhead, the lodge lights were suddenly blazing, an alarm was pealing, and I could see Kagiso dashing down the path towards us. "Move it!" he cried. "They have returned!"

"Where's Evan?" I could see his canoe still onshore but no sign of him anywhere.

"He told us to leave if anything happened," Justin told me. "So we're leaving. Get in!"

"We're not going anywhere," Peaches said, heading back up the path.

"You go," I told the men, following after her.

"Get back here, you stupid bitches!" Justin said in a harsh whisper. "Orders are to leave!"

Our feet never faltered. We kept low, watching out for movement ahead. Peaches tugged me behind a water barrel and pointed above where two men could be seen looking out toward the river, machine guns in arms.

"Hell!" Peaches whispered.

"They're watching the river for boats," I said. I pulled out my phone to check for messages, my heart in my throat. On the screen was a text from Evan: *Down by the river other side.*

"We need a distraction," I whispered.

Nodding, she crept towards the main deck, lifted her phone at the fire pit sunk into the decking, and aimed. The pit exploded into a mass of black smokey flames.

"Damn, I love this thing!" she whispered holding up her phone as the men jumped around trying to extinguish the fire.

We slipped beneath the deck towards the opposite side and in minutes were down by the water edge where we saw Evan beckoning to us. Two canoes lay upended nearby along with the body of a man face-up in the muck.

"Are you all right?" I cried.

"Of course. I tackled that one," he was pointing to the man prone on the shore—"and while I was stunning him, my phone flew out of my hand," he said. "There are four men all together, one down—"

"Two down," Peaches said.

"Good, so two left but more will be on the way. We should kill them."

"But you won't, will you? I asked. "These guys are just hirelings. Let's save our blasts for the real bad guys."

Evan gave me a look, half-indulgent, half-disapproving. "Very well, but we still can't leave without that phone."

And we couldn't. No way did we want that technology to fall into enemy hands, even if they didn't know what to do with it.

Peaches handed her phone to him and we set both both devices to *locate phone* mode, picking up the signal instantly. It had fallen into the water not more than ten feet away deep in the pampas grass lining the river where the green *find me* light would not show. And neither would the crocodiles.

Wading up to our knees in the water, we picked our way in the direction of the signal while Peaches stood guard on the bank. "Croc coming in on your left!" she hissed.

Evan swung around, aiming for the pair of amber eyes slipping through the grass. One zap later and the beast kept on coming.

"Full stun zap, Phoebe, on the count of three. One, two, three," he whispered.

We zapped the reptile at full charge, relieved to see it stop moving. "It's only stunned briefly, Phoebe," Evan said. The beast's stun took long enough for Evan to locate his phone, pluck it up from the water beneath the croc, and the two of us scurry back to dry ground. A machine gun rat-a-tatted above us.

It was at that moment that a canoe slipped around the corner and pulled up to shore with Kagiso manning the oars. The three of us climbed in and were soon sliding soundlessly through the water leaving, pandemonium behind.

"Destroyed all their boats. Don't know if this canoe will carry the three of us back," Kagiso said. "Justin waits downstream with other canoe."

"How did you convince him to stay?" I asked.

"I didn't convince him, exactly. The man requires handling, you see. I just reminded him that one does not allow one's employer to die in the interests of fiscal responsibility." And he laughed.

We found the hunter waiting not far from where we had first landed, tucked into the pampas grass with the second canoe roped to the first. Evan and I climbed into one while Peaches remained with Kagiso, and we proceeded back to our lodge.

This return voyage being downstream went much quicker. We rounded the bend to our lodge half-dreading what we might see following the chaos we'd left behind but all appeared quiet.

Securing the canoes, we climbed onto shore. To our right the staff huts were dark and peaceful with no sign of movement. Soundlessly we wove our way back up to the lodge. Just before we reached the deck, Evan turned to face the team. "We escaped by the skin of our teeth tonight. With a little luck, they may think they've been hit by thieves, since there's enough of those around in these parts."

"I knocked out all their security cameras," Justin said. "There wasn't much there worth stealing except for food, which might be reason enough for a burglary. Otherwise, I shot one man."

"Killed him, I suppose?" Peaches asked.

"Yes, darling, I killed him. You don't want him coming after you a second time now, do we?" Standing there with his golden-boy good looks, his rifle slung over his shoulder, I suddenly recalled his parting shot to Peaches and me when we returned for Evan.

Before I could respond, Peaches strode up to Justin and slugged him across the jaw, sending him staggering backward. "If you ever call me, my friend, or any woman in earshot, a 'stupid bitch', a 'darling', a 'sweetheart', or any disrespectful shit, I swear I'll do more than sock your ugly kisser."

Justin, holding his cheek, briefly stared at her in stunned silence before letting loose a howl of laughter and saluting her. "Yes, ma'am!"

Kagiso joined the laughter, saying, "I told you, man."

Evan just shook his head. "Don't mess with these two, Justin," he warned the hunter. "I can't be held responsible for your safety."

We returned to our quarters without encountering anyone, staff or otherwise. Our *Do Not Disturb* sign still hung on our door. There was plenty to say but we were nearly too exhausted to speak. Though Evan kept one arm around my shoulder for most of the way.

"Did you find anything interesting?" he asked as I flopped on my back across the bed.

"Yes, actually. We can go through it all in the morning," I murmured.

Evan sat down beside me and thumbed through his phone. "Dad messaged us to say that his distraction was an 'unparalleled success'. He said that in order to sustain the distraction, he found it necessary to create a power outage and, to that end, he broke the circuit in the generator to plunge the lodge into darkness. It lasted for only a couple of hours, he assures us, and then he had the generator back into operation."

"Your father is endlessly inventive." I sighed, closing my eyes.

A sustained silence followed. After a moment Evan said quietly: "Which means that for two hours tonight, our accommodations were unsecured."

I sat up. "Damn."

The two of us scoured the room looking for something out of place, checking our suitcases, our tablets, everything. Nothing unusual appeared.

And then I saw it, a flash of white where there shouldn't be anything white. On the balcony, what looked to be a sketch jotted on the lodge notepaper weighted under a rock on a basket footstool.

In seconds, I held it in my fingers, staring. It looked exactly as if someone had roughly sketched a giant ostrich track on the lodge memo pad.

I turned to Evan. "The witch doctor was here."

CHAPTER 18

The next morning our staff heard that the neighboring lodge had been raided by a band of thieves, putting everyone on edge. Word traveled as if by magic in these camps using what Jarvis referred to as "the bush telegraph."

Everyone remained so busy preparing against a similar attack that after breakfast we were left to our own devices. Meanwhile, our quarters had been turned into operation southern as the team members convened later that morning.

"It would be bloody helpful if you were to disclose exactly what we're looking for," Justin said while pacing back and forth on the balcony outside our room. So far, the new team members knew nothing about the Hopkins's historical involvement, nothing about the staves of the three kings, and even less about the agency except that we'd all been traveling under assumed names.

We were all studying the photos of the map Peaches and I had taken the night before, a map that covered the full length of Zimbabwe and several neighboring countries with several sites circled across a wide range of territory. It told us nothing except that Semenov's team were searching all over southern Africa.

"We don't really know exactly what we're seeking or where," Evan explained, "and I'd say by looking at this map, that they don't, either.

However, as I explained earlier, it could be some ancient African treasure secreted away by a string of tribal kings nearly seven hundred years ago."

"There have been many rumors of secret gold all over Africa, the most famous being King Solomon's Mines but there are other tales," Kagiso said. "I am not surprised to learn such a quest is afoot but what triggered this one?"

We explained about the Hopkins diary, the nineteenth century brother and sister team that followed on the heels of Livingstone, and the story of the three staves of the three kings while revealing Louise's illustrations.

"Good, so you have a new lead," the doctor nodded. "This interests me very much. These stories were forged long before the white man attempted to claim Africa for his own and they often have a grain of truth buried at their heart. Here I see a story of African nations banding together to guard something of great importance. This rings true to me."

"Louise Hopkins believed that each of these three walking sticks belonged to a leader of one African nation, and that when the symbology is read all together, this understanding would pave the way to the location of the secret treasure," Peaches explained.

"But she herself played a role. We just don't understand how." I shared how Louise had been told by a witch doctor that she was part of a great story.

Kagiso was studying the drawings beside the corresponding photos. "Those Nyami Nyami sticks are common around the Kariba Dam area there," he told us, pointing to an area circled on the map. "The story goes that the river god Nyami *Nyami* became angry when the dam blocked him away from his wife on the other side. From then on he would occasionally flood the land to express his displeasure, but this is a more recent tale. The one you describe is far older. Looks like our friends upstream have already visited this place."

"You say that these sticks were common around Lake Kariba area but would they have been used elsewhere?" I asked.

"Oh, yes," Kagiso assured us, "all over. A carved walking stick was the sign of status to the tribal leaders and many people use walking sticks all over the world."

He peered closer at my printed panoramic photo. "But this one is not from a king but a priestess." He was pointing to the carving of the two people, man and woman, apparently crouching over five pots. "Look, you see how this woman leans above the man? She does not wear the headdress of a queen but is the Bedyango and would be selected from the king's sisters and aunts to preside over births, marriages, and deaths. You might call her a priestess. She held great influence and would also be the Secret Keeper, She Who Knew All." He widened his eyes and lowered his deep voice to set the mood.

For a moment we were all in his thrall. "The Bedyango," I whispered. "The Secret Keeper, the priestess. I had no idea there were high priestesses here but that must have been the meaning of the 'P' Louise jotted over the illustrations of this person. P for Priestess."

"They are all gone now, all the Bedyangos." Kagiso placed one hand over his heart. "Time and change, they are the great eradicators but many centuries ago these women ruled with kings and queens to assure that the tribe lived on."

"How likely would it be for three African tribes to have created a league to protect their trade routes five hundred years ago?" Peaches asked.

"Very. Modern man paints the African people as primitive and unknowing because they lack what we consider education but this only strengthens their knowledge of the spirits. These sticks tell the story of magic, river magic here with the rings representing the river currents, and in this one, the carvings of the trees speak of the spirits of the forest. And you say that the third one is missing?"

"So Louise Hopkins believed," I told him.

"Then that may hold the final piece."

"That's what we're after," I said.

"And the possibility of hidden treasure?" Evan asked.

"Gold is mined here in Africa, diamonds and precious stones, too," Justin said. The hunter shrugged. "We've been shot at for a lot less."

"The story of hidden gold in African is very old," Kagiso continued. "Very old. The tribes that opened trade routes with the East gained great wealth. They believed that jewels held the spirit light trapped inside. Sapphires and aquamarines for river gods and the sky, topaz and citrine for the sun, emerald for the forest spirits and ruby for fire's heart. Look at this stave here—the aquamarine holds the river's heart. They treasured these magic stones most. They would not trade their greatest jewels for fear of angering the gods. It would be reasonable to think that the they established a safe place to secure their greatest treasures."

"Oh, my God," Peaches whispered. "The trove could be enormous! No wonder Semenov is invested in finding the treasure."

"But our mission is to ensure that whatever wealth is located stays here in Africa," Evan said. "As I have stressed when I brought you both onboard, this is not about anyone lining their pockets but helping the African people claim what is rightfully theirs. This treasure cannot fall into Russian hands."

"We are behind you," Kagiso stated, his deep voice booming. "I pledge my life to my people and Justin knows that if he does not, I will have to kill him."

At which point he let out a howl of laugher and slapped Justin on the back hard enough to pop the man's phone out of his shirt pocket.

"We're good," Justin said, recovering. "My friend here and I are committed. You can trust us, even if I do come across as a sexist idiot at times." He held out his lands towards Peaches's and me. "We can start over now, right?"

"Right," I said with a laugh. "No hard feelings, but Justin," I said, "I need you to help me with something else. Answer me this: are there ostriches around here?"

It was such a pedestrian question following on the heels of treasure and spirit talk that the man looked temporarily confounded. "The South African Ostrich is found in the open scrublands, yes, but poachers have nearly decimated their numbers in these parts. Now they are mostly farmed. Haven't seen one in the wild for years, even in game reserves. Why do you ask?"

I held out the photo I'd taken on my phone. "This. Peaches—I mean Kenyatta—and I spotted it during the safari drive yesterday." I made no mention of the sketch—yet.

He took my phone and studied the photo. "That's no ostrich, that's human."

"Human?" Peaches gasped, jumping to her feet.

Kagiso and Evan joined Justin to gaze over his shoulder. All tall men, they stood head to head. "The Doma here? They are out of their territory," he murmured. "This is very strange."

"This is only one of many strange things you can encounter in our company," Evan remarked.

"What are the Doma?" Peaches enquired.

"Not what, *who*," Kagiso said. "They are a tribe sometimes known as the Two-toed tribe or the Ostrich people but they call themselves the Doma. They keep to themselves."

"As in a secret tribe?" I asked, barely able to contain my excitement.

He smiled at me. Kagiso had the most arresting smile which he used as much to make a point as to express pleasure. "Have you heard of it?"

"Heard of the Doma? No, I hadn't," I said, smiling back. It was impossible not to.

"Then it is secret, at least to all who do not live in these parts. The Doma mostly live in the Kanyemba region in Northern Zimbabwe and they are the original hunter gatherers of our land, still keeping to the old ways because they live apart from the modern world. They have a genetic condition with three middle toes missing and the two outer ones come together like this." He held one hand up and pointed at the photo on my phone.

"How long have they existed?" I asked.

"For as long as anyone can remember," Justin said. "Originally they were shunned by the other tribes but now they prefer to live apart. What others consider infirmatives, they see as benefits which give them great speed in running and ease in climbing trees."

"The condition is called ectrodactyly," Evan said, now head down over his phone. "It is a rare genetic mutation that has been retained because of a tribal decree that does not permit them to marry outside of the tribe."

Our eyes met. "We must find them."

"But they don't want to be found," Justin said. "They are resistant to outside influences and change."

"Which makes them perfect for keeping a great secret safe for centuries. And why was one of their footprints seen across the river, anyway?" I demanded. "And how would they have gotten here?"

"By river," Kagiso said. "The Zambezi goes all the way up to Northern Zimbabwe to Mozambique close to their main settlement but there are rumored to be other bands living throughout the land. Some are nomadic."

"And now it looks as though a band of them are on the move," Justin countered. "That is a very strange thing right there."

I was still in an eye-lock with Evan. "It isn't the first time the Doma have wandered this far from their homeland." I knew now that this was the mysterious tribe that Louise had referred to in her diary, possibly who dragged her away from her camp over a hundred years ago. "They are hiding a secret, keeping it safe for centuries. We have to find them before Semenov."

Justin looked ready to protest but stopped himself.

Kagiso spoke instead. "They'd be easily overcome. They're not warriors but live off the land full of heart. They believe that the land provides but the land has not been so kind to them—or anyone—for many years. I do not believe they can protect themselves."

"We'll need a helicopter or, better still, a plane," Justin told Evan.

"I've already arranged a helicopter but the plane won't be available for at least another day. The helicopter will be waiting for us on the Zimbabwe side of the river by tomorrow morning."

"Then we must get everything together and be ready to travel by tomorrow." Peaches appeared willing to go anywhere at a moment's notice.

"One more thing," I said holding up the sketch. "What would you say if I told you that I found this in our room after we returned from our raid last night?"

Kagiso took the page between his fingers. "I would say that great magic is about this place or perhaps I should say great magic is about you. I can feel this. Did this drawing just appear?"

"I have a witch doctor following me. I met him in Victoria Falls and glimpsed him once since. I know he's here. I can feel him. He won't approach me unless I'm alone and for obvious reasons, I'm seldom alone."

Kagiso was studying me. "There is more here than what you are telling us. Perhaps you would explain what is missing from your story so we may better understand?"

"I guess it's time". Evan and Peaches gave me the nod and so I began, going all the way back to the beginning with my lost-art-sniffer-dog gifts and my brother, the timewalking—everything.

Justin and Kagiso listened intently, one's eyes pealed wide with amazement, the other sitting in silence shaking his blond head. By the time I had finished, the African contingent knew the full story, or at least the elevator view.

"You draw strong magic to you, Phoebe, and here you tread in a land of strong magic. We must take extra care to protect you." Kagiso's otherwise mobile features had settled into a look of great solemnity.

"That remains our prime objective," Evan told him, strengthening his point by drawing me close to him.

"Justin and I will go now and speak in depth with the staff to see if they have seen any odd occurrences like Doma tracks or have seen witch doctors about. They are already on guard but we must ensure they remain more so."

"One more thing," Evan said just before the men left our room. "I have been monitoring the surveillance trackers we planted last night, and though I'm not fully fluent in Russian, with the assistance of my translator app I have pieced together enough. Semenov's team are not convinced that thieves broke into their compound last night. Nothing important was stolen, I heard them say, and certain events like a suddenly exploding firepit and a guard falling asleep on the job cued them in on a possible connection to the London raid. We must secure this lodge immediately."

Everyone agreed and as the men left our quarters, Evan about to leave with them, Rupert and Rory arrived.

"I say, things went rather swimmingly last night, don't you agree?" Rupert announced as he strode into the room.

"Actually, I do not agree and I'll explain why in detail in a moment, but first I do have a job for you."

"Finally!" Rory exclaimed, rubbing his hands together. "Make us useful on this great adventure, please do."

Evan appeared to be making an effort to keep his temper in check, at least that's how I read that twitch in his jaw. While he was describing why he did not agree that Rupert's distraction was "an unparalleled success," Peaches and I crept away.

"Can you imagine living with father and son?" I asked.

She shot me look. "You mean as me or you? If you mean me, either Rupert or I would be in a constant struggle on a societal level every minute of the day. If you mean you, well, sure. It wouldn't be perfect but what is? Why did you bring that up? Are you planning on moving into old Foxy's lair any time soon?"

"No, of course not." I wish I hadn't brought it up. "It's just that I'm wearing a ring on my finger and it's making me think."

Peaches stopped in her tracks. "Think marriage, you mean? Woman, are you holding out on me? Did that love-sick man of yours finally pop the question?"

"No!" I assured her. "It's just that we're living as husband and wife at the moment, so my mind naturally goes there."

"Your mind better not go to Harold Thorne or the romance will be as dead as a deep-fried calamari."

How I wish I hadn't said a word. "Anyway," I said loudly, "I'm guessing that Semenov's men know we're here. If Evan's right and they've traced certain indicators from last night to the break-in at Semenov's mansion, we may end up on the endangered species list. Come on, let's go." I linked my arm with hers and steered her along.

"Yeah, Kaggy told me that thieves around these parts don't typically cause exploding fires or put guards to sleep instantly—tell-tale signs, in other words."

"Kaggy now?" I asked. Table-turning time.

"Well, yes. We've had several good talks."

"Only talks?"

"Who's had the time for anything else?" she asked with a look of mock shock.

"Good point," I acknowledged. "So, back to the other issue: maybe we overplayed our hand back there at Semenov's?"

"The Russians may do something to retaliate. How can we protect this lodge and all the staff then?"

"Evan will figure something out," I said, "but now he has Rory and his father to worry about, too."

We spent the rest of the day studying maps, rereading Louises's diary, and assuring Jarvis and Deek that we weren't up to a game ride that day and were happy just to lounge around the deck watching the hippos from a distance. Our poor safari guides were obviously relieved and did little to convince us otherwise. Meanwhile, the men worked with the staff to rig up extra safety precautions. By now, the entire lodge was aware that their guests were not the garden variety tourists.

By the time supper rolled around, we were one large extended family gathered together against both wild and human predators, more than ready for a little release. I had one glass of wine, which was one more than I should have had but I told myself that I needed to relax.

Thus, together we all sat by the fire under the stars, me leaning against Evan's shoulder, feeling weary and content at the same time. Tonight, I'd ditched the Juliewear to climb into jeans and a sweater, not completely out of character but more comfortable in the cooler evening.

"If we weren't in the middle of Africa surrounded by some of the world's most dangerous predators, human or otherwise, I'd say this was a perfect moment," Evan whispered.

I smiled up at him. "It certainly is pretty spectacular and romantic, too, but for the predators part. Perfect foe what?"

"For you and me, of course. And," he continued as if my remark inspired him, "I believe this is the ideal time for me to ask you something that has been on my mind—in my heart, in truth—for some time." He reached into his pocket.

"So, when does the lodge go into lock-down?" I asked abruptly.

Evan's hand stilled. "We already have, Phoebe. I've established an invisible electric fence around our perimeter that is operated by a tablet of which Dad is in charge and we've taught Rory how to locate problems on the grid in a few easy steps. I see him checking it every few minutes. He's a quick learner. Nevertheless, what I've patched together is not foolproof, not that any system is ever foolproof. Now, may I return to my original line of thought?"

"What line of thought?"

"The beautiful evening, the moon over the Zambezi?" He pulled me closer until my head rested against his shoulder.

"I think I need to pee."

"Well, that ruined the moment."

"What moment?" Yes, I know.

Meanwhile, Rupert sat sipping his whiskey and saluting Jarvis as the guide finished his story about being charged by a white rhino. He looked so relaxed, thoroughly enjoying himself while his pseudo nephew sat nearby clapping and cheering each storyteller on while keeping one eye fixed on his tablet.

"If you want to go to the toilet, you might want to make a dash for it before Kagiso launches his story."

"Good idea." I checked my watch. On top of everything else, it demanded to be recharged.

"I'll be right back," I said.

"I'll come with you," Evan said.

"No need. I'll use the loo off the bar."

Only, it was currently occupied so I wound my way back towards our room. I'd just bolt for our room.

"Wait!" Peaches said, catching up to me. "You're not going anywhere without your bodyguard."

I turned and caught Evan's eye . On his feet now and watching me down near the fireside it was obvious that I was to go nowhere without accompaniment. Right, got it. "Okay, but I do have my phone with me and I'm only going to the bathroom." I held my phone up to prove my point.

"Doesn't matter." We carried on up the planked path. "I think I'm in love," she finally admitted.

"At last you've found a man your equal," I grinned, turning to give her a hug which sent the narrow bridge swaying like an electric snake beneath our feet. "I wondered when he'd appear."

"Don't joke. I'm smitten."

"I'm not joking and I feel like dancing, I'm so happy for you. So, would Kagiso be willing to return to London with you?" I asked.

"Okay, so we haven't exactly worked out all the details yet," she said, casting me a mischievous grin, "but we're getting to it. I have some serious territory to cover first."

I swung around. "I just bet and, by the way, I think Evan was about to ask me to marry him."

"And you what?" she demanded, excitement in her voice.

"I said I needed to pee, what else?"

"What? Don't you love him?"

"I love him but that doesn't me I want to ruin our romance with matrimony."

"Matrimony heralds a different kind of love, you twit! How can you be so brave and yet a total coward at the same time?" She was still berating me when I unlocked my room and strode for the bathroom. "Make yourself comfy."

I slid my phone onto the counter, popped my watch onto the charger, shut the door, and did my business. While washing my hands moments later, I noticed that the outside shower door was ajar.

And then the lights went off.

"Peaches?" I cried.

CHAPTER 19

My limbs were encased in some tube-like thing with tape slapped over my mouth. Seconds later, I was dragged into the shower stall, felt something fastened onto the tube, and winched up into the air.

I kicked out, gazing down at two black-garbed attackers signaling to whoever operated the pulley above my head. The ground flew away. The huge ebony tree that formed part of our treehouse was now a prop for my kidnapping.

I couldn't move, couldn't cry out, but by the time I reached the first towering branch, I could look over the thatched roof to see Peaches splayed on her back on our deck, hear Kagiso's deep voice boom out across the river in the midst of his story, and listen to my brain screaming outrage. *Peaches!*

Within minutes, I had been levered down the other side of the tree and unhooked, my body as efficiently handled as if I was a precious cargo being passed from man to man into a waiting canoe. I counted five of them. They needed me alive.

Soon, I was faceup on the bottom of a canoe being paddled soundlessly downstream—*downstream*, not up towards the enemy lodge as everyone would expect! We encountered mini rapids along the way that splashed cool water onto my prone form but the men were expert paddlers and kept the boat steady during our soundless ride. I glimpsed trees and pampas grass flying by so knew they were keeping close to shore. I shivered.

How long would it take for someone to sound the alarm—two minutes, twenty? The security alerts hadn't been triggered because the breech occurred overhead. Evan knew that Peaches and I could easily get into long conversations which would keep us from returning right away. Our phone alerts hadn't been set because there were too many people around and our signals would indicate that we were exactly where we were supposed to be—in my room.

Meanwhile, the canoe pulled into shore. I was trundled out, one man carrying my feet, the other my shoulders, and transferred through the bush. Wherever they were taking me must have been shielded from the river because I saw the dark mass of a rocky escarpment pass as they wound around and through the trees.

A flash of electric light and suddenly I was taken in through an open door, heard a generator cranking away, saw a thatched ceiling overhead, and smelled woodsmoke. Then I was unceremoniously plopped upright onto a seat. My tube was removed but my legs swiftly secured to the chair, my hands bound together in my lap. Peeling off the duct tape from my mouth was the final step and provoked swearing on my part.

As my eyes adjusted to the light, I realized I was in a large mud rondavel furnished with multiple seats and a curved bar along one side. A fire burned in a grate in the center of the room, the smoke escaping through a hole in the thatched roof.

I blinked. A man stood up from the other side of the fire and strolled towards me. I recognized him at once. Though I had last seen him in a photo wearing a long cashmere coat telling the press that, no, he had no allegiance to certain political powers in the Kremlin, this was the same man. His hair had the recognizable short dirty-blond cut, slightly spiky on the top as was the fashion, but now he wore tall boots and jodhpurs with a belted jacket in a subdued shade of bush green.

"Semenov, I presume," I gasped.

He laughed, a brief "Ha!". He was in his early fifties, short, and fit. "Ah, yes, like Livingstone. Yes, I am Ivan Semenov and I recognize you, also. I hoped that we would meet under different circumstances, perhaps before you broke into my home and stole from me." Though his accent was noticeably Russian, his English was excellent.

"Do you mean as in retrieved the pieces stolen from your neighbor, Sir Hanley Hopkins before you caused his death?"

He stood looming over me, rocking back and forth on his booted heels. "How is old Hanny—still dead, I hope? Death happens to people who cross me. You crossed me, Phoebe McCabe."

"I thought you were in Belarus," I said.

"You were mistaken, see?" He lifted his hands. "Not in Belarus."

Enough of this. "What do you want from me?"

"You know what I want, Ms. McCabe. You are called 'the Lost-Art Sniffer Dog' and you will sniff out what I want or everyone you love dies." He held up a phone with the screen displaying a video of explosions and flames. "This is your lodge right now. As we speak, they are fighting fires and explosions, like those you set at my lodge but worse. There will be casualties. My men will do much worse to the survivors if you do not do what I want."

I hoped to God that he couldn't see me swallow or notice how badly I was shivering, but I knew a man like that could smell fear. "Don't hurt them. I'll do whatever you ask!"

"You will take me to the third Nyami Nyami stick and you will do it tonight."

"I don't know where it is!" I cried, clawing back my panic. "Why do you think I investigated your lodge last night? I was looking for information, too, and if I knew where the stick was, don't you think I'd have it by now?"

"Then you are not as clever as you need to be to survive. If you cannot use your great gift to find this third stick and the treasure, then you are useless to me—useless!" It was as though a brutal fire crackled behind his eyes. I felt one of the men standing near stiffen.

He knew all about me, knew about the timewalking. Hell, of course he did. Wasn't he in league with the late Baldi and probably every criminal art-stealing bastard besides? He might even know Noel. I needed to walk the fine line between telling the truth and withholding information. He'd know if I were lying and my only trump card was that he needed me alive, or so I hoped.

"I watched you break into my house but I let it continue because of your amazing gift. They say that you have a supernatural ability to find things lost in time. You I let live so you would lead me where I want to go. I knew you would come to me in time." Reaching over, he tilted my chin so that I met his eyes directly. "What did you see when you touched my Nyami sticks?" he demanded.

"I didn't touch them, not once! I refused to handle them in case I went somewhere I didn't want to go." Truth.

"Stupid." His hand dropped from my chin, his voice grating low and harsh as if harnessing a deep rage. "You bring an expedition to Africa equipped with the one tool that could lead you to what you seek and you do not use it? What fool is this?"

THE ZAMBEZI CODE

He had a point.

He snapped his fingers and a minion dashed across the space and returned with a bottle of clear liquid.

"Thirsty?"

"No!"

But suddenly my head was jerked back and a minion was dribbling something down my throat. It tasted like dirt. I coughed it back up. The man attempted again, only this time holding my neck still until some of it went down my throat despite my heaving efforts to dislodge it. Bastard was drugging me!

Though I coughed and sputtered afterwards, I knew something had hit my system. Already, the world tilted.

"What have you felt since you arrived?" Semenov demanded.

"Nothing," I gasped. Truth again (almost).

He swung away, taking two paces forward before turning back to me. "But you will use your gifts tonight. One part of the diary no one has read but me. A witch doctor told Louise Hopkins that one will only find the third magic stave by asking the river god."

Of course, I remembered that Semenov was into the occult so perhaps was spiritually attuned to the power in Africa. Unfortunately, being spiritually attuned worked for both good and evil, depending on one's set point. I was pretty sure I knew the direction his went. If he believed, it made him that much more dangerous. "Ask the river god yourself!"

"I am not correct person. You will ask."

"Ask what?" I asked quickly. Keep him talking. I was feeling dizzy.

"This I do not know. Only she who is willing to ask the gods directly receives their wisdom," he continued.

"She?" I asked.

"Yes, she. The river god, Nyami, misses his wife, the story goes. Through a priestess, the river can speak to her and in return grant special request."

Shit. "Okay..." I said slowly. "This is the first I've heard of that. Did Louise attempt...(getting really dizzy)...to talk to the river spirit?"

"Who knows? She did not write an—what do you call—epilogue? Maybe she died trying but she was no priestess. But you have a power. Maybe with your gift, you are close enough. We will see." He shrugged. "If you do not succeed, you die. That is the risk."

"What do you mean: *ask the river spirit in person?*" I didn't want to know and I was simultaneously desperate to hear the answer. "Am I supposed to stand on the riverbank and cast incantations over the currents or something?"

But he wasn't listening. Semenov snapped his fingers and barked something in Russian. Two men rushed forward to untie my bound feet from the chair legs and pull me to standing.

"Prepare to meet the river, Ms. McCabe."

"Wait, I'm no African priestess, Semenov. Maybe I have a heightened sixth sense but that doesn't mean…I can talk to African spirits!"

He wasn't interested in my excuses.

I didn't know what was happening but I was cobbling together a picture quickly: Semenov had information we didn't—a few pages of Louise'd diary. Had she known of a special ritual where the Bedyango addressed the river spirit? Had Louise attempted to do this herself and died trying? And since Semenov had yet to mention the Doma tribe, did that mean he knew nothing of them? Kagiso said nothing about rituals of river gods but maybe he didn't know, either. Maybe they were sacred rituals and therefore secret.

But I was preoccupied with my current situation as the men picked me up and carried me back to the river. I was placed alone in an inflatable boat as the world spun around, and watched from my trussed state as they tied my craft to the back of a motorboat. My hands were then unbound and Semenov shoved something into my palms.

"From Louise for luck." And he laughed as he waded up to another boat and climbed in. Now there were two motorboats accompanying me into the center of the Zambezi, one tugging me behind it. What the hell was going on? I was being dragged down the Zambezi like a sniffer dog on a leash?

What was I meant to do as this supposed priestess, address the Nyami Nyami asking for guidance? I'd ask anyone for anything at that moment because I was beyond terrified. Drugged—what did he give me? No friends—were they all right? Did they know I was missing?—no phone and totally plunged into this surreal world of a star-washed Africa on a voyage to the unknown. I tried bending my head low to get the blood back to my brain. I needed to think.

My boat began to rock wildly on its tether as we hit the rapids. As I grabbed the sides, something dropped onto the floor, something darkly gleaming like a stone in the moonlight. Whatever Semenov had handed me now lay under the seat but I was too occupied trying to steady myself in the craft to pay any attention.

I thought for sure I was going to retch. There were no oars and no motor. I was totally in the power of my keepers and, perhaps, the river itself, but the craft seemed made for waters like these and remained upright.

Overhead, the moon hung low in the sky washing a stark silver light over river and landscape alike as the boat bucked and twisted. The highway of stars overhead, the clutch of terror in my chest, my heaving gut, those were my real companions. The men in the boats ahead looked over their shoulder once in awhile but that was it. They were not with me.

At least Semenov could have given me instructions. Was I supposed to call out something? But I suspected he had no idea, either. I had never deliberately reached out for Louise Hopkins and I wasn't reaching out to her now. I would avoid timewalking at all costs. Whatever Semenov hoped to gain by tugging me down the Zambezi, I wouldn't give in to anything willingly.

And then it hit me. Oh, my God! They were dragging me towards the falls, Victoria Falls! Panic hit with such intensity that I screamed. I checked my feet and found them bound with something of tubal that encased my ankles to my shins. The only way to remove it was to slice through the elastic with something sharp which I didn't have. So, could I jump overboard with my legs bound, try to kick-swim to shore in the fast-moving currents, avoiding the crocs and who knew what else in the process? Not likely but it was all that I could do to keep from throwing myself overboard. I sat frozen in my seat, clutching the raft's sides.

We must have been traveling for at least twenty minutes, maybe more. Sometimes I'd glimpse the lights of lodges slipping by but my attempts to call out were drowned by the boat's engines and the drums. I wish they'd stop beating those drums, which seemed to grow louder by the moment.

Many islets appeared now, tiny rocky or grass-fringed worlds floating on the river's glowing surface. Are they waiting for me as promised? They must be, for they have pledged their assistance on this night and I put my faith in them as they have me.

If I have learned anything from this fierce land, it is that faith—faith in the spirit, faith in the people, faith in the land—carries us over all obstacles, that we must see obstacles for what they are: barriers on the always road. Do not fear for we never travel alone. Yes, I could see their torchlights flickering on the shore, from every islet we passed. They were with me, as would all the might of the world, all the spirit of existence, on this night. We do not go into the dark alone. There will always be the light.

And now the magnificent arc of silver is leaping over the sky to greet me, breaking open my heart with wonder as it traces a path beyond the stars. How small are we in the face of the great mystery and yet it enlarges us all. With the roar of the mist, the power of the great river spirit opens its mighty arms to lead me on.

I reach for the Eye of the Nyami under the seat, holding it up to the moon so the light fractures into diamond shards that pierce my heart with love. The drums grow louder, loud enough to challenge Nyami's roar, and the voices sing out to me, calling me home, calling me on. I feel no fear.

Ahead is the deep precipice that plunges us into another world, into the next world, one which we all must go someday. I am not alone. The voices sing in profound harmony, the drums reverberate to the moon and Nyami's roaring smoke blasts the air with almighty power.

I can see nothing now as the mist consumes the air but still I hear the voices and feel the drums and I understand Nyami's story. *Take me by the hand and I will follow, take me by the heart and I will lead*. The water moves swiftly, hurling me forward. Men are shouting but they hold no sway over me now.

All I can hear is roaring mist, throbbing drums, and singing before the screaming begins. That screaming sears my ears and sends me into a thrashing fury. My throat grows raw from the sound. I feel the craft dip and sway, see two men on either side of the boat holding it steady while the current tries to hurl me over the edge.

"What does the Nyami say?" one man shouts. "Tell me or boat goes over edge."

But there are other people, too. Many, many other people suddenly appearing all around as if from the river itself. There is shouting and crying. A gun goes off. A man cries in pain.

Somebody is holding me down—no, carrying me—many hands lifting me out of the boat as it…disappears. Now I'm in the water up to my waist. My eyes are blurred so I can't identify the figures carrying me but they are friends, friends keeping me safe. I glimpse the edge only once and even in the moon glow that churn of boiling water seems to suck me down before all goes dark.

CHAPTER 20

I found myself lying on my back on the ground wrapped in a blanket. An old woman crouched over a fire stirring something. Wizen, wearing a knit hat of what looked to be as holey as her blanket wrap, she seemed intent on her work. When I struggled to sit, she rushed to my side urging me back down. I couldn't understand her language or she mine but soon I was asleep.

The next time my eyes opened, I was in the same place but now could focus on the details, sense others present, smell something cooking. Jolting to sitting, I clutched the blanket to my naked chest asking: "Where am I? Who are you?"

The old woman jumped up and waved her arms, chasing three men out through the flap of a door. She returned to me nodding and smiling toothlessly, passing me a small bowl of something fragrant.

I smiled my thanks and sipped the warm meaty stew, tasting something I couldn't identify but so grateful for the nutrition that it may as well be a feast. While I sipped, the woman plucked my clothes strung from a rope by the fire and placed them at my feet. I put down my bowl and dressed.

"You rescued me," I said as I pulled one leg into my jeans. "What happened to the Russians?"

She darted to the door calling out: "Speak'a the English, Speak'a the English!"

In moments, a young man entered, nodded to me and said: "Hello, you are welcome here. You special guest." Dressed in rags, he couldn't be older than twenty but that was only a guess.

Suddenly, exhausted again, I collapsed back cross-legged on the ground. "Who are you? Where am I?"

"I Speakathenglish. They call me this when I learn English at the school. My true name is Bobo." He laughed and waved one hand. "This is my aunt, Nula. You are very special guest."

Slowly, my memory returned, though nothing in my recall seemed remotely feasible. "When last I remembered, I was being dragged down the river in a boat." Did I only imagine that?

Speakatheenglish translated for his auntie who nodded and said something back. "Auntie says you were caught by very bad men. We knew you would come. The mooti man warned us and we bring you here. We are waiting for long, long time."

"The mooti man?"

Nula went to the door and beckoned to somebody and soon I was facing my witch doctor at last.

Bizarrely, I was so happy to see him. "You helped me," I whispered. "Thank you!"

Speakatheenglish translated and soon I learned that my witch doctor friend had been following me since Victoria Falls, as I had suspected. He had alerted these people that I had come at last.

I didn't understand *the come at last part* and not much that he told me fit into what I understood about the world. How had he contacted them? Not by phone because it was clear that nobody had cell plans here, and yet somehow word had spread a great distance. And, how did they get to the Falls area so quickly? I sensed that this community didn't have cars, either, yet my protectors were waiting by Victoria Falls when Semenov dragged me to the edge.?

Still, I tried to make sense of it by posing more questions. When they attempted to answer, I ended up more confused. It was as though I had been dropped into a world where surreal memories of moonbows and drums were only the beginning. I was struck by the enormity of what we modern humans failed to understand and what those living close to the earth have always known. Overwhelmed by humility but still fishing for answers, I picked through my memory looking for something recognizable.

"Are my friends all right? I am terrified that something happened to them."

"We always fear for those we love but not all calamities (my word) are as they seem," our translator said as he listened to the witch doctor's words.

Okay... "Was I about to go over the falls?"

"The Great Spirit rescued you," the nganga said through our translator. "We have been expecting you."

"Expecting me?" It was then and only by chance that I happened to glance down and notice that Speakatheenglish's and his aunt's feet both had only two toes. Each appeared to have a split foot…like an ostrich… The witch doctor wore battered sneakers but Nula and her nephew were clearly from the same tribe. "You're the Doma!" I exclaimed.

Speakatheenglish beamed. "We are the Doma and you and Mooti Joe our special guests!"

Joe, my witch doctor's name was Joe? I still had a million questions for everyone: how did they find me; how did they know about the bad men? Were the bad men dead, and, most importantly, could they take me to my friends upriver?

But, as I was to learn, the Doma like the witch doctor, worked in their own mysterious ways and my arrival was somehow foreshadowed—another mystery. They did not appear concerned about the bad men—the Great Spirit would take care of them.

Maybe my questions would be answered eventually, maybe I had to intuit the answers from their dance because there would be a dance, I was assured, a great celebration that very night.

No matter what I did or attempted to do, it was clear to me that both Mooti Joe and I must first be properly welcomed, that it was very important that we watch this performance. I tried to warn them that these evil men would come after them as they had me and soon, that what they may hold a secret was in danger still. In other words, nobody had time for dances. That concept shocked them. No time for dances? What world did I inhabit?

Attempting to impress Nula, who I now understood to be the tribe's priestess, that danger was imminent was futile. Expressing my alarm to both the tribal leader Sam and Mooti Joe, equally so.

First things first, apparently. There were no phones, no signs of the modern world anywhere. This community worked on its own rules and lived much as the hunter-gatherers had for millennia only perhaps with fewer resources. Clearly, they were poor. Barefoot, dressed in rags and yet seemingly content, the entire village was now abuzz with preparation for the great feast. Even I was to wear special make-up accordingly and sat still while villagers fixed my hair and painted my face.

There couldn't be more than forty people living in makeshift bomas around a southern clearing surrounded by rocky escarpments and trees. They appeared ready to leave in a minute, everything transportable, nobody attached to possessions, except for the ritual objects that played a role in their celebrations. And yet this community was pulling together its meager resources for a feast that very night and there was no doubt that the community was more than ready to party.

I had slept away an entire day, an entire day where events had threatened everything I cared about and threatened them still, but there I was sitting on a rock waiting for a feast. It felt so wrong yet so absolutely right all at the same time. This push-pull of conflicting opposites would become my great teacher in all things African. Finally I had resolved not to swim upstream but to trust that I was exactly where I should be.

A fire crackled in the center of the clearing. The stars cast a brilliant ceiling overhead. Mooti Joe and I sat next to each other between Nula and Sam. These elders were not treated as kings and queens per se but as very special by virtue of their age and wisdom. We were the guests and therefore treated to best of what the community could offer—a feast of roast meat which I took to be some kind of impala or kudu served with roasted root vegetables. Giant leaves served as plates, our fingers as cutlery.

Once our meals were finished, I sat expectantly waiting for the dance to begin, my anxiety nearly lulled by the sweet-sour fizzy brew I was given to drink. It did not taste like the sludge that Semenov had forced on me yet the taste still had a fermented edge.

I forgot all else when the drumming began and others began playing an instrument made with gourds wired with nails, which was plucked into a haunting tune. The drummers were not in my line of sight but behind me, which made thrumming seem to come from everywhere at once. They beat on tin barrels and wood and skin instruments alike. The energy around the circle increased with the pounding and it was all I could do not to thump my hands on something, too.

Suddenly people came jumping out from behind the rocks dressed in masks, strange grass-fringed headdresses, leaping and crying while the music played. Were they fearful of something—animals, strong magic? They encircled the clearing singing and calling out while the music played. I let my gourd be filled again with more drink and sipped away.

Then everyone fell silent. The players bowed low as another figure entered the circle, a tall man wrapped in a blanket, holding a walking stick and wearing an even more extraordinary bird feather-fringed headdress which gave him the illusion of being six feet tall. Covering his face was a mask of dark carved wood, maybe ebony.

Other dancers stepped forward to set clay pots at his feet, bowing low.

This then, was a great king. Turning, the king waited until another man joined him also carrying a walking stick and wearing a similar headdress yet unique, too. His crown feature seemed entirely made of ostrich feathers with his mask fashioned from the same dark wood. More pots were placed at his feet.

Finally, a third person entered the circle and a hush descended the clearing. An old woman, stooped but proud, her blanket sewn with hundreds of feathers with strings of beads around her neck and bedecked with a fringe of green feathers on her head. She carried a stave like no other, this one richly carved and set with aquamarines, diamonds and emeralds that flashed in the firelight as she lifted it high. The two kings greeted her by lifting their staves as the drums began rolling again. I shivered with expectation.

Now a little figure danced into the circle, his mask fashioned from another dark wood painted in ochres, rusts, and black. Dancing and leaping, he waved his arms at the three leaders who lifted their staves in greeting as the tribe began to sing, everyone knowing the words, everyone in harmony. Now Mooti Joe was on his feet, his finger stabbing his chest, his face alight with an almost frenzied glee. He pointed to me but all I could do was sit and gape.

I remained in this half-stunned state when the next figure entered the circle. She wore a mask very much like the one Peaches had received—the same henna-red shock of dreadlocks curling in all directions above a light speckled wood, the mouth carved into a circle of surprise.

No, that was impossible—that wasn't me! I struggled to my feet, stumbling through the mist that had settled around my brain, feeling surer than ever that I knew this story, that I had played my part long ago and would do so again.

Somehow, I ended up standing before the priestess who offered me the remarkable stave. I gripped something in my fist. Opening my palm, I saw the stone that I had carried to the river god glinting in the moonlight, a huge diamond. I reached out and set it into the hole below the carvings as if it belonged there all along.

In the midst of the beating drums, the chanting voices, I gazed at the final chapter, reading it by heart. The other two sticks told of the distance we must cross through river and forest but here the snake wound its way up to the rocks to form what looked to be a round tower. A tower made of stones carefully articulated in the carved wood seemed to be curving round the top of the stave, extending out concentrically like a chambered nautilus, like a wall but not a wall. Snake, river, earth, air, stone, fire—all spirits from the same great source.

Three figures stood before the fortress near pots filled with treasure, the magic of Africa united to protect its heart through many hands, many spirits. Fingers carved into the stave's base now held the one enormous diamond charged by the great spirit that spoke of purity of spirit, unity of purpose.

I now understood that I was part of something far greater than myself, just one small element of a story, as had Louise been before me, both entrusted to help in the resolution. Swaying on my feet, my body moved with the music. Maybe I remained like that for minutes or hours, I didn't know but when the chanting turned to shouting and cries, I almost didn't notice.

When Mooti Joe began tugging me away from the clearing, I didn't know what was happening. Was it already time? So deep in the trance-like state was I that I didn't recognize those bright circles of light bouncing through the bush towards us. Even when the shooting began, I failed to grasp what was going on.

All I could do was run, duck, scramble, hide. Run. Run.

CHAPTER 21

Cold and bruised, my body had been crammed down into a cold dark hole and left raw and shivering. No, that couldn't be right. A fuse of disconnected images scrambled through my brain, none of which I could latch onto with any certainty. I knew that I had run most of the night, fallen repeatedly, and been lifted back up to run again. In the end, I must have collapsed but where I was at that very moment, was beyond me.

I looked up, no *out*. A man stood framed against a burnished sky and beckoned me to get up and follow him but my limbs refused to move. Finally, he half-tugged, half-dragged me to standing where I clung onto his arm and stared. I sort almost knew him but couldn't remember how or why.

We were on of a rocky outcrop looking down over an open grassland punctuated by clumps of trees and rocks. A rough track-like road wove in and around the savannah and far in the distance, a ridge of foothills smudged purple across the orange sky. Birds were flitting through the grasses screeching in a high-pitched call, their wings silhouetted in the rising sun.

My companion pointed at the headlights bouncing towards us across the plain. We had been escaping headlights all night long until my tangled brain saw them as demon eyes plunging through the night trying to devour us alive. Not demon eyes, I told myself now. It was all that I could do to force another perspective onto this addled reality.

He urged me to duck deeper behind the rocks. Gradually I began to recognize Mooti Joe. He'd been my protector over these long hours but where were the others?

I touched his shoulder and indicated with a shrug and a sweeping hand *Where are the Doma?* He answered me back with a fist thumped into his hand and his fingers spread. Got it: they dispersed, they hid, they ran. Throwing my hands up, I tried to ask if they were all right. He shrugged then forced me to focus back on our current predicament. Right, two truckloads of people coming. Headlights, not evil eyes.

But the throaty growl didn't come from that direction. The last thing we needed was to see that large cat perched on the highest rock behind us. A shock of terror hit my spine.

"Ingwe!" Mooti Joe hissed.

Oh, my God! We were easy pickings for a hungry beast in these rocks. Frantically, we began scrambling downward but I knew in my heart that the cat would win. What were we but fangless and defenseless creatures out here? Joe turned and waved a calabash and screamed, trying to frighten the cat away but by then it was leaping from rock to rock as if it recognized an easy breakfast.

I grabbed a stone and threw it at the leopard and screamed my throat raw. I knew survival tricks for bear attacks but came up empty in the leopard department. But the truck was closer now and knew exactly where we were. I didn't care. Evil Russians were preferable to being eaten alive.

Gunshots rang out in the dawn, bullets pinging against rocks. I turned to see the trucks barreling across the savanna toward us, somebody hanging out of the cab window poised to shoot again.

Joe screamed. I turned back to see the leopard leaping into the air towards him, heard a rifle crack, saw the cat fall in a hump on the ground. I ran over to that beautiful beast and cried my heart out while Mooti Joe stood by clapping his hands.

In seconds, we were surrounded by men in uniforms—park rangers, maybe. One man was saying something to me in what I would later learn to be in the Shona language but I only understood the lone woman who came running up behind him.

"We thought we'd lost you!" she cried.

Dressed in jeans and a jacket strode Sonny Baldi, rifle slung over one shoulder, approaching me as if I were the wild beast. "Sonny?" I gasped.

"Yes, me," she said moving in as if about to give me a hug but taking one step back when she saw me more clearly. "What happened to you? The hair! You look...like hell!"

I felt around my head, my hand touching nobs of straw or maybe roots sticking out everywhere. "I don't know," I whispered. "It was a rough night."

The rangers were now lifting the dead beast into the back of one of the trucks while Mooti Joe explained something to them that caused the men to nod and fire a battery of questions in return.

"I can't believe they had to shoot the leopard," I moaned, wiping my eyes.

"Better it than you," Sonny commented. "You're covered in mud. What's that on your face, in your hair?"

Like I cared. Confusion reigned.

Soon we were climbing into the back of a truck, Sonny keeping as far away from me as possible. "No offense but you stink!"

I cast her a baleful glance. "How did you find me?"

Sonny explained that they had been searching for me for hours—Rangers, staff from private game lodges, the army, everybody on the hunt.

"Is Evan, Peaches, Rupert—everyone—okay?" I asked, squeezing my heart until I heard the answer. If anything had happened to them…

"They have been searching for you, also."

"They're alive?"

"But of course!"

Semenov must have lied about attacking the lodge. I saw his video of an exploding something or other and bought into his story.

Then I started crying again. I was a mess, sobbing away, mourning dead leopards, my fear of losing everything that mattered to me, not to mention lack of sleep on top of wrenching myself from a drug-induced state. To learn that those I loved survived only made me bawl even harder, even it was with tears of joy. When your whole system tumbles into overdrive, every emotion responds the same.

Sonny gazed at me with pity tinged with distaste as she passed me a bottle of water. "Drink."

I downed the thing in one go. "Semenov showed me a photo of the lodge in flames," I said once I'd caught my breath. "Said he'd kill everyone unless I took him to the treasure."

"Bastard. Just like him to threaten. The lodge was burned but everyone escaped alive. Nothing but minor casualties. The gallery in London also suffered a big hit."

"What?"

"Your gallery—Baker and Mermaid? Gone. Big explosion. Good thing it was empty, yes?"

I stared at her aghast. The idea of the gallery being destroyed was almost too much for me to grasp but she just continued talking.

"I thought you knew? Anyway, your Evan doesn't know that I am here but soon will." She shouted out to one of the drivers who understood English. "Call helicopter! Have them meet us somewhere."

The man nodded and got onto his phone.

"How did you get here?" I asked.

"Same way as you—by plane."

"I figured that much," I mumbled sourly.

She grinned. "Gad you are feeling better. Is now a good time to tell you that I've seen the face you are wearing in Semenov's collection? You are the mask!"

"What are you talking about?"

"Later. Okay, so Semenov put a hit on me and on you, too, so I think, why not leave Italy, jump into the lion's jaws? I bring my people here and we stay downstream from you on Zimbabwe side. Did you think those disguises would work? Barman at your lodge was in touch with Semenov the whole time. Bastard has spies in all the lodges."

I didn't mention that the disguise bit wasn't my idea. Stand by your man and all that. "You could have told us," I complained.

"I was, what do you call?—excommunicated, not welcome, so I go on my own. It is easy to buy spies here. Everybody hears about the burning lodge and I learn that Evan's friends pull together a big search party. Do you know where the treasure is?"

Oh, look—dropped that in with all the subtlety of a bomb. I yawned and closed my eyes. "So tired," I murmured. *The gallery was gone! Had Max stayed, he might be gone, too!* I started crying and thought I might never stop.

We bounced along for another twenty minutes or so until the sight of the sun rising over the grasslands forced me to open my eyes and breathe in the day. Behind us, the second Rover rumbled along with Mooti Joe sitting in the backseat looking triumphant. I did not feel triumphant. I felt like hell.

When the whir of a helicopter thundered overhead, my heart pulsed some energy back into my system. The chopper was a big carrier and bore the insignia of the Zimbabwe armed forces.

The moment it touched down, I was out of the truck and running across the grass because Evan, Peaches and Kagiso were climbing out. Evan reached me first, embracing me so tightly that my feet left the ground. I clung to him while Peaches stood looking on and shouting over the whirring blades.

"The gallery is gone!" I whispered.

"I heard. I'm so sorry, love."

"What happened to your hair, woman? You look a fright!" Peaches grinned.

"Long story," I called back. "Tell you later!"

"We have to leave," Evan said, holding me at arm's length before briefly crushing me against him again. "Semenov has probably logged our position by now. Come, get into the helicopter, love."

Peaches took me by the arm while Evan moved away to speak to the pilot.

"Oh, my God!" she exclaimed. "Your hair! You are totally rocking the mask look Baldi sent."

"What?" I stopped and gaped at her.

Sonny stepped up holding a little cosmetic mirror: "Take a look. You *are* the mask!"

I gazed at my reflection, stunned. They were right: I *was* the mask. I had the same pale skin, the same wild banshee hair sticking out like lightening rods all over my head—the Doma idea of red curly hair?—with luminescent green feathers and the same startled expression. Shit.

"Looks like they formed your 'do' with animal fat, which is probably what smells so bad," Peaches added. "But you are really rocking those feathers, though."

"What happened back there?" Sonny demanded. "You and that witch doctor, you know where the treasure is, don't you?"

Peaches stepped between us. "Back off, Sonobitchi. You're as deep into Semenov's pocket as those thugs that attacked us."

"Not true!" she cried. "He tried to kill me, too."

"Because you're a double-dealing manipulator!" Peaches yelled back.

"Come on, time to get aboard," Evan called.

I scanned around and saw Mootie Joe heading in the other direction. "Wait!" I called after him.

But the witch doctor was backing away, in fact, he was almost in a full-fledged scramble back the way he'd come. I take it he'd never flown before and for whatever reason, refused to travel further with the game wardens.

"Joe," I called, running after him. "Come with us, please!"

He stopped, turned, glanced from the helicopter to me as I held out my hand.

"It's time to fly!" I mimed flying and reluctantly he lopped back next to me.

Sonny was standing by the helicopter with her arms crossed glaring at Evan when I reached them seconds later. "What about me?", she was saying.

"Did you think because I wasn't invited that I wouldn't show up here? It is because of me that Phoebe is alive so let me come or you won't learn what else I know."

Evan caught my eye as we approached. I nodded my assent. "She'll follow us anyway. May as well put her aboard."

CHAPTER 22

I learned very little on the flight since helicopter rides were not conducive for conversation. Remaining awake was my only goal, that and drinking from the thermos of hot coffee and munching on the granola bars they had on board.

Peaches passed me back my phone and my watch, both of which I gazed down at as if trying to measure their relevance. At that moment they seemed useless to me, to everything. I ended shoving them into my pocket and forgetting about them.

Rupert, Rory, and Justin would be waiting us in Victoria Falls, Peaches told me. They'd meet up with us later and would bring whatever clothes they'd managed to salvage. I had so many questions but no energy left for asking them. Finally, I ended up dozing, my head on Peaches shoulder while Evan sat up front with the pilot.

The first stop was an airfield back in Victoria Falls where we were to await an army plane. After we'd touched down, I was greeted by people I didn't know, including local officials and army captains who fired questions at me while Evan, Peaches, Justin, and Kagiso stood by fielding my answers.

Other than to say that I'd been kidnapped by Semenov, tugged to the precipice of Victoria Falls, and then rescued by the Two-toed tribe and the witch doctor, I had little to say. I mean, really, wasn't that enough? But the men posing questions pressed for more details, since the whole thing made little sense and my current state of attire signaled that something very strange was going on. Truth was, I had no details and something very strange was afoot.

I gathered that Mooti Joe wasn't more forthcoming. He spoke to them in Shona, hands waving in the air, facial expressions changing from stark fear to joy. Kagiso explained later that the witch doctor kept repeating an old legend about three tribal elders who had preserved a great secret across a big distance to protect the heart of the people. It all happened many suns ago. When they urged him to provide specifics, he just told the same story all over again. Finally, they gave up. In Africa, witch doctors were supposed to be inscrutable and Joe was playing the part.

One thing the authorities knew for certain was that the Russians were after African treasure and that I was somehow a key to finding it. They treated me like a special locked box that they feared to break open in case the secrets trapped inside were somehow damaged. Handled with great care, I was later given the best seat in the hanger,—actually the only seat in the hangar—while we awaited the arrival of the army plane and the others. Clearly, we had the Zimbabwean government's full attention.

Meanwhile, Semenov had apparently slithered underground, though rumor was that he was mustering mercenary forces somewhere in Zambia and Mozambique. He had burned two lodges, attacked a few officials, and stolen a pack of guns from a storeroom somewhere, not to mention kidnapped me. His cover was completely blown. Now, that they knew what he was after, an entire army had been mobilized to locate him. Only no one knew exactly where he was heading or even where the treasure lay. Except me, of course. At least, that was the theory.

I knew, yet didn't know. Whatever had happened in my dream state with the Doma, I had briefly seen the location of the buried treasure but was unable to identify exactly where that was. Everything lay entangled in dreams and probable hallucinations, locked down along with the phantasmagoric images that the drink had induced and the evening's events had intensified.

"That was must have been the local beer," Kagiso told me as we waited in the hanger for our plane to arrive. I had been led to a serviceable if grubby little toilet where one look in the grimy mirror told me just how hellish I looked.

"All the villagers across Africa ferment a variety of roots and herbs to create their own liquor and every tribe has its own recipe. If they were having a special feast, they probably gave you their prized brew. meaning the oldest and most fermented. You are lucky to survive it." He flashed a brilliant smile, all white teeth against dark skin. I smiled back.

"I almost didn't," I said as I sat there leaning against a sack of corn, "and I have a hangover like you wouldn't' believe." All around sat tins, barrels, boxes and crates with the southern space empty but for oil stains and a wire curling like a snake across the cement. A snake, always a snake.

Evan had gone to organize our next stop, which would be challenging since we weren't certain exactly where we were headed. Somewhere in the neighboring airport terminal, Peaches was rustling up something to eat and had dragged Sonny along to keep the woman from pestering me. Mooti Joe refused to remain indoors and sat outside on a barrel, waiting. Nobody mentioned how badly I needed a shower but those niceties would have to wait, too.

"Tell me what you remember," Kagiso asked me softly. He had stayed behind as my guard along with the army personnel posted beyond the hangar. "Take your time. No hurry. If you took part in a ritual dance, then that dance must tell the story of what you seek. I have spoken to Joe and understand a small part of the tale. Strands of these myths I have heard in these parts before but only now have I begun to piece them all together."

We were alone at the moment, the hangar quiet. He leaned against a wall, arms crossed, gaze steady and strangely comforting.

I closed my eyes. "I saw the stick of the third elder, a priestess, jeweled with the heart of the people which somehow Semenov got hold of and placed in my hand before dragging me down the river. I, in turn, put it into the eye of the snake god. It was a huge diamond, I think. The Doma must have been keeping the stave safe for hundreds of years and have it still. They passed it to me and I held it high, glimpsing these images of a stone castle, processions of people traveling great distances, a pact to preserve some great secret."

"Recorded history is sparse in these parts as there is no written accounts available but we know that during the 1500's or thereabouts a great trade route had been established across a swath of southern Africa involving many tribes and kingdoms. In stories I've heard, it appears that even the Zulu were involved, and certainly the Shona and the peoples who have since dispersed to other regions."

"I know that the image of three wise men, which let's call 'wise people' in this case, thrives throughout ancient mythology," I whispered, my brain beginning to clear briefly as I drained the last of the thermos. "Here we have the power of the three again—three staves, three tribal elders. Even Semenov was on to the three idea but nothing I saw last night makes sense to me."

"Perhaps you are not meant to understand it, only to remember it."

"But why a castle tower in southern Africa? The one I saw looked

JANE THORNLEY

European but not. It was as if the walls curved in and around, close together but not in a European style at all."

Kagiso straightened. "Did you say a tower?"

I met his gaze. "Yes, a stone tower but not particularly high and there was this image of a carved bird…"

He reached over and grabbed my hand. "I know what you saw! I know where we are headed!" Turning away, he pressed his phone to his ear and began talking excitedly to Evan as he strode away.

I got to my feet. At that moment, Rupert and Rory arrived with Justin and two soldiers lugging baggage. Seeing me, Rupert dropped his carrier and stopped in his tracks. "My word, Phoebe, you do look a fright!"

Rory's expression, however, was different. "Phoebe", he whispered. "You are the vision of Louise's mask!" He stepped forward. "That mask Terrence brought back from his travels, the one that was stolen. It was always referred to as 'Louise's mask' because it was supposedly made for her by some local tribe. It was given to my ancestor by a witch doctor when he sent his men out to find her after she'd disappeared. Apparently, it represents her red hair and shocked expression during some event."

I strode forward. "And you never told me this?"

"It never came up."

"And Louise had red hair, too?" I asked.

"I thought you knew?" he said, his expression almost as surprised as mine.

"How could I have?" I demanded. "I've only ever seen pictures of her under a pith helmet!"

And then Evan dashed in. "Time to go, everyone! Our plane has arrived and we have indication that Semenov is mustering forces on the border of Mozambique near a place called Masvingo."

"Great Zimbabwe!" Kagiso cried, spreading his arms wide. "My friends, we will journey to Great Zimbabwe!"

CHAPTER 23

I knew little about Great Zimbabwe, assuming as I did that any reference I may have heard previously referred to the country, not a specific place therein. "Zimbabwe," for instance, meant stone houses in Shona, I was to learn.

By the time I was belted into in a jump seat in the cabin of a military plane, I had discovered that Great Zimbabwe had once been a medieval city located near Lake Mutirikwe. Nobody knew much about the site but believed it to have been the capital of a great kingdom, probably the ancestors of the Shona, and that the stone city had spanned an area of hundreds of square kilometers.

"The early Europeans believed that there was no way for an African nation to build a such a magnificent drywall structure," Kagiso told us as we sat strapped into our seats. Rupert, Rory, Peaches, Sonny, and two soldiers sat on one side of the aisle; Evan, Kagiso, Justin, a trembling Mooti Joe, plus me and two more soldiers sat on the other. Travel on the jiggling and bouncing carrier was disconcerting though no one appeared to be as bothered by the lack of onboard service as Rupert.

"Surely we could have commandeered a private plane?" Rupert grumbled as the craft hit another air pocket.

"Oh, come on, Rupe," Peaches chided. "You can bear up without champagne service for an hour, can't you?"

"It's not champagne I miss but basic comfort," Rupert said.

Beside me, Evan sat grim. Normally it would be enough for him to have everybody he cared for safely within his line of sight but we had no idea what we were flying into. It was one thing to have the army on our side and another to deploy them against an enemy like Semenov. He fought through sleight of hand and secrecy, poisons and double crosses, in a country so desperate that it could be easy to bribe even one's allies.

Meanwhile, I was still attempting to sort through the discordant images cramming into my head from the night before. It was like trying to separate a pile of gummed-together stamps. What was real and what wasn't? Nothing hung together linearly. In my memory, the Victoria Falls event occurred after the Doma dance but I knew that couldn't be right. Why did I remember those events in reverse order? So much still didn't make sense.

Did I play the role of Louisa in the dance or did she play me in hers, the two of us playing a part in tandem across the centuries? Had she been tugged to the edge of the Zambezi to speak to the river spirit and, if so, by whom, and is that how she died? I needed answers but struggling to grasp them only increased my confusion. Being drugged by two different concoctions over a couple of days didn't help.

I shot a quick look at Mooti Joe, who sat gripping his hands between his knees, probably praying for a safe landing. He must know the answers and I was convinced that deep down, so did I. At some point, my tangled thoughts might loosen enough to unravel into my brain as clear thoughts. Meanwhile, the witch doctor only spoke in riddles and I only thought in them.

What I really needed was sleep followed by more coffee but knew it would take a long time before I had much of either. It was as though I treaded the border of two worlds without belonging fully to either.

The plane bounced and jostled as we began our descent. There were no windows to check the landscape, but once had landed, I saw that we had flown into a rocky, hilly, treed area unlike any other we'd experienced so far.

Soon we were in the back of a truck with an army convoy on the short drive to Great Zimbabwe. I sat wedged between Evan and Peaches in the back of of a large troop carrier staring out at the trees whizzing by on either side of the road. They had agreed to allow Rupert to drive in the cab up front but I doubt he would be comfortable wedged between the captains.

Evan was frequently on his phone. "I've just heard from Justin up front who says that troops on the ground at Great Zimbabwe say that all is quiet up there." Justin was in a truck up ahead.

"What do you suppose that means?" Peaches asked.

"Trouble," Evan replied. "If Semenov has mustered mercenary forces, he could be preparing some kind of covert attack. He may just be laying in wait for Phoebe to arrive in order to locate the treasure before making his move."

What if Phoebe can't locate the treasure?, I thought.

"Does that mean that somebody on our team may be a mole?" Peaches was leaning over me now.

"It has always been a possibility but it could be anybody," Evan remarked, staring straight ahead.

Peaches sat back. "Perfect."

Our military companions appeared trained to take their jobs very seriously. So far, none cracked a smile. What they thought of driving this white woman dressed in full ritual paraphernalia and her friends along with a witch doctor to a national historic site, is anyone's guess. Kagiso attempted to engage one or two but other than to answer his questions, they kept their eyes fixed straight ahead.

The road began to climb higher into the hills until it left the main road to form a narrow dirt track guarded by soldiers along each side. Though they waved us through, the public were clearly prevented entry at the moment. We continued along past a sign announcing a UNESCO World Heritage Site with the image of a bird, the same bird I had glimpsed in my drugged state. Glimpsing it gave me a jolt of excitement.

Finally, our truck lurched to a stop. A handful of other trucks painted in camouflage could be seen clustered around a graveled lot. We climbed out and gazed around.

"I knew as soon as you said it that this must be the place in your dream," Kagiso said, excitement percolating in his voice.

A man dressed in an officer's uniform ("a major general", Evan whispered) approached to shake Evan's and Kagiso's hands after which they began striding away with him deep in an earnest discussion. I could see Justin break away from a group of soldiers in the distance to join them.

"Oh, look at that. The men are having a manly confab," Peaches remarked, watching them stride away.

"They didn't include me," Rory pointed out.

"Nor me," Rupert muttered, "And, indeed, I have a great deal of expertise in the strategy department and could no doubt offer an opinion."

"Let's look around," I said quickly. Surely we'd be safe enough surrounded by soldiers?

That left Rory, Rupert, Peaches, Joe, and me to stroll around at the tumble of gray stone walls and the hilly terrain surrounding us. I was certain that the witch doctor had never been there before and yet being at the site appeared to electrify him. He seemed wired with energy while always looking around as if seeking something specific.

As the hillside slipped upwards into the distance, we could see piles of stones everywhere but, so far, nothing that looked like an intact structure.

Mooti Joe began beckoning to us so we followed him up a narrow path that wound up through the trees and ruins until we were high enough up to look out over the hillside. Now I could see walls and towers over in the distance. A tremor hit my gut. Abruptly, I sat down on the nearest stone.

"You okay, Phoeb?" Peaches asked.

"Still in revival mode. I don't suppose anyone has a leftover thermos of coffee in their bags?" Our luggage had been heaped into the back of one of the trucks down below and what lunch we'd had consisted of soda and airport buns.

"Sorry, no," Rory said. "Are you in need for a bit of stimulant?"

"I could sure use one plus a couple of pain pills." I rubbed the bridge if my nose trying to clear my thinking as well as banish the dull thud that had settled in since I awoke that morning. Whatever was in that beer delivered a vicious hangover.

"What about your tea things, Rupe?" Peaches asked as Rupert pulled his pith helmet forward to better shield his eyes and lowered himself onto a rock beside me.

"And where would I obtain a kettle, do tell, Penelope? Furthermore, I have no notion of where these lads may have tossed my luggage for I have no doubt that toss them they did."

After a few minutes, Evan, Justin, and Kagiso returned from their confab with the major general and joined us on the hillside.

"The major says that the place is wide open and impossible to secure. He's posted men across the seven hectares but fears that may not be enough," Evan said.

"Could an army or any troop contingent get across the border from a neighboring country and make their way here?" Rory asked.

"Bloody right they could," Justin told him. "Borders between countries in Africa are mostly unsecured with thousands of hectares of bush in between. Even by plane, the bastards can get in easily enough. These are mercenaries. They don't play by the rules."

"Perhaps it is best that we put Phoebe and you folk in a safe place for the night," Kagiso said, looking at Evan. Justin nodded his approval but Evan kept his gaze fixed firmly on my face.

"They're heading here," I pointed out, rousing myself. "They're looking for me. One way or the other, this is where I'll end up if we are ever to locate the treasure so I may as well stay put. Rupert and Rory, you go to a hotel for the night but the rest of us will camp out here."

"I agree," Evan said. "It will be easier to defend you with the army guarding the site than if we remained in a hotel. Meanwhile, we can get Dad to safety, along with Rory and Baldi, and dare I say, to a measure of comfort."

"Makes sense," Peaches agreed.

Justin erupted. "Those bastards will be swarming this place by tonight. It's not safe for her, either."

Her must be me. "Nothing's safe," I said, keeping my tone matter-of-fact. Nothing was, not for me. Besides, it appeared that Justin still didn't grasp the enormity of the situation let alone comprehend the secret I carried.

"They'll be looking for you, ready to nab you the first chance they get," Justin continued, "and you want to camp outside?"

I gazed up at him with as firm an expression as anyone can muster while wearing animal-fattened feathered cornrows. "Justin, I appreciate the work you're doing on my behalf, truly, but in my case as far as being safe is concerned, forget it. It's enough to help secure me until I find what we're looking for. Take Rupert, Rory and Sonny someplace comfortable back in town."

"I'm not going anywhere," Rupert protested, "but do find me a decent mattress and a spot of electricity for tonight, old chap, if you don't mind, there's a good fellow," he said to Evan.

Justin looked over at Evan who was technically his employer. "We'll arrange an army escort back into Masvingo where Rupert, Rory, and Sonny will spend the night. I'm certain the major will oblige and leave a couple of soldiers with them for security."

"Absolutely not!" Sonny sputtered once she had finally tuned into the conversation. "I'm staying with Phoebe."

"To do what—spy?" Peaches stated, thumbing her chest. "The rest of us are here to protect and support her, not use her!"

Sonny refused to look at her and fixed on me, instead. "You would not even be here if it weren't for me," she protested. "Phoebe, we have a deal?"

"Do we?" I asked. "You disclosed nothing about what was really going on here but, instead, tossed bread crumbs for us to follow. I'm done with you, Sonny."

"I'm still staying," the woman said between her teeth.

Immediately Rory and Rupert joined the protest which Evan quickly shut down with an uncharacteristic chop of his hand. He was in no mood for squabbling and neither was I. "The three of you are going to stay in town under an armed guard. Now, do as I say."

CHAPTER 24

In the end, Sonny, Rupert, and Rory were escorted back to town by one of the soldiers despite their grumbling. Apparently there were guest houses in town where they would be secured for the night. That left the rest of us to stroll the Great Zimbabwe ruins in relative peace. Men could be seen stationed all over the stony hills.

"We will go to the Great Enclosure," Kagiso explained. "I understand that parts of the surrounding ruins date back to the Iron Age and that the smaller similar structures you can see are scattered over maybe as many as two hundred acres."

"Wow," Peaches marveled. "And it was abandoned in maybe the fifteenth century?"

"That's what they believe but nobody knows for certain. There are no signs of an invasion such as scorched stones and what few artifacts that remain—European explorers in the past centuries mostly tossed them away thinking them insignificant—are mostly gone."

"Even so, they were looking for gold," Evan remarked. "But apparently they did not find what they sought."

"Because they were thinking like white foreigners instead of like Africans," Kagiso commented.

"But I'm a white foreigner, too, so why am I even here?" I asked. It was question I'd long been asking myself and had yet to find a satisfying answer.

"As far as I can understand, Louise never set foot here. She was kidnapped back in Victoria Falls which is where she met her end."

"I believe there is a deeper message here that we have yet to understand," said Kagiso.

"Or maybe we do understand it but have yet to recognize our knowledge as anything profound," Peaches remarked. We all stared at her which prompted her to grin. "Thought I'd sound mysterious like Phoebe and Kaggy to set you all to pondering. Seriously, though, look at this place."

We had arrived at the Great Enclosure which spread out before us in tall dry-stone walls that were a testament to the builders' mastery. I'd seen nothing like it in all my travels.

The stones were so expertly fitted together without the aid of mortar, almost as if they evolved from the living landscape. Unlike European construction, this massive enclosure obeyed no rules of classic architecture and disregarded the linear mores of geometry. There seemed to be few straight edges. Instead, the stone seemed to emerge from the earth almost organically like some living thing snaking over the hillside. Two conical towers reared above the walls exactly as I had glimpsed them on the Doma's Nyami stick. This was the place!

Mooti Joe scrambled forward clapping his hands and chanting.

"What's he saying?" Peaches asked.

"He's singing, which to him is much like praying," Kagiso replied. "As to what his song says, I am not too clear. Something about a snake that traveled a great distance."

"A snake?" I whispered.

"The rounded shapes represent the contours of the earth," Kagiso continued. "The circular energy of life itself, if you will. The people believe that the land is alive with spirit, and to honor this energy, one must build in its image. For this reason, all that is circular is believed to be preferable to anything square. Mooti Joe appears to be calling this place a great snake, another creature of circular energy."

I stared, something plucking at the back of my brain as if trying to latch on to a thread I could follow through the maze. But I couldn't grasp anything.

We carried on, leaving the witch doctor to sing alone while we slipped inside the broad enclosure. Here, the walls rose over eleven meters high all around us. By now my feet seemed to be moving by themselves as I picked my way past the tower into an area where two walls rose up on either side with a narrow path running between. No one asked if I felt anything, for which I was grateful but in truth the only sense hitting me just then was wonder.

I guessed that everyone was remaining silent to leave room for a moment of insight on my part. "The treasure is probably buried somewhere around here but I'm receiving no bolts illuminating exactly where," I said. I resisted the urge to apologize. "This amazing place has a special energy but I can touch these stones and not feel like I'm about to be drawn into another century." I turned to face them, Peaches, Kagiso and Evan all standing behind me watching intently. "I want to camp out here tonight."

That prompted a flurry of protests. "But Phoebe," Evan began, "this place will be challenging to defend. We had thought to sleep in one of the rondavels on the property, as the major suggested."

"It must be here." I gazed up at the walls overhead and to the overhanging trees. No ceilings existed. "This place was once a great sanctuary and if I camp out right here," I pointed to the stone floor between the walls, "I'll feel safe and might gain some inkling as to where the treasure is hidden."

Feel safe? Who was I kidding? But hiding would not remove the gridlock in my mind or move us one step closer to locating the treasure. Moving forward was the only way. Ironically, I needed to remain still to reach my mission. I needed to stay right here in this sacred spot while the images swirled in my head.

Once that was settled, matters moved quickly. The neighboring Shona village sent over bowls of stew for supper plus we had plenty of bottled water provided by the soldiers to wash it down. We borrowed blankets and used our luggage for pillows while wearing every warm article of clothing we had brought. Now that we were at a higher altitude, the nights were chilly.

Mooti Joe refused to sleep between the walls but camped within the broader enclosure next to the base of one of the towers. Despite our misgivings, he lit himself a fire as did clusters of soldiers up and down the site.

We stood outside where we were to sleep for the night, taking one last look at the surrounding hills.

"Aren't those fires like announcing to Semenov that we're here?" Peaches asked.

"By now they know exactly where we are," Evan remarked, gazing up at the stars. The sun had long ago dropped behind the escarpment, sending up the waning moon to hang low in its place. "How can you hide an army convoy? Besides, I'm sure those eagles we spotted far in the distance were drones staking us out."

"What eagles?" I asked.

"Don't worry, Phoebe, you were still spacey when we saw what looked like large birds of prey way up in the hills behind us. So," Peaches said turning to Evan, "the plan is to let the mercenaries swarm us tonight trying to nab Phoebe? Are the soldiers then supposed to round up and catch the bastards or what?" She turned back to gaze off towards the hills where fires now peppered the landscape like beacons in the night. "We're like sitting ducks."

"That's the idea," Evan told her. "We need to draw them out. Once we nab Semenov, his band of mercenaries will disperse. If their leader is caught, they won't get paid, and if they don't get paid, they won't work."

"That is the thing with bloody mercenaries," Justin remarked. "They're driven solely by money and not ideology. I'll be remaining with the soldiers tonight on watch right over there." He pointed somewhere off to the dark. "That way I can see anyone approaching."

"I intend to remain just outside Phoebe's campsite," Evan added. "Kagiso and Peaches, stay with Phoebe. No more dropdown operatives this time." He leaned over and briefly kissed me.

"We'll guard her, won't we Kaggy?" Peaches replied, looking up at Kagiso who was holding her gaze with a completely focussed expression. It appeared that the attraction was mutual.

"Of course, we will," he said. "I am honored to be Phoebe's private guard."

"Got an extra gun, Ev?" Peaches whispered to Evan without taking her eyes off Kagiso.

"Take my pistol. I'll use a rifle." Evan passed her a handgun, which she took without a backward glance. "But your phone is still the best weapon, remember that."

Peaches snapped her attention back. "Don't know if it's got enough juice left in it for a night of fun and games," she told him. "Come on, Phoebe and Kaggy. Let's try to get comfy."

I stifled a yawn. Something buzzed in my pocket and I pulled out my phone. I had forgotten about it. "It's Rupert," I said, scanning the text. "He's itemizing all the problems he's facing with his accommodations." I yawned again and shoved the phone back into my pocket. "I don't have the energy to respond right now."

"Neither does your phone. Did you see that red bar? You need to charge that thing," Peaches pointed out. "Here, give it to me and I'll share my storage charger. We might get enough life out of the two phones to get through the night."

I passed it over. "Anyways, if I don't lie down now, I'll drop standing up."

Kagiso led the way back onto the path between the enclosure's walls, his rifle slung over one shoulder. Our sleeping quarters promised to be lumpy and uncomfortable. Since we couldn't light a fire without scorching those ancient stones, it would be enough if we could remain warm.

Huddled in our layers of clothing, we shared body heat under a single blanket, me wedged between Kagiso and Peaches. If the chemical warmth of mutual attraction were manifested in physical heat, I'd be toast by morning with those two on either side of me. I got the sense that left by themselves, Kagiso and Peaches wouldn't keep their hands off one another.

Though expecting prickling anxiety to keep me awake, I actually dropped off to sleep quickly, my head resting on my backpack, one hand gripping my phone which Peaches had shoved into my palm while it charged, the permitter alert on high. I remained asleep for several hours or, at least, that was how it seemed.

My dreams were continuous and lucid. Over and over again, I envisioned snakes slithering across my brain. One was trying to lead me along. When I refused to follow, it would coil into striking pose and rear its head up to fix me with a piercing glittering eye.

Then it hissed.

I bolted up, feeling the stone ground beneath me. In seconds, I realized that I was shivering alone in the dark. I shrugged off the blanket and stood up, my heart thundering in my chest. Where were the others? At my feet, my phone pulsed red.

And then I heard it again, a hissing followed by the unmistakable cry of pain. Now shouting beyond the walls. And gunfire. In seconds, I had picked up my phone and was following the path between the walls towards the exterior, my heart thumping.

Outside, I kept plastered against the wall, trying to focus. Though I sensed activity everywhere, I couldn't see anything clearly, only the looming shapes of rocks all around, the moon now hidden behind the trees. If I flicked on my phone light, I'd give away my location, but without it, I couldn't see a thing.

Where was Evan? Where were Peaches and Kagiso? Nearby, I saw the embers of Mooti Joe's fire but the witch doctor had disappeared. They had to be in trouble!

I made to scramble around the edge of the tower but stumbled over something and fell to my knees. Pushing myself back on my feet, I recognized the body of a man face down—a soldier. To the right, I could just make out the shape of another and another. I stared in horror as my eyes adjusted to shadowy contours that weren't contours at all but bodies—bodies everywhere.

There was that hiss again. Was I only imagining it or were those arrows, or maybe darts, whizzing through the air? Something stealthy, almost invisible shooting, in any case. Damn!

I needed to reach higher ground so I could see what was going on. Turning, I clawed my way up the path almost on my hands and knees. keeping low behind the walls leading up the hillside. So far, I had not seen a single person moving. Our enemy had to be hidden behind the rocks farther up.

Another gunshot cracked way over to my right. A man called out in Shona. Some of the good guys were still standing, at least, but where was my team? I stifled a pang of fear and kept on moving until I had reached an outcrop of stony ruins. Wedging myself between the boulders, I peered down.

The moon was now visible, but even in its waning state, it cast everything into stark silvered shadows. Below, I could see the glowing embers of the fires, make out the shapes of the trucks in the parking lot, see two black figures scrambling low over the rocks. I watched as they approached the walls where I'd slept. No one tried to stop them and from the way in which they approached, I guessed they were Semenov's.

Then more men appeared, some scaling the walls with ropes, some swarming into the walled path I'd just left. Like ants, they seemed to be everywhere at once. Gunfire sounded overhead. Behind me, slipped a line of soundless troops descending towards the enclosure with their rifles poised.

This must be the ambush, then. Shit! I was right in the midst of the battle zone and could easily be mistaken as the enemy. I had to get away. Keeping close to the wall, I climbed farther upward, picking my way over loose stones, tumbling ruins and scraggly thornbushes. Finally, I pulled myself up onto a smooth boulder, a perfect viewpoint over the valley below.

Silvered rubble everywhere I looked. I crouched, gazing at the skirmish below. I could see nothing clearly—friend and foe were all just moving shapes —but I could hear the cries and the gunshots, hear the men shouting. Despite the pandemonium, my mind stilled. The hissing was stronger now. Slowly I turned.

Behind me, a large snake curled, its head arched above its body ready to strike, its eyes glittering coldly in the moonlight. I stared at it and it at me while I calmly clutched my phone. I felt no fear, just understanding.

A voice called to my right. "I want her alive!"

I turned toward the voice, watching as three men stepped out of the shadows, Semenov flanked by two henchmen. Strange how I knew that he would appear.

"Come any closer and I'll shoot," I said, holding my phone aloft. To the phone, I issued the command: "Activate sweep stun app."

"Sweep stun app activated," said the phone in Evan's voice.

"Do you think toy will stop me?" Semenov laughed. "I have men everywhere. I call them now." He paused to issue orders to one of his dudes who was soon reeling off a command in an African dialect I didn't recognize.

"This toy kills, Semenov."

"But you do not kill, Phoebe." Semenov took a step forward. "I know this."

My gaze flew to the snake still coiled as if ready to spring. Did nobody notice it? "In your case, I will make an exception." I was clearheaded for the first time in days.

"Tell me where the treasure is and I let your friends below live," he said stepping nearer. "I have them captive below. You know where it is now and you will tell me."

I wasn't falling for that again. "Yes, I know where it is, Semenov, but I won't tell you and you could never reach it, anyway. It isn't any place you can access with your mercenaries and hired thugs."

And then another figure scrambled into view, a gun held in one hand and stepped between us. "Bastard Semenov! Let her go!"

Seriously? "Get lost, Sonny. I have this under control," I said. Really, I would have stunned her where she stood had my phone had enough juice. As it was, I'd be lucky if I could blast Semenov. My thumb hovered over the app button but she was blocking my aim.

"What took you so long? You betrayed me!" Semenov gave a jerk of his head and one of his henchmen fired at Sonny. She fired back and both stumbled backward. The second man stepped forward to finish her off at the same time that Semenov made a grab for me.

Everything happened at once. A gun went off; I pushed *fire*; there was a screech in the dark; I saw the snake strike Semenov.

And then everything went still. I stared aghast at the carnage all around me and at Mootie Joe standing stone-still before me, his eyes glittering in the moonlight.

CHAPTER 25

The world had just become a richer place—larger, broader, deeper. Though still inexplicable as far as the big questions went, nevertheless I felt more at peace than I had for months, maybe years.

Certainly that morning in Zimbabwe, everything felt bright and new, even supercharged. We were winding our way up the path to Great Zimbabwe for the celebration, Evan and I plus Peaches, Rupert, Rory, Kagiso, and Justin along with numerous local officials threading up single file.

Everywhere, the air of festivity reigned as people clapped and cheered. Though only dignitaries were allowed up to the excavation site that day, since the event was being televised internationally, theoretically everyone could witness the moment when Zimbabwe unearthed the Treasure of the Three Wise Leaders, as it was now being called.

My only regret was that the Doma would not be in attendance. Their conviction that public scrutiny would destroy their secluded lifestyle only increased once the treasure had been announced. As for the witch doctor, Mooti Joe had disappeared the night of the attack ,and to this day, no one had laid eyes on him.

Kagiso believed that Joe was the manifestation of the river spirit, the snake that had been leading me all along but that explanation didn't align with my conviction. To me, the witch doctor was the conduit for all those mysterious forces that were still active in Africa, a power that couldn't be diminished by time or outside interference. Yes, he channeled Nyami but so much more. He was the magic that is Africa.

The most telling moment for me was that instant when I saw him standing where the snake had been and realized that the snake had never been real. Or maybe it had—medics claimed that Semenov had died of snake bite, bitten by the black mamba, a lethal snake found mostly by the Zambezi river. None of that made sense. Not only was the reptile far outside its natural habitat, but it should have been in hibernation, considering the temperatures. Yet snake bite was listed as the oligarch's cause of death.

I had blasted him, of course, but that charge alone wasn't strong enough to fry the bastard. As for Sonny, whose double game of treachery fooled no one, she suffered a gunshot wound to her shoulder that night; it would keep her out of action for awhile.

In her case, I was ambivalent. She had lead us here, had played a role in this story, if only as the instigator, but the fact that she had been on Semenov's team, even briefly, dropped the curtain on her for me. Besides, she had evaded her soldier guard that night and had made off with an army truck. I had to give her credit for chutzpah.

Meanwhile, Evan, Peaches, Kagiso and Justin had all escaped with nothing more serious than assorted bruising and one knife wound (Justin). Evan and Peaches had been shot with a tranquilizer gun designed for taking down game animals. They were lucky that the dose was low enough not to stop their hearts.

It turned out that Semenov's men did not have sufficient ammunition. He couldn't release enough funds to secure the necessary armaments from Africa's underground market so his mercenaries were armed with nothing but knives, slings, poisoned arrows, and rifles used as bludgeons. They had broken into a supply depot for the park rangers which gave them access to the tranquilizer darts that had downed so many the night of the attack.

As Evan had predicted, once their leader died, the mercenaries quickly dispersed, leaving Semenov's band of elite Russian henchmen to be rounded up and imprisoned by Zimbabwean forces.

Losing the gallery—Semenov's blazing act of retaliation—was the biggest blow. The entire ground showroom level had been bombed which destroyed the upstairs offices along with my apartment. It took weeks for Max and I to pick through the rubble, salvaging whatever was left of either our memories or our valuables. We had been devastated at first but then rallied, deciding to use the insurance money to rebuild. Our lives had changed so our living arrangements must, too. The gallery would be rebuilt above the agency laboratory but I would no longer be living on the premises. Time to move on.

Now, two months later, we were on our way to the celebration, special guests of the Zimbabwean government. On the night of the attack, I had glimpsed it all—the image of the walls snaking up the hillside, of the boulder that reared like the head of a coiled snake above the valley.

The ancient elders had secured their sacred treasure deep beneath the earth under that very rock where I had witnessed the snake. The story weaving through this land was the tale of many people who believed that natural elements like the river and the snake held the spirits of their ancestors, of the earth itself.

I now knew that Louise had died that night at Victoria Falls. The Doma had lead her to the brink of the falls believing that she was the one their prophecy had foretold, she who would reveal the secret of the river snake. They had not intended to harm her but the ropes had snapped, the canoe tipped, and the river claimed her as its own. She was me, I was she.

"I feel as though this act today will finally lay my father's ghost to rest along with Terrence's and Louise's," Rory said. "It was Dad's great obsession to discover what happened to his great-great-grand aunt and now we have the answers."

I squeezed his hand. "Louise's spirit will finally rest, too. Will you keep your father's secretary on?"

"I don't see what choice I have since Sydney is in my father's will, but that's all right. I've made my peace with the man and nobody can reproach him as much as he reproaches himself," Rory told me.

We threaded our way up the path past the Great Enclosure until we could see people gathering just below the rearing boulder on the hillside. An atmosphere of anticipation percolated everywhere. Film and news crews stood ready for the big reveal, attention focused on the hillside above.

A plastic tarp covered the area where a team of archaeologists had been working for weeks. We had been invited up the path to join the dignitaries standing around the tent. I was to make a speech on behalf of the Agency of the Ancient Lost and Found.

I touched Kagiso's arm. "Wait, please," I said.

He turned.

"Kagiso, I won't be speaking here today, no member of the Agency of the Ancient Lost and Found will." Peaches, Evan, Rupert, and I had already agreed to be present as supporters only so nobody looked the least surprised there. "Rory will go with you officially."

Kagiso, however, was baffled. "I do not understand. You need to tell this story, Phoebe, for you are the hero. This is such a wonderful tale and you are a living part of it."

I smiled but shook my head. "But I'm not—part of it, I mean. I'm only the agent, a kind of imposter because this isn't *my* story; it belongs to you and everyone here. It belongs to Africa. If I played a part, it was only to enforce the truth that as humans we must stand together against oppression—black, white, and a thousand shades between. We entered only to prevent an injustice as foreigners against another foreign force." I held up my hands. "Go tell the story, Kagiso. Rory will accompany you."

He held my gaze briefly before shaking his head. He understood. A slow smile crossed his lips. "Of course, Phoebe. I will be honored." And with that he turned to make his way up the path hand in hand with Peaches who had taken Rory's hand, too.

Rupert was gazing at me, aghast. "I say, Phoebe, at least you could do is watch when they open those pots. Surely that would not be too much of an imposition upon African sensibilities! Observe, we are not the only Caucasians in attendance besides Rory. Indeed, I see Justin and others among those VIP's."

"They're all African, Dad," Evan pointed out. "Rory will be in attendance because his ancestors found the Nyami sticks which he will officially repatriate to Zimbabwe today."

"As for the treasure, you will see it televised soon enough," I told him, "but I'll give you a hint of what I glimpsed in my mind's eye that night: gold nuggets, some pieces shaped into the Zimbabwe bird motif, and a solid gold Nyami stick inset with diamonds and special gems—that will be the star attraction, you watch. There were four staves, not three as Louise believed. The diamond in Nyami's eye will be one of the biggest anyone has seen for a long time."

"My word!" Rupert exclaimed. "I must nab a front row seat when they show that on the monitors." And he huffed over to the screens that had been positioned for viewing on the wall of the Great Enclosure.

"Phoebe," Evan began, drawing me away, "speaking of diamonds, I've been considering them carefully lately, taking advantage of African expertise and British design sensibilities."

He turned me around to face him. He looked so nervous and to see a man like him quake, even a little, moved me.

With the crowd surging towards the monitors we may as well be alone.

Now I could see that he was holding out a ring—gold filigreed leaves folding over a faceted sparkler that shot prisms of color into the sunlight.

But he kept on talking. "I tried to imagine a more romantic spot for this moment—a secluded garden, a boat ride on the Zambezi, a moonlit night blazing with stars—but any time we're alone in such magnificent locations, it appears as though someone is trying to kill us. I thought I'd ask you while we're here, instead. Phoebe, my love, will you marry me?"

All around the crowd began to clap and cheer, an exhalation of wonder as one precious artifact after another was lifted into view.

Evan was still talking, probably nervously, me barely fixing on his words. "I know I can't promise you a peaceful life and, until we locate a place of our own, asking you to continue living with me in my dad's house is probably a deal breaker. But I do promise to love, honor, and protect you, the latter probably full-time, given recent events and your abilities." He paused long enough to smile at that. "You are, after all, the most incredible woman to whom a man could be committed for a lifetime of loving and full-time security services, and I consider it my life's work just to keep you from being absconded, coerced, threatened, kidnapped—"

"Enough, please!" I said, laughing. "Just kiss me and we can discuss the details later."

The End

AFTERWORD

The Two-toed tribe or "Ostrich People" actually exist. My husband who grew up in Zimbabwe told me stories about the people who kept to themselves due to a genetic deformity that fused their feet into two large toes. Amazing, right?

Many elements in The Zambezi Code, especially tales of witch doctors, are based on his first-hand accounts. The witch doctor wanting a lock of Phoebe's red hair because it contained powerful "mooti" is my experience in visiting a market outside of Victoria Falls years ago. My brother-in-law and husband tugged me away before this transaction could be completed but it always left me wondering. Tales of witch doctors curing the sick beset with evil spirits abound in Africa and the account Louise tells in her diary is another based on reality.

I visited Great Zimbabwe long ago and marveled at how little we hear about such places in the western world. Though I've woven stories around and underneath the monument that are completely fictional, the magic of the continent and its people are real. Africa is truly filled with wonder.

ALSO BY JANE THORNLEY

SERIES: CRIME BY DESIGN
Crime by Design Boxed Set Books 1-3
Crime by Design Prequel: Rogue Wave e-book available free to newsletter subscribers.
Crime by Design Book 1: Warp in the Weave
Crime by Design Book 2: Beautiful Survivor
Crime by Design Book 3: The Greater of Two Evils
Crime by Design Book 4: The Plunge
Also featuring Phoebe McCabe:
SERIES: THE AGENCY OF THE ANCIENT LOST & FOUND
The Carpet Cipher Book 1
The Crown that Lost its Head Book 2
The Florentine's Secret Book 3
The Artemis Key Book 4
The Thread of the Unicorn Book 5
The Shadow of the Emperor Book 6

SERIES: NONE OF THE ABOVE MYSTERY

None of the Above Series Book 1: Downside Up
None of the Above Series Book 2: DownPlay

SERIES: TIME SHADOWS
Consider me Gone Book 1
The Spirit in the Fold 2 (companion to The Florentine's Secret)

ABOUT THE AUTHOR

JANE THORNLEY is an author of historical mystery thrillers with a humorous twist, mysteries, tales of time travel and just a touch of the unexplained embedded into everything. She has been writing for as long as she can remember and when not traveling and writing, lives a very dull life—at least on the outside. Her inner world is something else.

With multiple novels published and more on the way, she keeps up a lively dialogue with her characters and invites you to eavesdrop by reading all of her works.

To follow Jane and share her books' interesting background details, special offers, and more, please join her newsletter using the link below. All newsletter signees will receive an option to download *Rogue Wave*, book 1 in the Crime by Design Series.

NEWSLETTER SIGN-UP

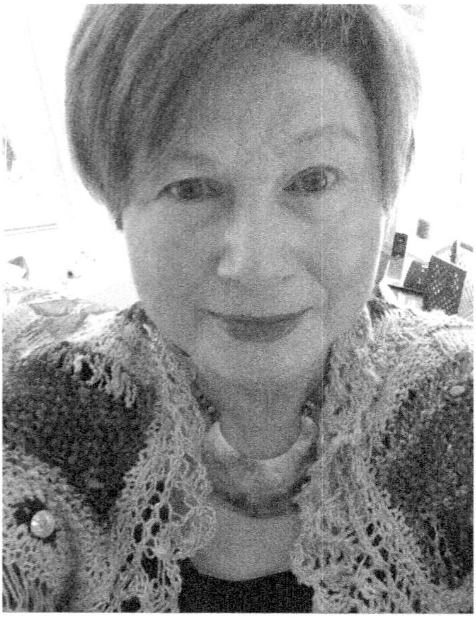

Printed in Great Britain
by Amazon